I0672535

The Minuscule Monk

The Minuscule Monk:
A Lizzie Borden,
Girl Detective Mystery

Richard Behrens

Nine Muses Books

Copyright © 2015

Nine Muses Books
New England, USA
www.lizziebordengirldetective.com
www.ninemusesbooks.com

© 2015 Nine Muses Books
© 2015 Richard Behrens

All Rights Reserved. Printed in the United States. No part of
this book may be used or reproduced in any manner whatsoever
without written permission from the publisher except in the case
of brief quotations embedded in critical articles and reviews. For
information write: lizziebordengirldetective@gmail.com.

ISBN-10:0991278402
ISBN-13:978-0-9912784-0-4

Chapter Title illustrations: Anna Behrens

Cover illustration & Lizzie Cameo: Marc Reed
www.marcreed.com

FOR MY FATHER, FRANK BEHRENS

THE CYRANO OF 6S

Also by Richard Behrens

From PearTree Press:

Lizzie Borden: Girl Detective

From Nine Muses Books:

The Agitated Elocutionist
The Forlorn Maggie
The Purloined Curio
The Melancholy Scion
The Sculling Boat

Acknowledgments

The Minuscule Monk is a work of fiction. The Borden family and their city of Fall River were very real. I have reconstructed them for my own purposes and sincerely hope those who have been resting in peace will forgive the liberties I allowed myself in this fantasy of their times.

Much love to my wife Anna who co-forged Nine Muses Books and has decorated this tale with her own version of the story in 23 objects.

Many thanks go to Stefani Koorey and Kat Koorey of PearTree Press for their generous support of this project and the Lizzie Borden, Girl Detective concept in general. It was in Stefani's magazine *The Hatchet* that my Lizzie took shape, a first phase effort culminating in the book *Lizzie Borden: Girl Detective* (PearTree Press, 2010) and it was Kat who took a very rough manuscript and shaped it with her tireless fact and continuity checking.

More thanks go to Shelley Dziedzic for giving me such a vivid image of the Widow Mrs. Borden at her dinner table and for other remarkable encounters in Fall River, as well as her most excellent guide to the city's necropolis, *A History of Oak Grove Cemetery*.

Also, much appreciation to the Mutton Eaters, The Fall River Chapter of the Lizzie Borden Society, and to the Pear Essential Players whose members, too numerous to name here, have been endlessly fraternal.

My gratitude to Ted and Lorraine Gregoire for being the first fans; Jinny Alpaugh for proofing and support; Ric Rebello for his documentary *Lizbeth: A Victorian Nightmare*; Michael Martins and Dennis Binette of the Fall River Historical Society; Lee-Ann Wilbur of the Lizzie Borden Bed & Breakfast; Deborah Allard for keeping the story alive; Marc Reed for his great illustrations; and a special thanks to Susan Behrens and Catherine Behrens for their many read-throughs and critical pencils.

Thanks to my friends John Walp and Heather Bernhardt, Emory Anderson, Craig Lange, Mark Walter, Seth Block and James Taddeo. Also to my sister Susan and her husband Tony Sarowitz, my cousin Janet Goldstein, Roy and Nila Gandhi-Schwatlo, the Taddeo family, my Aunt Margarete Pierce, my father Frank and stepmother Cathy, many thanks for making my transition to New England most endearing.

Last but not least to my mother, Shirley Hill, who loves mysteries and who I hope will like this one.

Table of Contents

MISS LIZZIE BORDEN

"*Yesterday, upon the stair*
I met a man who wasn't there.
He wasn't there again today,
I wish, I wish he'd go away...."

William Hughes Mearns

Prelude

The Last Hand

Black Bone, Dakota Territory. 1871.

Albert Duey had received word from an informant that there was no Faro more rewarding than the standing game at the Oriental and that if he were ever to catch up with the Minuscule Monk, it would be at that notorious establishment. Besides, the attested honesty of dealer Ambrose Fly, a native of Schenectady, gave a man some fair chance of beating the house with respectable odds. Sensing that he would be safer with the layout of a Yankee banker than that of a Dakotan bandit—not that losing money would be a problem while trapping the Monk—Duey decided to take the informant's lead as salient. Hoisting his leather satchel, bearing it burdensomely with both hands, he herded himself through the muddy and pestilent streets of Black Bone straight for the indicated saloon.

His mind, once so agile and open to a world of unending possibilities, was now, as if due to the result of some botched surgery on a head wound, fixed upon that monomaniacal purpose that had come to dominate his life and to which he had assigned his self-identity: the destruction of the Minuscule Monk and the confiscation of the outlaw's lifeless body. There had been a day in his optimistic youth when he had pledged upon the family Bible that he would never commit the sin of taking a human life; but here he was in Black Bone, thousands of miles and several decades away from where he had taken his oath, guiding death to its target. Very ironic, but life is peculiar that way, he quipped philosophically as he plowed through a gauntlet of working women, drunkards, desperados, Fort Laramie

1

scum, gold miners, Chinese laborers and stone-faced Indian scouts who filled the streets of Black Bone like so much human flotsam.

At the Oriental he found a smoky room with a crystal-mirrored bar along the back wall and a dance stage that was currently void of any discernible entertainment. The main action, as predicted, was around the Faro table where a game was in full swing. The players, huddled over the layout, resembled a sea of floating hats. He had never before witnessed such a wide variety of human headgear: bowlers, beavers, high tops, Mexican sombreros, Indian feathers, even a Jewish skull cap. The faces beneath the hats were swimming in cloudy swirls of smoke as if a fugitive octopus had cast up black plumes of ink to obscure its hefty dimensions from the eyes of a desperate predator. No one in this room wants to be examined too carefully, Duey reasoned. Myself included, was his honest addendum.

Upon this fetid landscape of gambling and dishonesty, Duey laid eyes on the Minuscule Monk for the second time in his life. The first occasion had been buried in memories so painful that he recalled nothing save a demonic face and a flashing gun. After all those years of obsession and nightmare, the demon now sat before Duey in the flesh. In this more mundane light, Duey was almost disappointed.

Amongst the Faro-playing prospectors and itinerant drummers, the small desperado seemed a shrunken parody of a Western shootist. His moustaches flared off his fleshy cheeks, stormy brows framed his eyes, and an over-sized leather belt strapped down his tiny rawhide vest. He was perched upon a toddler's high chair, his booted feet dangling, stubby arms reclining on the gaming felt, and small but thick hands holding a few precious coppers.

The air about the Monk carried an unmistakable and unbearable stench as if he had not bathed in several weeks. Duey had smelled that foul air about the roadside carrion and hapless human corpses that had populated the roads during the wars in Kansas. It was the stench of Death. The Monk's particular variation of it was an amalgam of all his victims' dying emissions, an intangible sea of noxious and odoriferous plenitude. Even if they had been innocent folk—women, children, school teachers, farmers, random travelers in the heart of the bleeding territories—the very act of having being killed by the Monk had sent their souls incomplete into the Hereafter.

Pray that I should be killed by a coward, many a prospective victim had pleaded, rather than taken by such a foul creature as the Monk.

Just as he approached the table, some significant play had occurred and the assembled punters bellowed uproariously. "Whipsawed by the Monk, I'd say!" came a shout. "I may have to give up my gold watch on the hock!"

"Whipsawed, my granny's false teeth!" shouted a drummer across the felt.

The Minuscule Monk, his eyes like small augurs drilling into the layout, let loose with a husky growl. "You want to contend my action, we can settle it in the alley with some serious leather slapping!"

"You called it, Monk," whined the now visibly rattled drummer. "I'm merely commentating. I ramble when I lose! You know me!"

The Monk acquiesced and returned to ruminating over his cards. Duey watched him patiently, standing just beyond the range of the lantern light, a dark shadow merging into darker shadows, until the conclusion of the game when the losers cast their scowls, hooted their curses, made their threats, and then roared off leaving empty seats for fresh blood to slap the felt. Duey took a position just across from and to the left of the Monk. He settled in, placing his satchel between his feet. From this vantage point, he could study the Monk without limit, watching his fingers, examining his facial muscles, discerning caution or fearfulness, or any other subtle gesture that a seasoned gambler may have failed to erase from his body's lexicon of unconscious movements.

In the first few plays of the game, Duey made some desperate bids—gambling was not his bailiwick, nor was winning his priority. Each and every penny that left his pocket was an investment in his dogged pursuit of the villain before him. His blind trust in the banker Ambrose Fly was critical to his strategy. Here was the type of man who had achieved that most valued state of a Faro dealer—the complete removal of the human personality as if by surgery. Fly stared down at the players with pin-pointed eyes, completely focused, his derby tilted over clean eyebrows that gave his oval face a cherubic motif. Duey needed such a man to ensure that no uncontrollable factors would be introduced into the game's dangerous maneuvers. The Monk must be seduced into thinking that he was participating in an ordinary Faro game presided over by an honest Yankee banker.

Through light conversation with his opponents between rounds, Duey discovered he was sharing the felt with other outlaws posing as drummers: the Rib Roasting Rabbit Killer, the Snort Bandit and the Jackass Kid. Most of them were ambitious amateurs saddled with imposing monikers who floated about the territory looking for trouble, trying to make a name for themselves in the yellow-backs. Once some print-hack back East got a hold of their reputations, the violent yarns would follow, even if they were just a pack of lies. The shootists often failed to contradict the more outrageous claims, knowing that their legends had taken on lives of their own. But the Monk, Duey had assured himself, was capable of every depraved and atrocious deed attributed to him by the lurid journalists.

After a few rounds and some fierce felt slapping, Duey learned that his opponents were predictable in their play, unlike the Monk. They showed no evidence of collusion. These were solitary men who knew no kinship, no loyalty, not even occupational courtesy to each other. Hence their actions, including their bluffs and sleights of hand, were absolutely predictable, just as Duey required.

An hour into the game, having lost almost every dollar he had budgeted for the occasion, Duey rose and pointed straight at the Monk's pug nose. "I'll be Shanghaied five times over!" he roared. "Don't matter a whoop if you place split bets, flat-foot it, or go three-way on a copper, this is no honest Faro, or I'm a hanging judge!"

The Monk grinned, then spat back, "You got some accusation dancing around on the back of your tongue, *boy?*" He shot the last word as if it were a poisoned dart.

The Monk's dusty vest was now parted an inch wider than it had been a scant two seconds before. There had been no visible transition. Two single-action six shooters were bucking at his hips, clearly visible, and within easy reach of his motionless fingers.

His responses are supernatural, Duey thought. He's more than good, and I'm a hair's breadth away from being roasted. I now cast off into that unknown country of living second-by-second on wits alone.

"Boy?" Duey laughed lightly. "You calling me boy? Why, a toddler who can't stand up long enough to fall down, he's a good foot taller than you!"

The Monk remained poker-faced, tapping his fingers on the layout felt. "I ain't as tall as your words," he said gracefully. "That's for Devil sure. What do you say, Fly?"

It was a deliberate act of nastiness to include the banker in the ribbing; the man's neutrality during the course of the game had been as sacred as a church altar. But Fly just gave a tight whisper of a smile. "I come in front of no man's bullet," he said tonelessly.

"Spoken like a true Yankee," the Monk said. "So I got a choice here, don't I? I can get down to some harsh leather slapping, or I can perform an act of charity. Which way do you suppose I'll go?"

"That ain't my call," Duey said, raising his palms. "But I'm not agitating you, Monk. I'm just trying to protect my here investment in this game, which you can see is considerable."

The Monk huffed. "I have a reputation for bucking the tiger with honesty. You want to contend that, we can go out into the alley and get down with it and be done!"

"I'm not contending anything," Duey replied, reaching his hands to his lapels. "I'm a right proud punter who just wants to make an honest jackpot. You can trust me as far as you can throw a New York barber."

The Faro table went ominously silent as the Monk stared back at his formidable antagonist. The Monk seemed legitimately shaken by the rib. A bleak shadow coalesced above his head, descended to his face, and covered it for a moment, masking the convulsion that gripped his features. The assembled outlaws began to withdraw into their separate shadows. The Jackass Kid pulled his hat brim down to his nose and the Snort Bandit pretended to be studying his cards. The cool directness of this unknown player from the East was breaking all the rules, a violation that made the air fraught with explosive potential. They dared not even glance at the exit door lest their eye movements be misconstrued as an aggressive act.

The Monk's face brightened and he kicked his feet in mid-flight, breaking the tension with a delicate chuckle. "Well," he said, "sit and play the layout for a while and when your last dime is in my grouch bag, I'll be happy to take that situation as a full payback for your insults and we can go our separate ways. Is that kosher with you?"

"You got it," Duey said, tapping his hat brim. "But by the way, Monk.

I got something to tell you straight."

"And what pray tell would that be?"

"Gobble-gobble!" Duey spat out, a hair-split second before a loud explosion rocked the room. Everyone present, seated or not, leapt about two inches into the air, and then plopped back down to where they had begun their journey upwards. All eyes stayed on the Monk as the cracking noise gave way to a harsh silence. The little man's face was twisted into a half-smile, but there was now a new mark on his forehead, one that grew in diameter with each passing second till it was clear to be the run-off from a bullet wound. The Monk slid off the highchair like an unattended child who had drifted off to sleep, tumbled towards the wooden floor boards and slammed against them with a sickening thud.

Duey stood proudly, his hands by his side, empty of any weapon. At first it looked as if he had had nothing to do with the shooting. Witnesses were too busy staring at his hands—an instinct natural to those that lived on the edge with gunslingers—so they were slow to notice the tiny face peering from just below his belt buckle. It was mean and stingy with a camouflaging walrus moustache. Tiny hands held up two ivory-handled derringers, one muzzle still whispering the residue of gunfire. The air over the table, already sickened with cigar smoke, was now mingled with the aroma of cordite.

To the desperados and drummers assembled, it looked like a small child was attempting to crawl out of Mr. Duey's denims, but upon closer examination, it was clear that a tiny man had been concealed in the satchel bag and had lifted himself up at the final second before the gunfire.

Duey hoisted up the body of the newly revealed gunslinger. The child-sized killer was several degrees smaller than the Minuscule Monk, although such a confluence of attributes—a diminutive height combined with the skills of a shootist—seemed hardly possible to occur twice in one reality. With a graceful arc, he kicked his feet down upon the Faro layout, kicking at the cards and coppers with legs that were swathed in chaps. His torso was corralled by a coarse buffalo hide vest. He lifted up his still-loaded derringer and posed in a quick-draw stance like a marble tribute.

Albert Duey twirled one edge of his moustache as the cards

scattered to all corners of the room, effectively ending the game. "To catch a Minuscule Monk," he shouted to the crowd, "you've got to hire a Mite! Folks, say hello to the Monongahela Mite!"

"Fiat! Fiat!" the tiny shootist whooped, firing the loaded pistol into the still smoking air. As he stamped his buck boots, the entire room, mesmerized by the pounding rhythm, began to clap their hands to his little dance, then broke out into shouts of approval and riotous applause.

Chapter One

A Fatal Concern

Fall River, Massachusetts. 1875.

Lizzie Andrew Borden, a woman shining with the ebullient optimism of one so young, emerged from the City Hall tower, her mind excited and racing with possibilities. She darted into the crowded bustle of the North Main Street foot traffic, flitted across the gutter through the onrush of horse-drawn carts and livery vehicles, and alighted on the west side of the thoroughfare as the tower clock chimed noon. Her imagination was feverish over the lecture she had just attended at the City Hall library on the process of Egyptian mummification by one Professor Bildung of New York.

For one shining hour, the erudite speaker at the podium had mesmerized his audience, preaching his dark knowledge and esoteric recipes for immortality. As he spoke, his wild black hair swirled about his craggy and scarred face, which was anchored by an eye-patch that Lizzie had found somewhat enchanting, perhaps even exotic. He spoke about the various techniques by which the ancients had attempted immortality. The oils, perfumes, linens and sacred ointments all felt palpably real in the wake of his vivid descriptions of the eviscerations, dehydrations, disembowelments and trepanations that accompanied the creation of an immortal being in the ancient world. He described human brains extracted with iron hooks through nostrils, of fingers and toes rendered jackal-proof with splints and bandages, and human flesh drying to the hardness of stone. He even related several romantic stories about Egyptian mummies, including curses upon their tombs and resurrections after thousands of years

9

of interment. The professor had taken his small audience on a manic trip past the deep abysses of history to a mythic afterlife, one of hope and wonder, convincing her that there was more depth to this mystifying world than the small glimmer she had witnessed from the dull confines of her life in Fall River.

Overwhelmed with glee, she couldn't wait to share her new-found insights into the dark mysteries of immortality with Andrew Jackson Borden, her hard-working father, at his place of business. "He will be very proud of me," she thought excitedly. "What with his grim opinions about the finality of death, he will delight that there is hope for us yet!"

In her excitement, she turned back towards the City Hall as if hunting for some way to lock the marvelous revelations she had heard there into her memory; but her eye was immediately drawn to a strange vehicle that was parked as if abandoned on the side-street, gray and spectral in the shadows cast by the building's tower. It looked to be a small circus wagon, tall with paneled sides, illustrated with garish paint. A chestnut horse lolled before it, his body harnessed to the wagon. The creature's nose was buried in a feed bag, but one lonesome eye stared at Lizzie as if beckoning for her sympathy. Descending from between his bat-like ears was a long white diamond, his only decoration. Despite his morbid gaze, he munched mindlessly on his meal with a continuous gnashing of teeth.

The painted sides of the wagon displayed no depictions of clown gangs, no bareback riders, no airborne acrobats spiraling, and no ring masters or elephant parades. Instead, a desolate stretch of desert sported one sandstone pyramid framed on the horizon. An Egyptian pharaoh, his arms crossed over his chest, risen like a resurrected ghost from the burning dunes. A strange pronouncement was scripted above the scene in hand-painted letters:

Professor Bildung's Death and Resurrection Show!
Boston—New York—Philadelphia

Lizzie chuckled over the comical image of Professor Bildung snapping his whip and driving his depressed horse on the same bumpy post road that had serviced the Commonwealth since before the revolution. Imagine travelling the seacoast in such a thing! And what use did a lecturer who relied on a lantern and some glass slides to project his mummy pictures have for a wagon?

She then gasped at the possibility that it contained the remains of an ancient pharaoh, his time come round at last to rise from the dead and walk the streets of Fall River, demanding the return of his kingdom. She was tempted to throw back its canvas door flap and take a peek inside—what mysteries may lie within! But pressed for time, she continued towards her father's store.

At the corner of Pleasant and South Main Streets, Lizzie paused before the tall construction of the new Academy of Music building, which was slowly rising against the bright, cloudless sky. From within the network of scaffolds and half-finished brickwork came the screeching of hacksaws and the clanking of carpenter hammers. The building gave off the sound of a laborious breathing, as if it were a living creature fighting to find its next lungful of air.

Once, in a newspaper drawing, she had seen the plans for the façade of this glorious structure, with its pilasters and columns rising in three-fold splendor over ornate windows, an artistic grandeur that towered above the block, casting a long shadow on the Second Street homes behind it. It widened above the town center like a giant stretching its angled limbs to a colossal height, attempting to gain some form of skyward immortality, determined to outpace death with architecture.

The Academy of Music was, in Lizzie's estimation, a great symbol of the new Fall River. Here was a building worthy of the ancient temples. In a town dominated by the dull and serious business of textiles, with its endless pantheon of mills and factories and operative housing, its dull fascination with account ledgers and bank accounts and economic growth, there was some deep need for the fabulous, the world of music and theater, of great artistic achievement and European aesthetics. No more shall quaint wives and dutiful daughters play their dreary Stephen Foster songs upon a family piano and call that culture; they will now hear the angelic choruses of Mozart and Verdi sung to the far flung corners of Bristol County, transforming all who hear the harmonies.

Lizzie saw the history of her city as the evolution of a child into an adult. Fall River had experienced a naïve infancy full of land expansion and Indian wars, then an adolescence of industry and wealth. Now it was time to enjoy the adult aspirations of life, to hear the music of eternity singing through the edifice of art.

Across the busy street, the furniture concern of Borden & Almy's, a narrow building fronted by display windows, stared upwards like a child defying the pomp and ceremony of the Academy. Hand-painted signs in the display window announced new armoires and pinewood caskets at most excellent prices befitting the dignity of the Commonwealth. Here business transacted its daily affairs with all its dull and repetitive rhythms. Such was the drab reality of Lizzie's life.

Her father, a tall, lean man with a bristly beard and dark marble eyes, was standing on the front doorstep, gazing at the construction site with a trace of envy twitching in his cheeks. The bright sun's rays hit against his dour complexion and outdated neckwear. He had been wearing that string tie ever since Lizzie could remember. It reminded her of old tintypes and war veterans begging in the streets.

Lizzie bounded into the horse traffic and alighted onto the sidewalk, diverting her father's attention with a skip step and a lopsided smile. "Daughter," he said, flashing recognition. "What brings you to my place of business? I would have thought that you had domestic chores to occupy your time."

Lizzie chuckled, "Father, I'm quite elated. I've made an important discovery about the immortality of the human soul."

The corners of his lips twitched. "Have you now?"

"Yes," she grinned. "Professor Bildung has taught us all about the secrets of the Egyptians. I have just attended his lecture at the library."

He shook his lean cheeks. "I had rather you not spend your time at the Athenaeum. If abundance of time vexes you, Mrs. Borden can assign you some chores, I am sure."

"Why do you not call it the library?" Lizzie asked, giving him a quick hug. "Father, sometimes I do swear you are living in another age."

"I am of this age," he said, pulling himself from her and gesturing towards the Academy Building. "The new architects, it is they who are abandoning our age."

"The Academy will be a grand addition to our city," Lizzie chimed gaily. "Soon you'll hear music like you've never dreamed."

"Nonsense," Andrew scowled. "Stephen Foster is good enough

for me. Did you ever hear his arrangement of 'If You've Only Got a Moustache'?" His fists clenched and his eyes rolled as if the song were being played by some fiddle band inside his head.

Lizzie frowned. "Many times. Father, that song is so dreary and outdated. There are great composers now: Verdi, Wagner!"

"There are also businesses to run," Andrew replied. "And not enough time for silly nonsense such as opera. Immortality of the soul! Apply yourself to more practical lessons, like sewing. That would be a good profession for you, to be a dress maker."

Lizzie shook her head. "No, it is a good thing that I study the funeral rites of the ancients. When I get older I'll join an expedition to the Egyptian valleys. There are many opportunities there for a young woman of ambition."

"And what do you plan to do in these Egyptian valleys?"

"Why, discover the last resting places of the Pharaohs. I am curious to discover how they outpaced mortality. Perhaps we too shall conquer death."

Andrew's eyes widened. "Daughter, I can charm that ambition away from you. Come with me into the basement and you will see a Valley of Death from which no man can escape."

Lizzie glanced towards the open door. The store's dim interior was filled with cabinets, sideboards, and feather beds; but beyond, in the basement, there were boxes for the dead. "Well, I have other appointments…" she mumbled.

"They can wait," Andrew said harshly, taking her by the wrist and leading her across the showroom to the back steps. They scurried down into the lamp-lit interior of the basement, where a sharp hammering grew in intensity as they approached the workshop. Mr. Darling, the store's squat and clean-shaven assistant, labored with a claw hammer, driving nails into a fresh pinewood coffin. The box was mounted like a ship in dry dock on the backs of two large wooden sawhorses. Mr. Darling drove down his tool with each puff of his swollen cheeks.

Lizzie felt a dim shudder at the sight of the assistant. He was a colleague's nephew, possibly dim-witted and largely silent. The way he peered up at Lizzie as she stepped into the room made her uncomfortable, and she looked quickly towards a heavy business desk where Mr. Almy, Andrew's longtime partner, hovered over a ledger book. With his rosy cheeks and close-cropped beard, he was a welcome sight in the midst of the dreariness. "Andrew," he said cheerfully, "you've come just in time. I checked the level on all the corners and was just about to lay the lid in place. Miss Lizzie, how do you do this fine morning?"

"I am doing exceedingly well," she announced. "After an informative lecture at the library, I am now convinced that we are immortal beings who do not have to die."

Mr. Almy lowered his spectacles. "Hmm. Immortality isn't quite good for business, especially now, eh, Andrew?"

"Gaze, Lizzie," Andrew commanded, extending a hand towards the wooden coffin upon which Mr. Darling labored. He then pointed towards an identical unit that stood upright against the rear wall of the basement, its slender form tapering down to the floor. "No, we shall have no resurrections while we remain human. This is where it all ends with a frightening finality. Gaze upon the last resting place of all mortal flesh."

Lizzie huffed. "Father, you're a spiritual man; you attend church services and read your Bible. You know your stories of the Risen Lord. Why is the possibility that something survives after death so unsettling to you?"

Mr. Darling's hammering came to a sudden halt. The assistant glared eerily and then intoned, "Only the dead know the secrets of dust," before resuming his work.

The dark pronouncement brought a chilled silence to the room. Mr. Almy coughed into his hand and chuckled, throwing off his discomfort. "Do you believe in an afterlife?" he asked his partner.

Andrew's face twisted up. "Whatever form we assume after death will not resemble that which we currently inhabit. For all practical considerations, it will no longer be us. There will be no treats, no succor, and no oasis of delights. I cannot imagine anything more meaningless or absurd."

"So what is this life all about then, Father?" Lizzie sighed. "I surely don't want to think that ten years of schooling and a lifetime of ironing a husband's shirts are followed by an eternity of boredom. It doesn't seem like a just reward."

"No, perhaps that is not an enviable existence," Andrew consented, and then dramatically pointed to an old single-wheeled, wooden wheelbarrow, which sat unused in a corner. "But life, Lizzie, is all about that!"

"What of it?" Lizzie asked, puzzled.

Andrew's eyes softened. "That is the first transport that Mr. Almy and I had when we opened this business almost thirty years ago. We were young carpenters then, weren't we, William?"

Mr. Almy nodded with a distant glint in his eye. "Yes, Andrew, we were."

"Neither of us could afford a horse team back then, so we made do with what we had. We were laughed at in the streets as we delivered our cabinets and caskets in that one-wheeler. But thrift and persistence paid off. We became master craftsmen, quite respected, and none dare laugh at us now."

"But all things must pass," Lizzie reminded him. "We know not the hour, but one day your entire business will be as motionless as that barrow that has not seen movement in many a long year."

Andrew smiled down at her. "It may pass, Lizzie. But there shall be men after us who will look back and say, Andrew Jackson Borden and William Almy built this city with the labor of their own hands. Their craftsmanship is in the walls of the houses, the sitting rooms, the docks at the court, the desks at the police station, the book shelves of men's libraries, the cabinets in the homes of kindly folk, the tables upon which they all eat, and the beds upon which they slumber at night. I may be gone, but my works shall remain. Therefore, it matters not into what mystic afterlife I ascend, my legacy will be right here in the daily life of generations to come."

Mr. Almy thumped his ledger book. "Regardless of where we go when we pass," he said, "we do have these coffins ready to be picked up within the hour. Shall we move the first unit, Andrew?"

"Why yes, William," Andrew replied and joined his two associates where the coffin lay propped against the wall. Together, they struggled to move it into a horizontal position, their faces expressing surprise at an excess of weight. In an instant, it slipped from their hands and crashed noisily to the ground. The men stood back aghast and bewildered, then knelt down in unison to lift it once more against the wall.

"I can swear," said Mr. Darling, "that we have misjudged the weight of the wood."

"Wood be hanged," Andrew barked. "I believe we have a stowaway!" He released the lid locks and pulled the top panel outward to reveal a startling sight. Within the coffin, a man in a crumpled suit and a floppy silk tie stood, his knees bent sideways, his nose pressed flat, his head slowly deflating towards his chest. Crooked hands were fixed at his abdomen around a dusty hat that toppled and rolled to the ground as he sank.

For a brief moment, not a sound disturbed the room. Andrew lifted his palm towards Lizzie's face, expecting to stifle a scream that would prelude a womanly faint. Instead, he found Lizzie frozen with rapt fascination. "I am gazing," she whispered, "into a wonderful abyss."

All stood at silent attention, weirdly reflecting upon how after all their pompous musings upon the finitude of life, Death itself had come to pay tribute at Borden & Almy's.

Chapter Two

Memento Mori

Even in her childhood, Lizzie had sensed wonder in the smallest of things. Darkened doorways became portals into undiscovered dreams; the slanting of light through a window traced an illuminated visitation from another sphere; and a scene as commonplace as her father reclining on a couch, his jaw bristle twitching as he snores away his afternoon nap, echoed a composed tableau: a bearded king sleeping in a golden bower. Thus, her imagination would take the most commonplace people and events and find their mythic counterparts, making the world one of endless magic.

This inspired Lizzie to great vision, but it also made her feel misplaced amongst serious-minded folk who led lives devoid of fancy. Only little Lizzie would see her father snoring upon that couch and think of Old Hamlet the King of Denmark, about to be murdered by a trusted member of his own family.

Once the pinewood coffin had been placed flat upon the sawhorses, Lizzie was able to examine the face of the unexpected corpse, and the mythic process resurrected in her mind. The sad droop of the lids over motionless eyes, the sullen collapse of the pale cheeks, the hard stubble on the chin that had stopped growing at the moment of death, and the hideous stitches that held the lips together all conjured up the drawing she had seen not one hour earlier of an Egyptian King who had been unburied after thousands of years. Was this nameless corpse truly a Pharaoh of old? Or was it a wandering spirit who had overheard her argument with her father about the afterlife and had decided on materialization to prove some pedantic point? Was he half-resurrected, brought back to physical life but still dead, as if the great power behind his rising had lost interest before the final miracle? What else could explain such a sudden, almost supernatural, appearance?

Mr. Almy peered in closer, pointing a finger. "The mouth has been sutured shut, and you may observe there is something pushing out the cheek."

Andrew snapped his fingers at Mr. Darling, and the carpenter grabbed needle-nosed pliers from his tool box. With a grunt and a shrug, he snipped the filaments that held the lips together, then deftly prised open the mouth. A rolled strip of vellum extruded from the dry cavity.

"What manner of man," Andrew puzzled, "passes with a paper within his mouth?"

"Let's see what it says," suggested Lizzie, pulling at the vellum. She unrolled it with delicate fingers, half expecting to read the hiero-glyphics of the ancient tombs. The lettering was not pictures of lotus flowers and kneeling gods, but her own native alphabet. Yet, the orthography was flowery and strange. She read the inscription aloud:

Vita brevis breviter in brevi finietur,
Mors venit velociter quae neminem veretur,
Omnia mors perimit et nulli miseretur.

Her last words yielded to eerie silence. They all gazed upon the corpse whose open mouth, wounded from the suturing, appeared to be screaming its hidden secrets at the ceiling.

"What does this mean?" Andrew whispered.

"It's Greek to me," Mr. Almy laughed nervously.

"Latin, to be exact," Lizzie corrected him. With a small frown, she conjured into memory her personal study of the classical language. During one dreary high school semester, she had worked solely from books obtained at the library, conjugating irregular verbs in her bedroom while her friends shopped for clothing and gossiped about the boys they fancied. This labor, combined with her regular courses, had made that autumn an intellectually exacting season.

She read in a voice filled with foreboding:

Life is short and shortly it will end,
Death comes quickly without respect,
It destroys everything,
And has mercy for no one.

The hairs on the back of her neck bristled as she turned the vellum around. More script peered from behind. She finished reading:

Si possunt ratiocinari possint suffragium

Suddenly the basement room was smaller, darker. Lizzie placed the vellum down on the work table as if she couldn't bear the responsibility of its secrets. The darkness of the poem and the uncomfortable call of its cryptic meaning provoked her dismal composure. All magical association fled: this was not a mythic journey to the Egyptian past but a very real dead body in her father's basement, perhaps deposited by a murderer. It was time for the Mythic Dreamer to take a nap and for the Girl Detective to awaken.

Andrew had turned pale. He attempted to raise his hand to his face, but stopped halfway, seized by a paralysis of will. "What can this mean?" he shivered.

"If they can reason, they can vote," Lizzie translated. "That's what it says."

"What?" Andrew stammered. "Is that all?"

"Yes," Lizzie confirmed. "If they can reason, they can vote."

"Vote?" Andrew's eyes almost crossed. "A suffragette killed this man?!"

"Less a matter of what it means," said Mr. Almy sharply, "than how this man came to be within our coffin."

"I shall take the fellow who did this and twist off his head," Andrew sputtered. "I shall do this!"

"Father," Lizzie cautioned, "let us not resort to hasty measures. I am sure there is a perfectly rational explanation."

"Rational?" Andrew's fingers groped before him at the empty air. "A dead man appears in my basement swallowing a poem? That's rational?"

"We will determine *that* in time. Meanwhile, we must examine the man's clothing and any possessions therein. Mr. Darling, would you be so kind?"

Darling peered hastily at her and then set about the grim business. Before long, the contents of the dead man's pockets were spread out upon the carpentry table, a scattered fan of loose ends, metallic scraps and unrelated geegaws. Lizzie turned them about with her finger tips, picking up pieces of paper and inspecting the writings scripted upon them, turning about the rings and pegs, raising a cigar stub to her nose, examining an oddly curved knife, sniffing some grit and powder that came off a few strips of leather. Then she stood in paused contemplation.

"This is most perplexing," she sighed. Straightening her collar and adjusting her pansy pin, she continued. "I would suspect the gentleman has come from out West. The train ticket announces his arrival last night and the pocket watch tells a different time than here in the East. These rings without their keys, I trust, have been used for a purpose other than the obvious, perhaps to hoist something of considerable weight, most likely with a good amount of sailor's rope, the frayed fibers of which are present in the lining of his pocket. His time piece is one of distinction but shows a significant neglect, so I deduce that he is a man who has put on airs of aristocracy but has been forced to procure his living through a less respectable means. I believe that he was in Fall River on a business venture, one of considerable risk."

"How do you determine there was risk?" Andrew asked.

"He lies before you dead," Lizzie said, waving a hand over the body.

"Oh," Andrew replied, glancing downward.

"Further, the presence of small pegs and needles stuck in cotton gauze shows that some medical procedure had been necessary in the course of his business. I don't suspect the darning of clothing since these needles and thread are of specific gauges that befit an undertaker rather than a tailor. But this curved blade is most assuredly a fleshing knife, one used to scrape tissue from animal hide. The absence of any blood stains perplexes me. Perhaps… Yes, perhaps…."

Mr. Darling smiled slyly as if anticipating Lizzie's pronouncement. "He was a mortician!" he said triumphantly.

"I don't think so," Lizzie said. "But he has dealt intimately with the dead." She peered closely at the man's wrists and then smiled. "Yes, we have a strangeness here that will complicate matters considerably. Notice that he is not wearing his own clothes."

"What kind of statement is that?" Mr. Almy protested. "Of course he is wearing clothes."

"Yes, he has clothes on. But they are not his own. They are awkwardly fitted, and the sleeves and cuffs do not match the position of his ankles and wrists. I cannot imagine that his tailor would have made so many mistakes."

"Perhaps the clothing was second-hand," Andrew snapped. "He may have been a thrifty fellow."

"Regardless," Lizzie said, "he must have gotten in here somehow." She peered about the room, searching for anything that would explain how a corpse could infiltrate a private concern's basement and wind up inside a coffin wearing another man's clothing. She inspected the floor, stamping her foot against the bricks. Her eyes then fell upon a small window near the ceiling, the pane of which was angled into the room, allowing for some daylight and the sound of the horse traffic on Anawan Street.

"That is the only entrance to this room other than the doorway?" she asked.

"Yes," Mr. Almy replied. "And the door to the basement is locked at night. It is simply impossible for anyone to have broken in during the night, not without visible damage."

"How do you know that he was not put here before you closed yesterday?" asked Lizzie.

"We worked on that coffin up until closing," Mr. Almy explained, "finishing it just as we locked up. No one could have entered this room except by that window, and that would not allow anything larger than a monkey, as far as I can see."

Lizzie rubbed her chin and then asked pointedly, "Who placed the order for the coffin you were constructing?"

A haze descended on Mr. Almy's face, and then he answered, "Mr. Pell. A most peculiar request."

"Pell?" Andrew said, startled. "What's this, William?"

"Yes, Mr. Jimmy Pell. I have had no direct contact with him, but he wired ahead ordering a coffin, this very one in fact. He claimed that there was no deceased person as of yet, but the coffin was merely for decorative purposes. He was quite precise about the wood to be used, the thickness of the lid, and the exact measurements."

"I would call that suspicious," Andrew said sourly. "Why did you not bring this to my attention?"

Mr. Almy remained silent.

Andrew peered suspiciously at his partner. "Could this Mr. Pell have offered a small gratuity to assure discretion?"

"Andrew, you know me better than that. I did not think you would approve of letting your workshop for such an affair, so I hid the details to guarantee the coffin's sale."

"And here is the conclusion of your choice," Andrew said, jerking a thumb at the dead body.

"Nonetheless," Lizzie intercepted. "We have a coffin that was being built for no one and then suddenly someone appears in it, albeit not properly embalmed." She ran a finger along the lips where signs of decay had already begun. "I suspect this Mr. Pell will never come to claim his coffin. The box was solely a means to deliver the remains of a grisly murder."

"Was this murder?" Mr. Almy said, his eyes widening. "I don't see how it could have been achieved."

Lizzie leaned in and sniffed the face of the corpse. "There is a strange mixture of odors," she announced. "Amongst them whiskey, if I'm not mistaken. And I detect a faint trace of almond, perhaps prussic acid. I would say a dime's worth, available through the corner drug store if you have means enough to procure a script for it."

"Murder!" Andrew choked. "In my concern! I cannot abide it!"

Lizzie turned to Mr. Darling. "Law enforcement should now be notified. Please go fetch Deputy Sheriff Wixon, who may be on duty at Central Station. He will suffice for now."

"See here, Lizzie," snapped Andrew. "Are you sure about this? If you fetch the sheriff, there will be hundreds of people all over this store and my reputation shall be ruined!"

"Patience, Father," Lizzie assured him. "Deputy Wixon and I share an understanding. Perhaps we will resolve this issue discretely, without fanfare or public spectacle. Trust me."

With this, Mr. Darling was dispatched from the store. For ten long minutes, the occupants of the grim basement waited while the Girl

Detective worked pensively, examining the victim's face, studying the inner lining of the coffin, and inspecting the dust swirls on the floorboards. She moved purposefully and deftly as if each point of detail were another character in a set of hieroglyphics that lined the lintels of some vast mausoleum of the regal dead. Every crime scene, Lizzie had been known to proclaim, was a signature waiting to be translated back into the hand that had drawn it. No one dared interrupt her concentration.

In time, Mr. Darling came back down the stairs, followed by a thin wispy deputy whose pencil moustache framed two fearfully pressed lips. The lawman wore a cloth cap and a belted coat upon which was pinned the badge of his office. "How now, what's this?" asked Deputy Wixon, pointing shakily at the figure splayed on the carpenter's table.

"It's a dead body," Andrew answered.

"I can see that," nodded the deputy. "But my question is more about how he came to be lying there. And who made him dead?"

"We don't know much," Mr. Almy confessed, "just that he is a man with no name who may have been poisoned while he was wearing another man's suit, and we found him in a coffin we were building for someone who may not even exist. And he was killed by a man who knew Latin poetry. That is all we know."

Wixon raised an eyebrow. "Ah, yes, well…perhaps if I leave and come back with a fresh mind." He angled towards the staircase.

"Stay, Deputy," pressed Lizzie. "No need for that. I will determine the meaning behind this all, but I'll need your help."

Deputy Wixon stepped forward, tilting back his cap, and glanced at the frayed stitching around the dead man's mouth. "He's been slaughtered by a maniac!" he exclaimed. "The Sheriff should be notified," and he turned his boot heels for the stairs.

"There is no need for that," Andrew said, flashing his hands. "I implore you to keep this quiet until we get to the bottom of it."

"But I have to report it. This is a murder, Mr. Borden."

"Yes, I know. But give me two hours…one hour. I don't want this out on the street."

"Deputy," said Lizzie, "we already have a good deal of information. We know that the victim came from the West by train, that he has been poisoned with prussic acid and deposited here in the middle of the night by persons unknown. He is wearing the clothing of a man who may be an undertaker of sorts. He has no identity as far as we can tell, but we may be able to track him through a train ticket."

Deputy Wixon removed his cap and scratched his head, as if the stimulation of his scalp would draw forth some understanding. "From out West you say? There was a nasty foray just yesterday afternoon at the train station, the peculiar coffin that came in on the six o'clock from Chicago. A man was transporting it, and he made it very straight that he came from the Dakota Territory."

"That is our man!" Mr. Almy shot forth. "But a coffin you say? He brought his own coffin with him? Is that even legal?"

"Did you take his identity?" Lizzie asked.

"He called himself Albert Duey. He tried to clear the coffin by saying that it was for a business concern and he was not at liberty to declare its contents. But then we opened it over his protests and found a wax figure of a man. After much of a whoop-de-doo he confessed that he was on the Lyceum circuit and the enclosed dummy was a prop."

"How did you know it was a wax figure?" Lizzie asked, glancing at the corpse. "Perhaps he was transporting our unknown man here."

"No, I inspected the body myself. The limbs of the coat and trousers were stuffed with knotted rags. The head was solid wax."

"Did he say the subject of his tour?" Lizzie pressed.

"Well, he was a bit vague on that. But he did mention a bit of fluff about mummies and being a professor of sorts. Yes, I do think that is what he said. Peculiar, isn't it?"

"Where is this Professor Duey now?" asked Lizzie.

"He packed off to destinations unknown and we have not heard from him since." Deputy Wixon then peered closely at the dead man. A pale light grew over his face and broke out into a radiant glow. "Until now, Miss Borden!" he shouted. "Dear God, until now!"

"This is the man?" asked Mr. Almy.

"The very soul! Why only yesterday, he walked and spoke and—"

"Professor Albert Duey," said Lizzie, as if testing the name. "And Jimmy Pell who commissioned the coffin was his executioner."

"You know the killer's name?" asked Deputy Wixon incredulously. "Jimmy Pell! Sounds like a rubber man from a dime museum."

"A man by that name commissioned the coffin," Mr. Almy explained. "We did not think it would be put into such dark service before it even left the shop."

Deputy Wixon blew hot air through his cheeks. "The poor man only wanted to lecture upon mummies. Who deserved such treatment?"

"I attended a lecture on mummies this very afternoon by Professor Bildung," said Lizzie. "There was no mention of an Albert Duey. I suspect this man was lying to you about his profession." She pressed a finger to her lips and bent in concentration over the paper retrieved from the corpse's mouth. Her eyes then rose, dancing in a mellow shine. "Deputy, would you be so kind as to accompany us on an errand upstreet? I do believe I can lead us to the solution of this mystery."

"By all means," he said. "I am at your disposal."

"Very good," she replied. "While we are off making our inquiries, would Mr. Darling stay here and stand vigil over this unfortunate man? That will allow Mr. Duey the respect he deserves, and ensure that no more dead bodies appear within the pine coffins of my father's basement."

Mr. Darling answered in a near whisper, "I'm afraid to be down here alone."

"Never you mind," said Andrew, paternally. "We'll close the shop and lock you in. It shall be perfectly safe."

"Afraid to be alone," Mr. Darling repeated, his eyes darting towards the dead man. "With him."

But Andrew had turned, engaged in heated conversation with Mr. Almy. Together, they ascended the stairs to the showroom, followed by Lizzie and the deputy sheriff. The last view Mr. Darling had of them was Lizzie looking back with a sly smile of knowing upon her lips.

"If he speaks," she commanded, "make sure to record all his words." Then she passed upward into the store.

When all was still, Mr. Darling, Lizzie's chilled directions rattling in his imagination, turned to the dead man laid out upon the carpenter's table and sighed. "So what's it like then, eh?" he asked. "Being dead?"

The corpse stayed rigidly still, his mouth grotesquely opened like a cracked egg.

"I figured as much," Mr. Darling finally sighed.

Chapter Three

The Truth-Telling Dog

The small company marched across South Main Street into the presence of the City Hall tower and the rising Academy Building. Lizzie lifted her eyes towards the looming hulks and smiled. These are our modern cathedrals, she mused, twin pillars of government and culture. They preside over a city crawling with life, grocers going about their commerce, house maids scurrying with laundry, cart peddlers driving their mules, street boys clutching coins tossed to them by gentlemen for errands various. The business of empire goes on as it has for thousands of years despite the ever changing generations. It starts with a wilderness and grows into this.

A butcher in a stained apron paused his street sweeping and blinked in nervous recognition of Andrew Jackson Borden and entourage thundering down the pavement accompanied by a deputy sheriff. Andrew returned the attention with a sickly smile, then whispered to Lizzie, "How much farther do we have? Tongues will be wagging."

"Up Bedford," she pointed, and marshalled them along the pavement. Presently, they were standing before a regal building of red brick and white pillars. Its rocky presence spoke of steadfastness against the changing times, an architecture that promised to outlast the wooden trivialities of the rabble. The name of the building's tenant was nobly chiseled into white marble over the front doors:

THE FALL RIVER ANIMAL SUFFRAGE LEAGUE

"Why bring us here?" Andrew asked with a puzzled frown. "These people are not sensible."

"You will see soon enough," Lizzie promised and led them into the front lobby, a formidable and expansive entry lined in veined marble. In the exact center of the foyer on a waist-high pedestal, posed like a statue, was a hairy and boldly erect Labrador retriever, one paw raised as if lurching forward, his eyes wide in some seizure of loyalty to an unseen master. His expression still sparkled with life, bathed in the sunlight that slanted through the front windows.

Andrew peered at the monument with suspicion. "We have found one of your Egyptian gods, the dog-headed one."

"Nonsense," replied Lizzie. "This is a noble servant who has been granted an eternal remembrance for service to his master. He stands guard at the entrance to a charitable organization that aims to alleviate the suffering of all animals."

Deputy Wixon sniffed at the dog's head and fell back with a grunt of disgust. "Stuffed, I should say."

Stuffed? Lizzie froze. She could hear the slashing of the fleshing knife, the threading of the stitches.

"Most decidedly stuffed," came a sonorous female voice, accompanied by the tiny tapping of heels on marble tiles. Strutting towards them along the corridor was an elegantly dressed woman in dark blue taffeta. As she approached, the light of the vestibule made visible a face lightly painted with cosmetics. Her hair boasted a chestnut coloring that seemed too dark against her patchy, aging skin.

"Good day, Miss Turpin," Andrew said shyly. "I did not think to see you here."

Noticing her father was uncharacteristically tipping his face, Lizzie asked, "Do you know her?"

The woman stretched out a hand which Lizzie touched briefly. "Evangeline Turpin," she announced. "You must be young Lizzie. Andrew has mentioned you often."

Lizzie frowned. The woman did seem familiar; her countenance emerged from a dim memory of her father's showroom many years before. Whatever had happened at the time had been so trivial that it had made little impression, but its residue was still in her mind, some vague trace of embarrassment. There had been a misunderstanding, or a difference of opinion, a moment of outrage, and then the woman was gone from their lives.

"It-it has been some time," Andrew stammered.

"Why of course, Mr. Borden," Miss Turpin replied with a confident smirk. "When I left your employ claiming that I had greener pastures ahead, ones that excluded the chore of posing alluringly in front of your feather beds to attract customers, I did not lie. Here I am the General Secretary for a well-endowed society which, I may add, represents an ethical cause and does not exist solely to accumulate personal wealth."

"And what cause may that be?" asked Andrew, his crinkled face conflicted. "For I'll be hanged if I can puzzle it out."

Miss Turpin drew in her breath, her small bosom heaving outwards, then said in a rapid stream of words: "The general suffrage of our mammalian four-legged cousins the world over; the process of Democracy extended to animals."

Andrew muttered dismissively as Miss Turpin turned from him. "Has there been a disturbance?" she asked, glancing towards Deputy Wixon.

"No disturbance that is directly connected, Ma'am," proclaimed the deputy.

"Miss Turpin," Lizzie said, bowing slightly. "I recognize this is a venerable organization, well-funded by anonymous philanthropists, and we do not wish to be any inconvenience. Only a few simple questions will suffice."

"Animal suffrage," Andrew said, staring down at his feet. "Of all the time-wasting rot!"

"Andrew," Mr. Almy said, touching his forearm. "You're trembling. I've never seen you so agitated."

"Leave me be," Andrew snapped, pulling back his arm. "I don't like being in the presence of lunatics. Animal suffrage! Can you not see the absurdity?"

"Don't rush to judgment, Father," Lizzie said. "There are sound philosophical arguments for involving animals in the civic affairs of humanity. Perhaps after our visit here we will walk away true-hearted converts."

"I'd sooner be a Papist!" Andrew snorted.

Miss Turpin coughed into her fist. "We do not discuss religion at the League," she said solemnly. "It tends to disturb the harmony."

"Would it be possible," Lizzie asked, "that we gain an audience with President Root?"

"What may I say is the nature of your business?" Miss Turpin asked, glancing nervously at Deputy Wixon.

"Just tell him," Lizzie answered, "that Andrew Jackson Borden of Second Street is calling on a matter of urgency. I am his daughter, Lizzie, and this is Mr. Almy, my father's business partner. Deputy Wixon you may know."

The woman's face relaxed. "Yes, I believe President Root has a few moments, if there is urgency and the police are involved. We have nothing to hide and perhaps it is best that we practice full disclosure and help bring your investigation, whatever it may be, to a conclusion."

"Then Mr. Root will give us audience!" Lizzie announced proudly. "Let us know as soon as he's ready to receive us!"

Miss Turpin nodded lightly before tapping back up the corridor, leaving Lizzie and her companions in a semi-circle around the stuffed Labrador. Andrew scratched his jaw bristle and asked, "What's your game here, Daughter? I see no similarity between crazy folk who want dogs in the ballot box, and a murderer who sews poetry into a dead man's mouth. How did you draw that connection?"

Lizzie raised a hand to a scarlet banner that dangled above their heads, stretched between two tall Ionic columns. Until her small gesture, they had not noticed it. On its broad front it read in bold lettering:

If They Can Reason, They Can Vote!

"The motto of the Animal Suffrage League," she announced. "Perhaps our killer was a member; perhaps the victim was a member. Perhaps we have been led here for a purpose or by chance, but for now it is our best clue."

Her eyes lowered to the sight of the stiffened creature on the pedestal. "Once in life he had the dignity of a name," she sighed, "and a master who loved him, and a favorite stick he would chase upon a sunny afternoon. I can only assume that the League mounted him in an attempt to preserve the charm, the beauty and the grace that he possessed in life." She thought for a moment, and then let out with a gay chuckle. "Father, you can clearly see that death was not the end for our brave Labrador. He lives on, in death, ready to defend the hall of animal dignity. Gaze upon it, for it is a death that could not be contained by any of your hand-built coffins."

"It's a stuffed dog," said Andrew, exhausted.

Miss Turpin had shuffled back into the room and was announcing that Manchester Root, President of the Fall River Animal Suffrage League, was ready to receive them. "But I warn you," she said. "He is in ill-humor. No doubt a peptic displeasure."

They advanced up the dim corridor into a main office which they found dark with mahogany panels and cigar smoke. Behind an enormous oak desk sat a rather corpulent man, bedecked in a lumpy worsted suit, his head a round extension of his shoulders, an oversized monocle twisted into one eye. His forelocks were plastered down upon his temples and his unadorned eye lost in the folds of his face. As Miss Turpin led them into his office, he let out with a sigh.

"Andrew Jackson Borden of Second Street," he intoned with an uncomfortable familiarity. "Come in man, bring your coterie! I have been an admirer of your craftsmanship ever since you built an armoire for my private chambers. Fine quality work, sir! I salute you!"

"Manchester," Andrew nodded. "I finally get to see your cloud cuckoo land."

"Ah," the large man chuckled. "A skeptic! Did you not ever in all your days consider the natural condition of man? We are but beasts ourselves, stuck upon this great rock of a planet, on the bits of it that are not consumed by the uninhabitable oceans, scraping shreds of nourishment from the dusty surface to continue our exhausting existence. We may doll ourselves up with symphonic orchestras and art galleries, but in the end we are beasts grunting and snorting for crusts of bread."

"Mr. Root," Andrew answered, his jaw bristle raised. "I just hang up my fiddle on anyone who talks that crazy."

"I do believe, Mr. Root," Lizzie interrupted, "that orchestras and art galleries are the very things that make us higher than the beasts. Humans are capable of so much more than mere survival."

"But we don't exercise our instincts!" Root said, banging a fist on the desk and setting a cigar tray into a half spin. "We cloud over our natural feelings with a layer of rationality, or with our self-deluded opinions that only obfuscate the reality of what we see around us."

Mr. Almy tapped Lizzie on the shoulder. "He belongs in a nervous hospital," he commented pitifully.

"Hush!" Lizzie said. "Listen."

Root twisted at his monocle. "Dogs and cats use their instincts to survive. They know danger and evil directly, not as abstract concepts from a minister's pulpit. They run when they sense that dark god of falsehood coming. They can spot him a mile away!" His eyes darted to the far corner of the room as if trying to catch some perceived danger.

"And you mean to say," Mr. Almy asked, "that a canine is more capable of accurately assessing the virtues and vices of a campaigning politician, more so than us?"

Root rose to his feet with a grunt of heavy breath, pressing down upon his cane. "Why this is axiomatic, sir! I discern that you, like all the rest of Fall River's finest minds, are skeptical about my cause. I shall prove my theory empirically, if you please."

Root snapped his fingers while producing a tremulous whistle through pursed lips. From the closed door of the room came a fluttering noise. A small square of wood, just above the panel's base, flapped and shifted on a vertical axis. A squat dark-haired Boston terrier came trotting out through the panel, his eyes ablaze with wonder in the midst of his square head, his tongue flapping between flabby cheeks, and his feet scuttling over the floorboard, the nails scraping on the ground. The tiny creature fled to Root's ankle and sat, closing its mouth, its red tongue darting outward and then withdrawing.

"May I introduce," Root said with a grin, "Herr Hugo von Trotter, my most valuable employee. Loyal to his master, ready to serve, and most important, eager to betray the confidence of any human being who is telling a lie. It is Herr Hugo who exposed the evil machinations of Shove the Gubernatorial candidate. If it weren't for this noble beast, that man would have robbed this commonwealth blind."

"Is that…" Lizzie began, then gasped. The downfall of Troilus Shove had been buried in murky rumors, one of which involved a strange new canine breed. There had been some sketches in the *Herald*, some publicity for the Animal Suffrage League, Manchester Root paraded through town, and then silence. It was hard for her to imagine how such an opulent building could have been funded from so small a political victory.

"Yes," Root said proudly. "Herr Hugo von Trotter attended a Shove stump speech and stood defiantly before the man on the podium, stared him straight in the eye, and commented liberally with bestial howls upon his colossal lies. It cost the man the election."

"Do you mean to tell me," Andrew said blinking, "that creature knows whether I'm telling a truth or not?"

"Why don't we demonstrate, eh Hugo?" The dog licked its chops afresh and shuffled his front paws with anticipation. His tall ears spiraled about trying to catch all vibrations from the room full of humans.

Root raised a finger and divulged to his guests, "The truth session must be preceded by the magic word, the only word that determines the range of time in which he can be attentive to truths or falsehoods. The word he learned from his previous master, a New Bedford confidence trickster. Such is the word!" He raised a finger over the dog's upturned nose. "Balderdash!"

All was silent for a pace, then Lizzie said innocently, "Balderdash is the word that starts the process?"

The dog dipped its head, rapidly losing any interest he had in the proceedings. Root stared sourly, and then said, "The word that starts it also ends it. You have inadvertently interrupted the process. I speak it again. Hugo! Balderdash!" And the dog's head lifted with a tail wag and a cracked pant that doubled as a happy smile.

"Now what?" Mr. Almy spoke. "I suppose one of us must tell a lie to see the dog's reaction."

"Such is the truth," Root confirmed.

"By all that is correct," announced Mr. Almy, "Borden & Almy's is the finest furniture establishment within Fall River, if not the entire Commonwealth of Massachusetts. So say I, William Almy!"

All were silent again. Herr Hugo von Trotter merely blinked. Finally, Root thumped his desk. "You have heard in the dog's profound silence that Borden & Almy's is indeed the finest furniture establishment in the Commonwealth. Now you must tell a lie! And tell the lie with true passion!"

Mr. Almy pressed his lips together, then said, "Yes, something that cannot possibly be true." After a pause, his face brightened and he said with a flourish: "The hair upon my head is not my own for I have fashioned a wig from the under-fur of the upland mountain yak!"

Without warning, the dog went into a spasm of yelping, one so violent that its head seemed to split in half. Its body half-spiraled about with each forceful outburst of breath, its forepaws dancing off the ground. It was as if the creature had swallowed a nail and was attempting to alleviate the wretched pain within its gut. Everyone in attendance, including Mr. Root, took a step back at this violent spectacle.

"A lie apparent only to the mind lacking rationality," Mr. Root announced proudly. "A very useful detection in the midst of a political election rife with corruption."

"How do you get him to stop?" asked Wixon.

Root snapped his fingers high above the dog's pointing ears. "Balderdash!" he shouted and the creature came to a rest, his only motion being the sinking of his tongue in a furious pant and the rapid rising and falling of his chest as his breath ran to stillness.

"A most impressive display," Lizzie said, chuckling. "I see how this animal can be useful in many cases of human affairs, not just politics. Crime detection, for example. But Mr. Root, the motto of your league applauds the animal kingdom for possessing reason. Yet, you tell me that Herr von Trotter's ability is a subversion of reason, a vote for instinct."

Manchester Root took another puff on his cigar. "Herr von Trotter's uncanny abilities are as yet a mystery to us. To the ordinary mind, he is possessed of enough reason to deserve a share of civic responsibilities. I believe he has proved himself, most notably in the Shove affair."

Lizzie pondered his evasion then decided to move on. "Mr. Root, we have had an unfortunate occasion. There has been a murder."

Root's eyebrows twitched visibly in the cloud of cigar smoke. "I do not think that I should be a suspect?"

"No, sir, we are merely following a lead. The slogan of your league was found sewn into the mouth of the deceased...on a strip of paper."

"A strip of..." Root stammered, then fell silent, his monocle falling from his eye to dangle before his chest. He turned to face an imposing oil portrait on the wall, one that had previously been obscured in the dim light of the office. It depicted a man almost twice as large as Root, his mutton chops flaring off the sides of his face, his strong hands hanging like giant hams by his side. For a moment, Root seemed to be in deep communion with the subject of the painting, and then he broke his silence: "Crapulous creeds! The folly of the human race! My most esteemed father Horace Root will be shamed in his grave."

Andrew asked meekly, "You are the son of H.B.E. Root?"

Root stood before the portrait in a strange imitation of the painted man's stature and raised his cigar. "Why, I have that honor, sir. His spirit dwells within me yet, and is just as appalled to hear about this murder as myself. May I inquire as to the identity of the misfortunate?"

"We have suspicions that he is a travelling professor named Albert Duey," explained Lizzie. "Does that name mean anything to you?"

Root's cigar trip flared while his flushed face betrayed that some inward search was being mentally performed. "No, Miss, it does not," he concluded.

"Can you perhaps recall any benefactor or contributor who is, shall we say, of a medical nature. Perhaps one who performs surgery on animals?"

"I do not catch your meaning."

Lizzie took a deep breath. "Perhaps it would be more pointed to ask if any of your associates felt the need to preserve the physical flesh of animals after their natural or accidental death."

"Miss," Root said darkly, "you are talking about taxidermy, are you not? We at the Animal Suffrage League prefer to call it immortalizing. It is a sacred act that allows the deceased to enjoy the open air and freedom of life. We do not believe in stuffing them into boxes and burying them in the ground. We find that…unnatural. We prefer to hand over our dearly departed pets to be prepared by an immortalist."

"I noticed your Labrador," Lizzie said, pointing towards the office door. "Does this mean that the League has a private, uh, immortalist?"

Root drummed his fingers against his chest, then announced, "But yes, there is such an individual. Jack Pratt, a former cloth doffer who not only immortalized the dear Lab but does odd jobs about town. Many a parlor room is graced with Jack's owls and deer heads. He also services our wealthy patrons when their pets cross over to their happier hunting grounds."

"He takes part in the debate as to whether animals suffer?"

"He has taken such a debate to fantastical extremes. He claims that the animals suffer even in death, not in a metaphysical sense, but as actual flesh, that their remains must be preserved and honored with reverence to alleviate their pain. Not everyone at the League subscribes to such an extreme belief, but we do not bar him from acting upon his conscience."

"Mr. Root," Lizzie said. "I need you to take a look at this knife that was found in the coffin with the dead man. I want you to tell me if you have seen it somewhere before?" She waved a hand towards Wixon, who brought forth the fleshing knife, which he extended towards Root for inspection.

The large man went pale, his eyelids fluttering. "You found that with the dead man?" he asked.

"I am afraid yes."

He turned away, unable to touch it. "I last saw that in the hands of Jack Pratt."

"It is no wonder!" said Andrew, feverishly. "All those macabre items in his pockets told us this tale. I say this Pratt is our man! Wixon, do your duty and arrest him!"

Deputy Wixon advanced with a visible shudder, and then spoke calmly to Root. "I suppose I must now consider Jack Pratt a suspect."

"No surprise," Root huffed. "He comes to our meetings and tends to our dead. True, he does make some folks nervous with his strange disposition, but no one can deny that he is a fine immortalist, most skilled and learned in the art. I would be sorry to hear that he has committed a crime."

"We cannot yet prove it," Lizzie said. "And perhaps we are wrong in assuming his guilt. But we must find him and interrogate him. Do you perhaps have his address?"

"In light of this situation," Miss Evangeline Turpin answered, "we must supply you with whatever information you need to bring this affair to its conclusion. You may forgive me."

She tapped down the hallway, her shadow trailing behind her as she slipped around a corner. When she had gone, Wixon let out with a hoot, "My word, Miss Lizzie, you have led us right to the murderer!

What instincts you have!"

"This case is far from over," she said bluntly. "We haven't even met Jack Pratt."

"You say this piece of paper was in the dead man's mouth?" Root asked nervously. "And it led you to my doorstep?"

Lizzie reached inside her jacket and produced the vellum, which she held out for Root to inspect, the motto-side upwards. The director screwed his monocle and inspected the lettering, then fell back with a sharp grunt. "Unbelievable," he said forcefully. "To think that the man would stuff such a thing into his victim's mouth and inadvertently lead you right back to the place of his employment. I had conquered the mind of the liar, but I'll be damned if I can fathom that of a killer's."

Miss Turpin tapped back before them, holding a card on which was written elegant cursive. "You may find him here," she said. "But never mention my name. I do not wish to sleep at night with one eye opened upon the door."

"Your anonymity is assured," Lizzie said.

Root passed Miss Turpin the vellum, and she inspected it with an unblinking face. "Sewn into the victim's mouth," Root declared. "Our motto! And a verse that denies immortality, no less."

"Yes," Miss Turpin whispered, then turned the vellum over and stared at the words. She handed it back to Lizzie with a snap of her wrist. "Nonsense," she said. "All it proves is the murderer can read a Latin Primer. Even a Fall River tradesman can recite the *Memento Mori*."

Lizzie slipped the vellum back into her jacket. "Shall we proceed to the Academy building and pay a visit to Mr. Pratt and discover if he is missing a suit of clothes?"

"The Academy?" Wixon said, astonished. "That's still under construction; how can he be residing there?"

Miss Turpin smiled slyly. "He is working as a carpenter on the theater. They have given him a room in exchange for labor. Such is the plebeian fate of the itinerant."

"Let's pay him a visit," Lizzie announced. She rotated, about to leave, but paused and fluttered her eyes. "Mr. Root, is Jack Pratt bald by any chance?"

"Jack? No, he is the possessor of a fine shock of black hair that goes from his brow to the nape of his neck."

"Hmm," Lizzie said. "That does make things difficult." Her eyes fell on Herr von Trotter who glared ahead with slackened jaw and bobbing tongue. "May I indulge myself for a moment?" Lizzie asked, and Root nodded with assent. She raised a hand high over Herr von Trotter's nose and said in a loud booming voice, "Balderdash!" The dog stirred imperceptibly and then stared fixedly at her as if awaiting instruction.

"Jack Pratt," she continued in a flat voice, "is the murderer of Albert Duey."

The dog went into a wretched spasm of yelping, its body spinning around like a compass trapped between two giant magnets.

Deputy Wixon breathed beneath his moustache. "Here's a how-dee-doo! I thought Pratt was the killer for sure!"

Andrew frowned. "We should confront the dog with a decided fact. I declare: Professor Albert Duey lies dead in the basement of Borden & Almy's." The dog stared at him as if he were a boring insect. "You see," Andrew scowled. "It is no competent mentalist."

"Unless," Wixon exclaimed, then snapped his fingers to get the dog's attention. He gazed deep at the terrier, watched it swallow twice, then spoke plainly: "Jack Pratt is *not* the murderer of Albert Duey."

At that statement, Herr von Trotter went into another contortion of barking, saliva trailing from his jowls.

"Both statements are falsehoods," Lizzie murmured. "How can that be? It's a logical contradiction. Gentlemen, please let us retire back to the furniture store. Based upon conditions there, we can evaluate the veracity of Herr von Trotter's mentalism."

As if galvanized with electrified wire, the company went rushing out the door, leaving Manchester Root alone with his secretary and his prized terrier. He bent over the dog and snapped his finger. "Balderdash!" he shouted, and the dog was still.

Root looked up at Miss Turpin, who seemed distracted and perturbed. "What is the matter, Evangeline? The revelations our friends bring have been too much for your nerves?"

"Perhaps," she said, stroking her throat.

"Then I will give you a task to distract you from your reverie." He took a pen off his desk, scribbled upon a scrap of paper and handed it to her. "Find that man. Tell him to be at the Academy stage in half an hour. If anyone in Fall River can help us at this hour, C.B.M. is our man."

She looked at the scrap and drew a finger to her lip as if trying to make sense out of something invisible. "Now, Miss Turpin!" Root said, and she was gone.

After a pause, he looked down at the small dog upon the rug whose tongue was bobbing over the hump of his lower fangs. "If not for my profound respect for your canine dignity," Manchester Root huffed, "I would have licensed you long ago to a freak circus, I swear."

The dog drew in his tongue and closed his mouth, and the room fell into silence.

Chapter 4

The Tell-Tale Hat

Lizzie Borden had always struggled with her ambiguous place in the world. The last child of a dead mother, raised in a city of wealthy men by a well-intending but ultimately unfathomable father, and continually subject to her stepmother's and older sister's unwarranted authority, she was forced to exploit her innate intelligence as a means of personal survival. Her intellect and reasoning powers, not any family fortune or privilege, would shape her destiny. She secretly wished, as she walked the streets of her Fall River, to hear the citizens whisper: "Pay no heed to the bank manager at his desk, look not towards the mill owner in his mansion, cast not your attention to the operatives and street urchins meandering in the dirty gutter, nor remain fixated upon the pompous and strutting shadows of the mansions on the Hill. For here, walking before us, in our lifetime, is the Girl Detective!"

Lizzie had solved many complicated cases for private clients, as well as the police, and with each passing success, her need for publicity had subsided. She eventually asked law enforcement to keep her involvement discrete, not because she did not crave reward, but the simple pleasure of having healed the crime victims' wounds through her ingenuity was rewarding enough. Their appreciation was all she desired, accompanied only by a good hearty meal and an evening's friendly banter in a cozy sitting room.

But racing back to South Main Street with her father, Mr. Almy and Deputy Wixon, her mind was in a muddle. Nothing about this case was ordinary, as if whoever had perpetrated the crime were deliberately acting against all the rules. And the carnival antics of a mentalist dog were now derailing the train of her logic. The simple clue that had appeared in the dead man's mouth, a direct link to the Animal Suffrage League, now seemed vague and misleading. Was it beyond her abilities to discover what had happened in that midnight basement?

Perhaps it was time to hand authority back to law enforcement. A coroner and his jury could determine whose body it was, whose clothes he was wearing, and why he had a fleshing knife in his pocket. Like a violinist who had collapsed in humble defeat before Paganini's Caprice No. 24, Lizzie may have to accept the Adventure of the Entombed Egyptologist as her first professional failure.

The company thundered down the steps into the basement where Mr. Darling was leaning against the workbench, his hand plastered behind his skull. His face was locked in a grimace as if so many fists had been beating upon him. Something had gone terribly wrong.

"Where is the blasted body?" Andrew shouted. The pine coffin was gone from the sawhorses. The second coffin that had been propped against the wall was also missing. "Our commission! And the taxidermy tools! All gone!"

"Mr. Borden," the assistant stammered. "Forgive my delinquency, but I have been assaulted."

"Assaulted?" asked Deputy Wixon, his cheeks puffing.

"A person most unknown came into this very basement while I was standing guard and confounded me from behind. As you can see, all traces of the body are gone!"

"But the door was locked!" Mr. Almy shouted.

Mr. Darling stroked his sore head. "I cannot tell how the fiend took me by surprise. I was standing right there, before the work table. He could not have come up behind me."

Lizzie examined the table, lowering her face until it was level with the surface. She reached forward and picked up a ball-peen hammer. "Perhaps this is the weapon. You can see there is human hair stuck to it."

"But how..." Mr. Darling began, his face shaking. "There was no room between me and the table."

She looked upwards, examining the ceiling beams. "Yes," she marveled. "Most mysterious."

Mr. Darling held up a dull copper key with a flared head. "What about this?" he asked.

"My Lord!" Andrew shouted, and reached out, snatching the key. "Where the Devil did you find this?"

Darling pointed towards the coffin. "There was a distended bulge in the neck of the corpse. I forced open the throat, and found that inside."

"You mean the dead man," Andrew shivered, "swallowed the key to my store?"

"Followed by the vellum," said Mr. Almy, adjusting his glasses.

"My employee attacked! My coffins stolen!" Andrew shouted. "And some corpse-snatching ghoul had unlimited access to my workshop! Wixon, I care not for the public shame I will endure. Take over this investigation! This business is far beyond the abilities of a young girl!"

As her father spoke, Lizzie was lifting the hat that had fallen from the dead man's head, the only artifact left behind after the pins and wires and fleshing knife had been cleared. She turned it over in her hands, staring at it with a strange fascination. It was a new style she had not seen before. The felt was creased on top in a German manner and it sported a silk band around its circumference. She turned her attention to its vacant cavity and was examining the fabric carefully when her father's words finally registered in her mind.

"Beyond the abilities of a young girl?" she exploded.

"Mr. Borden is all correct," said Mr. Almy pointedly. "This is no parlor game, but a heinous act that must be avenged." He coughed into a fist and stepped forward, a thumb creeping under a lapel. "Wixon, you are a seasoned lawman. What do you make out of this strange affair?"

The deputy stroked his beading forehead. "I must admit I haven't had time to collect all the facts within my mind, but I'll venture a guess."

"Please," Lizzie said quietly.

"Well," the deputy continued, "we have this man, Duey. He's from the West and he comes into town with a dummy in a coffin. That's oddity enough for one afternoon, but the next day, the poor man turns up dead in Mr. Borden's coffin…er, wearing another man's suit… with…er…poetry in his mouth."

"Which leads you to believe?" Lizzie prompted.

"Believe? Why, it seems obvious that the killer needed some new clothes. You said yourself that the suit was threadbare, like the owner had fallen on hard times. Perhaps Duey was a right dandy, and duded up like he…er…owned the shop! So the killer wants his clothes, which also serves as a get-away disguise." He paused awkwardly, and then his face lit up like someone had ignited a lamp. He snapped his fingers. "This man Pratt who works for the Animal Suffrage League… makes a living stuffing dogs, doesn't he? And the implements in Duey's pockets were the very tools of Pratt's trade. Pratt, therefore, is the killer no matter what that crazy dog said."

As Lizzie's eyes widened, the deputy's aggressive nods slowed, then turned into an ambiguous shaking of his lower face. "Or perhaps not," he trailed off.

"Deputy Wixon," Lizzie said patiently, "we can reasonably assume that the killer would have put Pratt's clothes on the body, but why would he? Surely such an act would lead law enforcement directly to him. To do so would be a certain invitation to the gallows, don't you think? Have you ever heard about a murder where the killer dresses his victim in his own clothes? More likely he intended that we should *think* that Pratt committed the murder."

"Well," Wixon grumbled, "I do follow you on the point about the clothes. But perhaps it wasn't so simple. Perhaps Pratt…er…exchanged clothes with Duey…er…by accident."

Lizzie stared at him.

"Maybe not by accident, but sort of in a forgetful state. Like he didn't mean to, but it was something he…well, you know…he wasn't thinking."

"He wouldn't be alone in that," Andrew said, pressing a palm to his beard.

"Yes," Lizzie affirmed. "Thought is important in this case, but our sight is just as crucial." She held up the derby for all to inspect. "What do you see?"

"The man's hat," Deputy Wixon stated. "Or more precisely, the hat of the man who killed Duey and dressed him like a taxidermist."

"Yes, yes," Lizzie snapped impatiently, and thrust the hat into the deputy's hands. With a swift upswing, she bent his arms towards his face, bringing the felt hat to just before his nose. "Look! Observe! Can you not see?"

"It smells like paraffin, I dare say."

"Yes, it does. But I did not ask you to smell, but to look. What do you *see*?"

He stared deep into the hat as if seeking oracular guidance. "I see nothing but the lining."

"Good," Lizzie said. "Now you must answer the question: What do you *not* see?"

He shook his head diagonally as if trying to dislodge her question from his ear. "Blast it, Miss Lizzie, you order me to see something; then you get upset that I'm not seeing something that isn't there. I wish you would just have out with it." He thrust the hat back into her hands.

"It is dusty as if worn on many a journey," she said plainly. "But there are no hairs anywhere inside the hat. The man who wore this so many years upon his head was bald."

Wixon's face sagged. "I'll be hanged if I can argue with that." He removed his own cap and stared into it. "I'll be hanged," he repeated. "And this Root fellow said that Pratt was not bald?"

"Precisely. This means that if the dead man is wearing his killer's clothes, and that killer is Jack Pratt, then he is wearing the hat of a third man."

"I don't like that," Andrew said tersely. "Our list of people who are losing their clothes seems to be expanding,"

"Bald or not," Mr. Almy sighed, "the killer is gaining valuable time to escape while we stand around embarrassing our noble deputy. What say we do, Lizzie? Find Mr. Jack Pratt and confront him with the situation?"

"That we may," Lizzie said, adjusting her own straw hat. "We will question this Mr. Pratt, or the Devil take us for fools!"

"Then let him take you!" came a booming voice from across the room. All eyes turned towards the open doorway where the wide shape of Manchester Root, his face twisted around a monocle and framed by a drooping moustache, descended, wobbling upon his cane. At his feet came the fluttering of a canine tail. Herr Hugo von Trotter danced across the dusty floor, his tongue distended and bobbing in the humid air. "For you need not labor to locate the mysterious Mr. Pratt," Root announced. "I have made arrangements for you to confront him where he lives!"

"Root!" cried Andrew. "Who invited you into the shop?"

"Who invited you to my office?" the heavy man roared. "I come to help you with your investigation. But I must take you to see someone first. He has cost me a pretty penny, but his services are invaluable."

"Who may that be?" asked Deputy Wixon.

"A detective, of sorts. I had him investigating a private matter related to my business. But now I see we can use him most effectively."

"Why…" Lizzie stammered, her mouth tightening. "You have a detective. She stands before you."

"With no offense meant to you, Miss Lizzie," Root proclaimed, "the man I am speaking of has more knowledge of this case than yourself."

"More knowledge?" Lizzie asked, startled. "How is that possible?"

Before Root could give an answer, their attentions were drawn to the Boston terrier who had somehow gotten on top of Andrew's workbench, just below the angled window of the basement. He was sniffing the air and taking small jumps towards the opening. As all eyes turned towards him with amazement, the dog succeeded in nipping the window jamb with his exposed teeth. Then he buckled down and began to bark into the empty air.

"Do you see that?" Andrew said, holding out an open palm. "The Truth-Telling Dog is exposing the window as a lie. What do you make of that?"

Root huffed and stomped towards the stairway. "I encourage you all to trust me and follow me to the Academy Building. Gentlemen and lady, come!" He gave a peculiar whistle with his cupped lips, upon which Herr von Trotter abandoned his assault upon the window and bounded from the table after his employer.

Andrew waved to Darling, implying that he should remain in the shop. When the assistant gave a pained frown, his employer patted him on the back. "All right, you may take the afternoon off."

"That is most kind," Mr. Darling responded, and grabbing his coat scurried madly for the stairs and disappeared in a flash, leaving whispery dust in his wake.

"Poor fellow," Mr. Almy sighed. "He has been through an ordeal."

"It is not his reputation on the line," Andrew blustered. "His name does not adorn the masthead of this concern."

"Come," Lizzie commanded, and led them all up the stairs into the shop. Once more they alighted onto the pavement, where horses and wagons and foot traffic streamed briskly through the crowded downtown street. Yet again they passed by the attentive butcher who scowled at Andrew with pursed lips.

Andrew tipped his hat and chuckled nervously, "Morning, Borden."

The butcher growled, "What trouble are you in this time, Borden?"

"Just tending to business," Andrew replied. "You wouldn't have seen a bald-headed man dressed like a taxidermist entering my shop this morning, would you?"

The butcher stared back, refusing to answer, and the entourage moved on.

As they crossed South Main towards the towering edifice of the Academy site, Lizzie peered into the small alley on the side of City Hall. As it vanished from her view, she was able to catch something that seemed a bit meaningless, but somehow tainted her mind as a buzzing fly in one's ear would stain the performance of a piano concerto.

The mummy wagon of Professor Bildung that had earlier seized her imagination, but had since faded from her mind, was no longer there. Only the horse's feedbag lay crumpled on the cobblestone where the horse no longer stood.

Chapter Five

The Lord of Imbecility

The Academy Building, cradled by scaffolds, rose above Borden & Almy's furniture store with terrible self-importance. The frontwall of towering pilasters, still lacking windows, framed itself majestically against the white clouds drifting above.

Mr. Almy halted. "If only," he breathed, "I could have the honor of building such an edifice. What a glorious achievement."

"Pay it no heed, William," Andrew scoffed. "he Tower of Babel was once considered an achievement but that just led to confusion, all because of vanity or some such rot. Soon the whole town will be filled with these abominations. They mean nothing and will go nowhere but to mortgage court."

"But the lasting value," Mr. Almy considered. "The pride in knowing what we have done. When we were youthful, Andrew, we dared not dream of such a commission."

"Our own humble achievements are more lasting. One day, the buildings of Fall River will be demolished by their own flatulence, but our sideboards and cabinets will be used by our grandchildren, and our coffins will be interred with our bones forever."

"Father," smiled Lizzie, "this city has grown too large for the quaint houses of your youth. We must look towards the future: architecture such as this ennobles us, gives us hope!"

Manchester Root, holding his canine employee with one hand and balancing his bulk on his cane with the other, interrupted. "Regardless of the ennobling potential of the building, we have business within."

Passing the open doorway, they walked across a large lobby and ascended a grand staircase, not yet decorated with velvet carpeting or railings, just a sweeping frame of risers and newel posts. As Root struggled to achieve the top step, they paused and marveled at what lay before them. Two large doors were opened onto a cavernous space where what appeared to be a theatrical stage was under construction. Planks of wood were stacked to the window frames; empty wheelbarrows were scattered like random spectators looking for their seats. In back of the stage was a series of ladders that all gestured upwards towards some heaven-bound destination. The company halted at the back of the auditorium.

Lizzie couldn't help but think that some Grecian-robed actor, his face garishly made up for Athenian theater, was about to wander out into a cross-fire of limelight to deliver a beautifully metered speech telling the tale of some ancient king. Soon, she thought amusedly, the wonder of stage art will be revealed in this very room to a mesmerized audience, actors animating a long-dead playwright's imagination. And I will be there, in the front row center. Perhaps.

"What are we here for?" Andrew asked impatiently. "I surely did not come to watch idle tools in an unfinished room."

"Quiet," Root commanded. "We did hear the two o'clock toll upon the hall tower. Soon, by my reckoning, he will appear."

"Who?" Mr. Almy asked.

"One of the greatest minds in Fall River. A man capable of discovering that which eludes even the best of our intellects."

"This had better prove worth the trouble," Andrew threatened.

"Oh, it shall!" Root said boisterously, adjusting his monocle as Herr von Trotter took small tongue darts at his cheek.

And so they waited, and the room waited with them. It seemed to be breathing imperceptibly with subtle inhalations. Light slanted through the windows and struck the dusty floor where a chalk grid marked where rows of seats would soon be planted.

Then came a clang somewhere in the darkness of the stage wings. This was followed by a clomping of shoes and finally a strange man appeared on the planks, walking skewed as if one foot were slightly out of alignment. He was well-dressed in a double breasted woolen coat and a brand new bowler hat. His face was pursed and pointed, his eyes heavy and mouth full, the upper lip decorated with a thin moustache. He stopped in the center of the stage and peered about into the darkened auditorium. Lizzie, her father, and the others moved silently back into the shadows.

"Ladies and gentlemen!" the young man cried out with a flourish, extending his bowler towards the empty balcony. "Thank you all for joining me tonight for this, my first engagement in your fair city. I have greatly pondered my repertoire for tonight and have settled upon a dramatic speech from Troilus and Cressida by the English bard. The speaker is the great warrior Ulysses."

He raised a fist to his mouth, burped and then flung out a hand. His voice bellowed across the empty space with an forced British stage accent:

And therefore is the glorious planet Sol
In noble eminence enthroned and sphered
Amidst the other; whose medicinable eye
Corrects the ill aspects of planets evil,
And posts, like the commandment of a king,
Sans cheque to good and bad: but when the planets
In evil mixture to disorder wander,
What plagues and what portents! what mutiny!
What raging of the sea! shaking of earth!
O, when degree is shaked,
Which is the ladder to all high designs,
Then enterprise is sick! How could communities,
Degrees in schools and brotherhoods in cities,
Peaceful commerce from dividable shores,
The primogenitive and due of birth,
Prerogative of age, crowns, sceptres, laurels,
But by degree, stand in authentic place?
Take but degree away, untune that string,
And, hark, what discord follows!
Strength should be lord of imbecility,
And the rude son should strike his father dead.

What a paradox, thought Lizzie. I imagined such a scene, just a few brief moments ago. The stage cried for a tragic chorus to capture the grand scope of some ancient king. And now this strange, petty man squawks about sick enterprises and imbeciles. Is this some prophetic actor? A confused visionary? A mad man?

The speaker, still oblivious to his audience, caught a curious twinkle in his eye, gazed out into the empty space and began a dainty little step dance, transforming from an Elizabethan actor to a pigeon-toed idiot. "Bow before me!" he bellowed, imitating an ill-tempered child on a throne. "I'm Master of Fall River! Lord of you all! I have lots of money! I have lots of money!"

"C.B.M.!" Manchester Root shouted across the space, his voice piercing like a thunderbolt.

The man on the stage yelped and froze in mid-step, the panic and embarrassment on his face distinctly visible.

Root moved from the darkness towards the stage, stepping awkwardly between the wheelbarrows. The actor nervously climbed down the side stairs to join him, his hands pressing down on his suit as if ironing out his dignity.

"I apologize for my little performance," he said. "I thought myself alone."

"Your dramatic debut was quite dynamic," Root noted.

The young man smiled weakly, then darted back a step when he saw the rest of the company approaching the stage. "Ah," he said. "Yes."

Lizzie clapped her hands briefly. "Marvelous performance. Encore!"

"I didn't really mean that I want anyone to bow before me," the man Root had called C.B.M. stammered. "I'm quite an advocate of workers' rights, you know. I was performing a parody."

"I'm sure you were," Root added, as the young man trotted quickly down a wooden ramp to join them on the floor of the theater.

Andrew inspected the newcomer with narrowing eyes. "And who, Manchester, is this? What does he have to do with the mystery?"

Root chuckled. "May I introduce Mr. Charles Borden M. Borden, son of Richard Durfee Brayton Jefferson Borden."

"Would you be the grandson of Henry Jefferson Borden?" Andrew asked.

"No," C.B.M. stated with a shake of his narrow face. "That's the other Borden."

"Charles is also the son of the widow Mrs. Opportunity Borden," Root explained.

"This is a great honor," Mr. Almy said, grinning and reaching forward to shake the young man's hand. "I had admired your father's career, from his humble origins as a general goods clerk to his rise in the banking industry."

"Do you have two Bordens in your name?" Lizzie asked.

C.B.M. nodded. "Yes, I do have that distinction. My father added the letter B between my first and second name and never had it fleshed out. When I came of age, I took the liberty of completing it."

"What does the M stand for?"

The young man rolled his eyes upwards, retrieving a rehearsed answer from his mind. "Mutability," he revealed. "True, not a common name, but my mother was upon my birth overwhelmed by the transient nature of reality and was compelled to make a statement."

Root raised his cane and pointed at the man's heavy-lidded eyes. "Charles here has no tolerance for banking. He's an aspiring detective."

"I fancy myself a bit of a sleuth" the young man said smugly. "And if it is a mystery that you bring here to me, then I will play the part to the hilt!"

The wide man smiled broadly. "C.B.M. is a great mind, a philosophical monk if you will. He has studied deeply in the labyrinths of metaphysics."

C.B.M. puffed up his chest. "Subjective idealism to be exact. It is a strong passion of my mother's and she introduced me to its beautiful structures and beliefs."

"Subjective idealism?" Lizzie asked, touching a finger to her lip. "I don't suppose you could explain."

"I direct you to the works of Bishop George Berkeley, a most excellent thinker, and one who postulates that the entire world is in the mind, that there is nothing but thinking makes it so, and that the very nature of being is to be perceived."

"That man is a bishop?" asked Andrew dismissively. "What kind of homily is that?"

"It is a positive argument," C.B.M. replied proudly. "For what do we have beyond the mind? We cannot see or think beyond it.

Matter as we know it does not exist."

Root nodded impatiently. "Yes, I do appreciate that, my good boy, but remember that this is not what I have paid you for."

"Paid?!" Deputy Wixon jumped.

"Yes," Root nodded. "Cash retainer, to ferret out the dark secrets of Jack Pratt. I suspected sabotage and an attempt to discredit my League. Now that there is a dead man, I am more convinced than ever."

"Where is this body?" C.B.M. asked, his nose twitching with interest.

"Uh…" Wixon started. "We can't—"

"It has disappeared," Lizzie interrupted. "As soon as we discovered it, it vanished."

"So the body is not sensible," C.B.M. said. "You don't have perception of it. Well, that must be the very reason why you came to see me. I specialize in things that don't exist. Or don't appear to exist."

"But he does exist!" Mr. Almy shouted. "We saw him with our own eyes."

"But you don't see him now," C.B.M. nodded assuredly. "He is no longer apprehended by your perception. Therefore, he does not exist."

"Why, that is madness," Andrew thundered. "If I were to think that way, I would believe that the entire world would disappear if my eyes happened to be shut."

"You begin," C.B.M. smiled, "to sense the beautiful and terrifying conclusions of subjective idealism."

A harsh silence fell across them. Lizzie thought about her options, to engage this wealthy scion of one of Fall River's most respectable and prosperous families, despite his challenge to her claim to be the town's most excellent detective; or to dismiss him as a lunatic who had fallen under the charm of a maddening thought system, rendering him useless in so serious a matter. She weighed the possibilities, then announced: "C.B.M., we wish to hear your thoughts on this affair. I cannot penetrate its mysteries on my own."

C.B.M. laughed. "Yes, I would like to hear about this dead man who doesn't exist. Indulge me."

With a measured breath, Lizzie carefully explained everything that had transpired since noon, sparing no detail, not even the truth-telling dog. C.B.M. Borden listened voraciously, scratching his chin. When Lizzie had finished, he paced the floor, tilting his head to the side as if trying to distribute his thoughts more evenly within his skull. Finally, he postured as would an orator about to address some political body, rocked on his heels and spread his hands at his lapels.

"Why, I have solved it!" he announced. "Here is my reasoning. We have a body that doesn't exist wearing clothes that are not his own, arrived in this town by train yesterday with a coffin that contained a man who wasn't real. Do you follow me so far?"

"Strangely, yes," answered Mr. Almy.

"A mysterious entity has shuttled his body about, first to the basement of Mr. Borden's woodshop, and then out to locations unknown. The name and nature of this villain we do not know. Nor do we know the motive or the method of murder. We suspect a connection with the Fall River Animal Suffrage League simply because of the parchment found within the body's mouth. What this connection is we do not know. There is a fleshing knife which points to an immortalist who works in this very building, but his whereabouts are unknown, nor do we know anything of his involvement besides the fact that his trousers and coat were on the dead man's body. All these we do not know."

Deputy Wixon shook his head. "That's what you call solving the case?"

"Ah, this is where we must adhere strictly to the dictates of Bishop Berkeley," said C.B.M. "A very learned man, albeit Irish. When we approach things from his perspective, we find the forms of the world are mere flickering shadows that cast their umbra upon the earth and quickly vanish, like the dead body of Mr. Duey, who may just be a shadow in a dimension that we cannot perceive. Therefore, I deduce that the body doesn't even exist, that the murderer is even more subjectively elusive than the victim, and that the event never even took place. Q.E.D." He beamed with friendly eyes.

All stared at him in a hushed silence until Andrew began a strange series of wheezes that sounded like nervous attempts at laughter.

"C.B.M.," Lizzie said, her voice cracking. "I have no doubt that in some manner of reasoning treasured by some great philosophers, subjective idealism has some value. But we are hunting for a killer who is, unfortunately, all too real. We must not waste our time with intellectual acrobatics, but must produce something tangible."

"Produce something!" the young scion said with a laugh. "Yes,

Miss Borden, I can indeed produce something tangible. You see, while you may think me mired in thought, detached from the real world, I have actually produced something that can be submitted as solid evidence." He bent a finger to indicate that they should follow him back onto the stage. There he led them towards an area under a hanging scaffold. The boy millionaire pointed down at the stage.

"Do you not see that pine knob? If I pull it, we will see the real evidence in this case."

He knelt down and pulled the hatch upwards, revealing a gaping hole into the sub-stage below. "Voilá!" he announced, "a hiding space for actors playing ghosts!" He reached down, yanking at something that he lifted with a grunt. Before everyone's astonished eyes, C.B.M. Borden had raised from the trap a tiny but heavy coffin, seemingly fitted for a child. He heaved it to the stage boards.

"How-dee-do!" Deputy Wixon said with astonishment.

There were gasps of amazement from the assembled, and Lizzie calmed them with outstretched hands. "We must not draw attention from the workmen," she cautioned. "Open that coffin immediately!"

Andrew knelt down, scrambling to release the latch on the box and prised open the front board, revealing the strange cargo that was nestled within. It was a human-shaped log with bow legs and a flat, blackened face, dressed as a garish parody of a cowboy in rawhide and denim. C.B.M. raised it gingerly from its tomb and put it down on the backstage floor, where it lay like a frozen corpse, no more than three feet in length from spurred heel to its rough leather hat. A savagely large pair of moustaches hid its mouth, and on either side of its pug nose were eyes that stared like dark marbles.

"Is that real?" Mr. Almy asked in a whisper.

"If you mean is it human," C.B.M. responded, "well, not exactly. As you can see, it is made entirely of wax, excepting the clothing and accoutrements." He rapped the skull with a buckled fist.

Deputy Wixon knelt to inspect the crushed face. "It is the likeness of a midget."

"It is the Minuscule Monk!" C.B.M. announced. "And the man who gave it its likeness has been dead for some time."

"The Minuscule Monk," Lizzie repeated, her voice almost a whisper. "The Western shootist who was murdered while playing poker?"

"Murdered, yes," C.B.M. grinned. "If you classify a gunslinger's shoot-out to be murder. And the game was Faro, the perennial table sport of the West."

"And this waxen statue is his very likeness?"

"Why, down to the bullet hole in the forehead. Whoever crafted it must have been a great artist."

"A midget gunslinger?" Deputy Wixon mused. "Is such a thing possible?"

"Haven't you heard the doggerel that has been circulating through the streets?" Lizzie said. "I hear it on Annawan Street amidst the songs of the disadvantaged children." She swallowed lightly and broke out into a tempered singing voice:

O! have you heard of the shortest gun
Who ever roamed the West?
His guns they roared
As the death toll soared.
By the Devil he was possessed.

He met his end at the hands of the Mite
Who caught him unaware.
O! God hates the skunk
Who shot the Monk
When no one else would dare.

Andrew's eyes flashed some recognition. "I have heard the urchins singing that, too. One hears all sorts of tear-sheet jingles, I paid it no mind."

Mr. Almy nodded. "I recognize the name from the posters that circulated after the war. There was a great price on the man's head. But who is the Mite? I cannot understand that line."

"Perhaps," Lizzie suggested, "the Mite stood to the Monk as David did to Goliath."

Mr. Almy stared down at the three-foot-long body. "The Mite must have been very small indeed."

"The Monk," C.B.M. explained, "was whisked from the saloon in which he was killed to an unknown location, only to appear the following year as a petrified body in a side-show. This wax dummy seems to be an exact replication, down to the clothing, of the real man. A carnival huckster may have wished to double his earnings by having two Monks in circulation."

Deputy Wixon snapped his fingers. "Look at the clothing, the stitching, the sewing together of the body parts. Jack Pratt has performed his art of taxidermy on a non-living thing. Perhaps he even..." He halted, then swallowed hard. "Dear God, can it be?"

"I suspect," C.B.M. proffered, "that there is a real Minuscule Monk in existence, immortalized by Duey. Rare is the Western town that does not claim to have seen the Monk on display these past few years."

"He would have rotted long ago," Mr. Almy conjectured. "No man can halt the decay of the flesh once life has fled."

"Unless," Andrew said gloomily, "he was embalmed with arsenic. That would make him hard as a tree stump, I imagine."

"As indeed he was," C.B.M. confirmed.

"How did you know this was here?" Lizzie asked him.

"I have been spying on Pratt for several days now, as ordered by Mr. Root. Many times he has sacrificed his meal breaks to come to this hatch and check upon his possession. He talks to it as if it could hear him. It is my theory that Albert Duey's death and Jack Pratt's tending to this waxen man are somehow related. Dare I say that Albert Duey was bringing the real Minuscule Monk to Fall River and somehow Jack Pratt was engaged in the business of swindling him, perhaps attempting to swap the wax dummy for the genuine mummy?"

At the sound of that last word, Lizzie stiffened. The magnitude of what she was looking at finally registered in her mind. Before her lay a mummy, albeit a waxen imitation. In the mottled brown face with its pressed nose and crushed lips, designed from the aspect of the agonized death gasp of a very real human being, she could sense the hopeful quest for the attainment of immortality. Whatever artist fashioned these contours must have been looking directly at the grim original, marveling as any craftsman would in the silent utterances of an interrupted eternity.

She shook herself from her meditative trance. "Marvelous," she said. "C.B.M., you have impressed me greatly. This is fine detective work."

The young scion lowered his head in a small bow. "I thank you, my Lady."

"But," Lizzie cautioned, "before you get too big in the head about this, I must point out that the body brought in to Fall River Station by Professor Duey was just a dummy, and a life-sized one at that. Deputy Wixon personally inspected it. No, it is more likely that Duey came here for other purposes, bringing the dummy for some sort of exchange."

"Perhaps," C.B.M. replied. "But you cannot deny that this dummy is your sole physical evidence that anything out of the ordinary has even occurred. Without this strange artifact, you have nothing. No body, no death, no murder. Except for this, and it is not even human."

"That will be up to our immortalist!" Root huffed. "And I would encourage you, Mr. Borden, to put the damned thing back into its trap and leave it there. It now behooves us to spring the trap on Jack Pratt."

"An excellent plan," said Lizzie. "The workers on the eastern wing will be having their meal break in a moment. Let us retire behind that curtain and stand vigil over the hiding place."

Root coughed for attention. "First, I'd like to perform a little test if no one has any protest." He leaned down, holding Herr von Trotter airborne over the pressed face of the dummy. The dog's shiny nose quivered and sniffed at the dusty and pock-ridden wax cheeks. "Hugo!" Root shouted. "Balderdash!"

The dog's eyes went into an eerily focused stare while his employer intoned: "Did Jack Pratt murder Professor Albert Duey?"

The dog's stare continued, his whiskers shaking nervously. Finally, Root shouted, "Balderdash" again and the dog's body sagged comfortably at ease.

"So it seems you are pursuing the wrong man," Root concluded. "We cannot assume his guilt in a murder based upon his possession of a wax statue!"

"Nonsense!" Andrew said with a phlegmatic wheeze. "Truth-telling dogs! I say let us grab this Pratt about the neck and squeeze from him whatever sense we can!"

"That's enough for now," Deputy Wixon announced. "We're not a lynch mob. First will be the investigation. An arrest on a reasonable cause can come later."

"Then we'd best retire behind our curtain right away," C.B.M. said, "for here is the meal bell ringing in the east wing, and Mr. Pratt will be back to check on his treasure in just a few moments."

They quickly shuffled the waxen dummy back into its casket and slammed shut the trap. Everyone then withdrew quietly and briskly behind a large hanging curtain in the wings. They pressed themselves in a single line against a brick wall, holding their breaths and stilling their bodies. Only Herr von Trotter, nestled in Root's corpulent arm, twitched and sniffed, a few gentle grunts and snorts emanating from his stubbed nose.

Chapter 6

The Immortalist

After a few hushed moments, something clattered and a wooden door to the side of the stage swung open. A man, small and thin, his eyebrows beetling over his face, his limbs steady and controlled, strolled into view. He was clothed in dirty and stained workman's denim with a tweed flat cap on his head. His trimmed beard gave a mannered hint out of style with his laborer's attire. Moving down-stage, he stopped and peered thoughtfully at a far window and then removed his cloth cap, revealing to his concealed audience a thick, bushy crop of graying hair.

"Ah," he murmured contentedly, and then walked directly to the floor trap, raised the hinged lid, and peered down into the hole. "How are you, my little friend?" he asked in a voice that was deeper than his thin frame should allow. He waited eerily as if listening to an answer. "Just one more day, my long-suffering friend. Your torment is nearly at an end."

Behind the curtain, Andrew whispered, "He is talking to the waxen man."

"So I gather," Lizzie responded.

"Did you hear what he said?" hissed Mr. Almy. "He is about to play his trump card. We should spring upon him."

"Stay," said Lizzie, holding up a hand. "Let us wait and watch."

Jack Pratt, for so it was he, slammed down the trap and sat on the edge of the stage under the proscenium; his bony legs, crossed at the ankles, dangling. He reached into his pocket, and drew forth a red handkerchief, which he spread out on his lap, and then a single egg, which he stared at, smiling, as if the small pleasure of the tiny bit of food was dear compensation for a world of stressful woe. Feeling into another shirt pocket, he produced a tiny brass spoon that he proceeded to knock against the edge of the eggshell, cracking it to reveal the hard-boiled meat within. Not a minute had passed before Pratt devoured the egg, leaving the shells to fall crumbled and broken into his handkerchief. Then he swiftly cleaned up and, stretching his back, burped so hard his moustache twanged. As he rose to his feet, bits of shell shuffled off his overalls.

"The man is mad," Andrew huffed.

Lizzie silenced her father with a reproachful finger. Inwardly, she mused upon the tableau they were witnessing: How solitary is this being who is nothing but a cipher, a zero? Is he a murderer? What does he hide behind his mask? He struts his hour upon the stage of life, playing his role to the hilt, wearing a common costume of denim and cotton; but we witness him here, with no audience, in his genuine state of being, beyond the slings and arrows of petty performances. There he sits, without his mask, feeding his mere hunger, hurting no one, content in his being with a simple hard-boiled egg.

Pratt held two fingertips to his ovaled mouth and let out with another burp. He peered into the darkness, his eyes closing into slits. For a moment, it seemed as if he would fall into sleep, so tight was his face, but at too late a moment, Lizzie understood that he had withdrawn his sight to add power to his hearing. He was listening for intruders and when he had satisfied his suspicion, he yelled out:

"Balderdash!"

Herr von Trotter squirmed in Root's arms, his warm nostril-breath charging the air. Lizzie stopped breathing as if that act would eliminate her presence.

"The sky is red!" Pratt proclaimed, and the Truth-Telling Dog began to yelp and squawk, causing all those hidden behind the cloth to break rank and fall forward into the fly-wings. Lizzie was pushed forward by Deputy Wixon and stumbled on the hem of her own dress, crashing to the floor and rolling over on her back.

Pratt scratched his chin with amusement while Manchester Root struggled to stifle the barking dog. "I should have guessed," he said calmly. "Root has brought along his boy spy and a coterie of misfits."

Lizzie was looking upwards at the ceiling, feeling quite helpless and floundered. She turned about onto her stomach and raised her head. "Jack Pratt!" she shouted. "Do not attempt to escape us!"

Deputy Wixon stammered, "I'm from the sheriff's office, and I demand that you stand your ground for interrogation!"

"Yes," Pratt said. "I know you, Wixon. You can drop all pomp with me; I am not harmful to you."

Lizzie scrambled to her feet, pushing down her skirts along with her indignity, and moved forward, leading the small crowd towards the man on the stage. Herr von Trotter danced around them, his stubby tail wagging furiously, his tongue twirling as he ran.

"Hell and thunder!" Mr. Almy exclaimed, raising his hands. "Here is our murderer!"

"What?" said Pratt, confused, struggling to focus in the dimness.

"There is no point in spouting any lies now," Mr. Almy declared. "We have seen your little man in the cubby hole!"

Pratt stared at Root, all the peacefulness brought on by his hard-boiled lunch having vanished, replaced with a virulent sneer and red pin-pointed eyes. "I should have known that you would bring the law," he snarled. "Did you sell out, Root?"

Root pulled at his moustache and sneered, then grabbed Herr von Trotter by the scruff of his mane, lifting him to his folded arms. He tapped the dog on the head and pointed at Pratt. "I had nothing to do with the dead man in the basement."

The dog panted and stared.

Pratt's face lengthened. "What dead man? What basement?"

All eyes turned towards the dog, the auditorium falling from crazed commotion to a deathly stillness as if a courtroom were awaiting a verdict from a jury. The dog kept its calm, staring lazily.

"There," Root proclaimed. "Proof of innocence in one moment of canine silence!"

C.B.M. thumped his chest. "That is no proof. We only have Root's word that the dog's reactions are genuine."

Root peered at him. "And who would you believe? An animal who has ferreted out corrupt politicians with a one-hundred percent success rate, or this boy detective, who doesn't even believe the world exists outside his own head? Who has more credibility?"

"I am merely pointing out," C.B.M. retorted, "that your dog cannot reason, and therefore his interjections or lack of interjections are meaningless."

"And while you all babble about dogs and philosophy," Deputy Wixon said pointedly, "we have a suspect to interrogate. We found your waxen midget, Pratt."

Pratt swaggered protectively towards the trap door with a fierce glow on his brow. "And what of it? That is my property. I bought him from a collector. He is my retirement security."

"A man came to town to do business with you," Lizzie informed him. "And now he is dead."

"What does that have to do with me," Pratt hissed.

"Professor Albert Duey," Deputy Wixon announced. "You killed him. We found your clothing and work tools on his remains."

"Why would I want to murder a man who I was doing business with? And who are you all anyway?" He glared at Andrew and Mr. Almy, then directly at Lizzie. "Who is this girl?"

Andrew pointed an angry finger. "That is my daughter, Lizzie. You'd best answer her questions."

"To whom were you planning to sell the waxen man?" Lizzie said hotly.

"Not to this professor of yours!"

"To whom then?"

"I'll be damned if I'm going to tell you."

"We can arrest you and force the answer out of you," Deputy Wixon threatened.

Pratt folded his arms. "You'd be wasting your time. I am bound by oath never to reveal his name. But I can assure you, he is no murderer either. I don't know how you connected me to this dead man you talk about, but I proclaim my innocence, and the innocence of my client!"

"Why don't we ask the dog this?" The deputy leaned towards Herr von Trotter's wet nose. "Hey, doggie! I'm about to say something and you tell me whether it's firm or not. Here goes: Jack Pratt is a murderer!"

Herr von Trotter stared for a moment, then leapt forward and swept his tongue across Wixon's lips. The man fell back blubbering, rubbing his mouth on his coat sleeve. "How-dee-doo!" he blurted.

"Balderdash, Hugo," Root murmured, rubbing the dog's head.

"We're playing nonsense games," Andrew interrupted. "I say wring this man about the neck until he tells us what we want to know. Here, I'll strangle him myself!"

There was an outburst of angry voices and a flailing of arms. Deputy Wixon plunged forward to prevent Andrew from colliding with Pratt, but only succeeded in entangling himself within their melee. Mr. Almy shouted, then pushed C.B.M. forward and the two nearly tumbled to the boards. Lizzie witnessed this all with a feeling of horror. Violence seemed imminent and beyond her control. She marched to her father and drove a fist into his shoulder, effectively silencing him. He stared at her with that chiseled face that had commanded her all her life.

"We will bring Jack Pratt in for questioning," Lizzie announced. "Let the police take over, just as you suggested."

Her father peered at her, his manic gleam dissipating. "Well, that's a sensible solution. Yes, we shall have that. I do not think there to be a more sensible solution. Wixon, do your duty."

"I am innocent of anything you are accusing me of," said Pratt sneeringly.

The deputy shouted, "There was a dead body at Mr. Almy's that was dressed in your clothing!"

The man's eyes twinkled. "Ah, yes. My clothing."

"Mr. Pratt," Lizzie said cautiously. "If Pratt is truly your name…"

His words were calm and careful. "I do not pretend to be anyone else."

"You are in an unenviable position here in Fall River, an outsider accused of murder."

"And what is the proof that I have committed murder? That a dead man wears my trousers? I want to ask you honestly, if I did kill this man, why in the name of Heaven would I dress him in my clothing? I may as well have invited the police to come witness the murder itself. Why would I have been so foolish?"

"That is what we are trying to determine."

"It is simple," Pratt shouted. "I had nothing to do with that murder! Now, Root, tell these buffoons to let me go so I can get back to my trade. I'm in trouble enough with my foreman."

Lizzie stared intently, ignoring Pratt's last comment. "Do you have any clothing missing from your possession?"

"Yes, my cotton fall suit, plus the brogues."

"When did you last see this suit?"

"I may have brought it from my closet not one week ago and shuffled it out to get some air into it. The shoes I have not seen for longer; they used to be at the bottom of my tallboy."

"Do you make a habit of carrying around taxidermy tools in the pockets of that suit?"

"I have not performed immortalizing for a long time. The League's Labrador was my last commission."

"And along with your fall suit, are you missing any of your tools? Any needles? Sutures?"

"Yes, my kit bag, including my knife. I noticed it missing last night. I suspected the thief who took my suit also grabbed the tools."

"Why did you not alert the police? Or at least your landlord?"

"What does it matter now? This deputy here thinks that he has solved the theft for me, that I myself had procured the kit bag and the clothing and wrapped them around someone who was conveniently dead. Can you not see the absurdity of this all? I am innocent of both crimes!"

"Hardly a crime if you took the bag and the clothing from your own tallboy," Lizzie pointed out. "But Mr. Pratt, I have to ask you two important questions, and you must beg my indulgence if I ask the question under the aegis of Herr von Trotter."

The dog stood at the sound of his own name, his nostrils quivering. Pratt stared uncomfortably at the terrier and inched back on the floorboards. "I have seen this creature many times at the League. Don't let him near me."

"Mr. Pratt, my questions will be fair if you are honest—oh, excuse me, I need to activate the dog: Balderdash!" Herr von Trotter twitched and his eyes glowed as if an inner light had been turned on. "There now, I can proceed," Lizzie said contently. "Mr. Jack Pratt, did you murder Professor Albert Duey?"

"No," Pratt answered.

Herr von Trotter nestled placidly in Root's arm. "There," Pratt shouted. "The dog is silent, that proves my innocence. I am not lying."

Immediately, Herr von Trotter went into a spasm of convulsive barking and scrambled from Root's embrace, falling to the floorboards where he spun about in a manic circle. Lizzie shouted out, "Balderdash!" and the yelping simpered into soft whines.

"What the devil?" Deputy Wixon shouted.

"Incredible!" C.B.M. Borden bellowed.

"I am innocent!" Pratt began to rant. "I did not kill that man you call Duey! I did not kill him! Activate that dog again, and I will prove it!"

Deputy Wixon stepped forward and clapped Pratt on the shoulder. "Mr. Jonathan Pratt, you are an official suspect in the death of Albert Duey."

"On what grounds?" Pratt spat. "That the dog barked? Who at Central Station is going to believe that? Root here is the laughing stock of all Fall River, him and his four-legged freak show."

"I must admit this is a bit thin," the deputy nodded, removing his hand.

"I am a private citizen, so I can go back to my job and ignore you," Pratt huffed. He edged towards the back of the stage and paused to point fixedly at the trap door in the boards. "And don't touch my wax dummy; I paid a lot of dosh for him!"

Then he was gone, his footfalls receding into the darkness of the construction site, leaving a confounded and gap-mouthed audience behind.

All were silent, until Lizzie stammered, "Who…?" then fell silent. "What…?" she began again. "This isn't fair," she said. "I'm trying to conduct an investigation, but someone keeps taking away all my evidence!"

"Perhaps," C.B.M. added, "we never had the evidence to begin with. It may very well be that the fragility of existence, being a phenomenon of the temporal and fleeting mind…"

"Shut your gaping maw!" said Mr. Almy hotly, raising a fist. "Or so help me, I'll shut it for you."

"Mr. Almy," Lizzie hushed, "be still. It isn't Pratt that we are concerned with right now. Somewhere behind the scenes of this little melodrama is a bald-headed murderer who walks through solid doors. It is he we must seek."

"Then Pratt is not our man," Andrew said.

"I don't know what to think at this point," she confessed. "Maybe

Pratt has an accomplice: Jimmy Pell for example, the man who ordered the coffin."

"Shall we search the theater?" Andrew asked, staring into the darkness of the wings. "Perhaps he is watching us, seeking the dummy in the trap, and we led him straight to it!"

"No," Lizzie said. "Whoever our culprit is, he is very clever. I say we retire to the Animal Suffrage League and with your blessing, Mr. Root, I need the use of your office for the interrogation of Miss Evangeline Turpin."

"The Devil you say!" Andrew erupted.

"A splendid idea," Root said haughtily. "And may I make a suggestion? Perhaps if we brought along Pratt's gunslinger there, it may serve as an oracular guidance. One can never know: a waxen midget may very well be the best thing for our inspiration."

"That is the property of Mr. Pratt," Lizzie said. "It would be quite unethical to remove it."

"Let me take responsibility for that," Root sneered. "A man who can lose his clothes and the tools of his trade in a clap and not care a jot will not miss his waxen midget despite his lofty thundering to the contrary. He need not get all in a twee if I snatch it for you."

"You'll take responsibility for this?" Mr. Almy asked. "I don't want any lawsuits."

"Of course," Root beamed. "Pratt is touched in the head. I believe the artifact to be safer in the hands of someone more responsible. Besides, I'm the one who paid for the damned thing."

All fell silent. Root lowered himself and scooped Her von Trotter off the floor. He noted their rapt attention and asked, "Why do you think I hired C.B.M. here to find where Pratt was hiding it? That's my property!"

"One incredible revelation follows another," Lizzie said breathlessly.

Root added, "I have a bill of sale at my office for a three-foot tall gunslinger made of wax by a Mr. Burbage, a circus arts promoter, of Providence, Rhode Island. If that doesn't suffice, I'm a monkey's uncle."

Lizzie nodded and gestured towards Deputy Wixon. "Bring the dummy with us. Perhaps Mr. Root is all correct, and its presence can give us oracular guidance. Yes, at this time we can use all the help we can muster."

Chapter Seven

The Little Beasts

The street vendors of South Main who had previously witnessed the strange entourage of a furniture salesman, his daughter, his business partner, and a deputy sheriff being followed by a corpulent man in a tweed suit holding a wide-eyed, big-headed dog, now were presented with the same parade marching north past City Hall. The law enforcer was staggering under the weight of what looked like a child's coffin. Lizzie, decidedly self-conscious, did not return any incredulous stares, proceeding with her chin aloft, projecting a quiet dignity.

They marched through the front doors of the Animal Suffrage League and passed the retriever, still frozen in its aspect. Its darkened eyes were as wide as before as if it had not blinked, nor ever would again. Miss Evangeline Turpin appeared in the hallway leading to Root's office, fish-mouthed, pointing a nervous finger at the coffin. Her employer gave her a dark wag of his heavy face.

"Meet me in my office, Miss Turpin," he instructed. "Ten minute's time." Before disappearing, she did not return his directive with any evident emotion.

"This is nonsense," Andrew barked. "Miss Turpin knows nothing about this."

"There are some points I wish to touch upon," Lizzie replied, and led them into the inner office. Once inside, she ordered Deputy Wixon and C.B.M. to perform a quick re-arrangement of the furnishings, exiling to the far corners a potted plant, a lectern and a hat rack. She left in place the director's tremendous leather-back chair, his large oak desk, and a small gilded seat, which she placed before it.

"Our waxen effigy will preside there," she directed Wixon, who propped the small coffin against the window sill. She examined its position for a moment, made a minute adjustment, and then rubbed her chin. "Yes," she said, "You are the specter of death, forever hidden but forever hunting."

She turned to Root and grinned. "I wish to have your office."

"What?" he exclaimed. "You can't—"

"I wish to interrogate Miss Turpin on her own. When I am done with her, I will call you back."

His face whitened; then he twisted his monocle and turned to leave. Lizzie coughed to get his attention and motioned for the dog. Root muttered, "If you must," and handed over the canine.

She planted herself down behind the desk, sinking in the soft leather, and planted the Boston terrier like a desk decoration before her. The dog panted and sighed, his heavy jowls lowering, as Lizzie patted between his ears.

"Herr von Trotter," she instructed, "in this court you may be the judge. And Deputy Wixon may be the scales of justice."

"And what may I be?" C.B.M. asked, his eyes twinkling.

"You," Lizzie said, "are the court jester, licensed to confound us with whimsical platitudes, no matter how absurd or illogical. Remind us often that the world is not always dictated by logic. Now, the court of inquiry is open. Constable, bring in Miss Turpin."

Deputy Wixon went to fetch her, leaving a hushed room. There was a soft tapping of heels against the marble and Evangeline Turpin returned with the deputy, her eyes calmly set on Lizzie.

"I believe you have some questions for me." Her comment was not itself a question.

"Yes, I do. Miss Turpin, please be seated."

The woman pursed her lips and began to sit in the chair, but her eyes froze on the coffin. Then she sat delicately down, her knees drawn together to preserve the dignity of her taffeta.

"I understand that several years ago you were employed by my father?" Lizzie asked.

The woman's crooked mouth curled into a semblance of a smile. "If I remember all correctly a small precocious girl who was always pilfering from the candy jar on the counter, I think you can answer that question as well as myself."

Lizzie almost blushed at the memory, but judged it would not become the dignity of the court she had established. "I confess I am young," she replied, "but since I have been that small precocious girl you mention, for the sake of my health I have curtailed my fancy for sweets."

Miss Turpin's eyes flared like coals. "My emphasis," she stated, "was on the pilfering itself, not on the candy."

A cold silence fell between them, and then Lizzie asked bluntly, "Why did you leave Borden & Almy's?"

"Because I was being treated like a subordinate."

"You were a subordinate. A sales clerk, I believe."

"There is subordination, and then there is exploitation."

Mr. Almy twitched uncomfortably. "You do not subscribe to the teaching of German socialism, Miss Turpin?"

"I am referring to the liberties which your father and his employees took with my dignity."

Andrew, silent up till this moment, gasped and stammered, "Don't play loose with the facts, Miss Turpin. Everything was handled in the most—"

"Such as?" Lizzie asked.

Miss Turpin stared directly at Andrew. "*I* was handled in a most unmannerly way by Mr. Darling, but my employer refused to take my word against his. I believe this was because I am a woman and not a man."

"Nonsense," Andrew blurted.

"Andrew," Mr. Almy pleaded. "Your daughter is—"

Lizzie ignored their interchange and continued her questioning. "Were you dismissed, or did you quit of your own accord?"

"After a most singular outburst of Mr. Borden's, who insisted that I was spouting lies, I stormed out the door, never to return. I even left my kid gloves and my best bonnet in the office. Your father never had the courtesy to send them round, and so I lost them."

"What had been your duties at the store?"

"To stand in front of the furniture made by your father and…let me see if I can recall his instructions to me on my first day of work… oh yes, I was to stand before the furniture and stare like a Jezebel, to bewitch the Pockets."

"Pockets?"

"Your father had flowery words for customers. That was one of them."

"I never," Andrew insisted. "Daughter, even you can see how full of balder—" He clutched his mouth as if trying to stifle the word with his fingers. He glanced disturbingly at the panting animal on the desk. Herr von Trotter glanced back with blinking but inscrutable eyes.

"Was that all you were to do?"

"I also had to clean the shavings in the workshop and to arrange the office."

"Were you often there after hours?"

"Many times I had to stay late to finish my duties, sometimes to the detriment of my health."

"At which point you would close up for the night?"

"Yes, Mr. Borden was deadly intent on security. There were locks everywhere. Six of them altogether, for which I had three separate keys on a chain."

"Such is the case now, I believe."

Miss Turpin blinked. "I cannot say, for I have not worked there for some time."

"How did you find your employment with Mr. Root and his League?"

"I watched an exhibition of the Truth-Telling Dog at a political fund raiser, two years ago, I might recall. I boldly introduced myself and offered my services."

"Mr. Root was just back from his European tour, I believe."

"Yes, and the dog seemed miraculous. I still believe that he has the potential to revolutionize politics as we know it. To restore truth and honesty to public discourse."

"And have you hoped that other animals can join Herr von Trotter in ferreting out corrupt politicians?"

"As far as I know, Herr von Trotter is the only of his kind. When I first came to the League there were dozens of little beasts. It was practically a zoo. Mr. Root was spending money on testing the Boston terrier. He reasoned that if there were a new breed of dog, it had new faculties of the mind. Herr von Trotter convinced him of this."

"But the experiments were not restricted to canines?"

"Indeed, no. There were cats that sometimes hissed at laywers, but otherwise they remained taciturn. A howler monkey seemed to be attentive to lies, but its savage growls were arbitrary and then contradictory, and we declared it finally to be insane. At one point Mr. Root had a horse that would strike its hooves on the ground every time someone told a lie, but we discovered that its owner had placed a thorn in its fetlock and the timing of the lies was purely coincidental. The horse still races under the name Root's Folly. Not one of our finer experiments."

"So Herr von Trotter was Mr. Root's sole accomplishment."

"Not at first. There was an Amazonian parrot, a brilliant thing with marvelous plumage. At first we thought it had precognitive abilities because it could repeat the speeches of politicians in what seemed to be a wry and cynical manner. There was much promise there."

Lizzie smiled and asked, "And what become of the parrot?"

Miss Turpin stared at the dog before her interrogator. Herr Hugo's head bobbed in time with his panting. "We made the mistake of leaving Herr Hugo alone with the parrot cage. The bird did not survive and we did not seek a replacement."

Lizzie looked at the back of Herr Hugo von Trotter's head, imagining the scene. "So the efforts of the League resulted in one animal trained for suffrage."

"Yes," replied Miss Turpin. "With money from our private investors, we hope to breed more like him. Then the face of politics will change, and we will accomplish more with a litter of canines than all the armies of anarchism."

"No doubt, but it stands as a fact that with the money that has been poured into this League, paying for its marble entry and mahogany walls, you have only produced one such animal."

"We have accomplished a great deal more than that," Miss Turpin glowered. "If Troilus Shove had been elected governor, this com- monwealth would—"

"Perhaps," Lizzie said. "But for now, Miss Turpin, you must indulge me in one small formality. I hope you don't mind."

The woman stared nervously at the dog. "You are going to put me to the canine truth test."

"Just once," Lizzie said, then snapped her fingers. "Balderdash!" she shouted. The dog stiffened, his wet nose trembling. "Miss Evangeline Turpin," Lizzie spoke to the braced terrier, "did not kill Albert Duey."

For a moment the dog's eyes sparkled and shot to and fro. Lizzie could clearly see the calm resolve in Miss Turpin's face. Then he let out with a tiny whine, a small stream of sound that almost erupted into a bouquet of barking, but fizzled into a sloppy tongue swipe along his whiskers.

"How do you puzzle that one out?" C.B.M. said, astonished. "That dog is endlessly fascinating."

"I am no murderer," Miss Turpin insisted. "I am shocked that you can even imply as much."

"Now I have a question for you," Lizzie announced, stroking Herr von Trotter's ears. "When you left my father's employ, did you return the keys to his store?"

Miss Turpin's eyes fluttered shut and her lips pursed as if she were about to utter a silent curse. When she opened her eyes, she explained, "I cannot but tell the truth before the dog. I never returned the keys."

"Then where are they?" Lizzie said sharply. "Last night we experienced a break-in at Borden & Almy's where no lock had been forced, no window had been broken. Your keys to the store are the only ones *not* accounted for. How do you answer for this?"

"I cannot," Miss Turpin said resignedly. "I do not even know where they are anymore. I have moved three times since leaving the firm." She glanced at Andrew, whose forehead was turning visibly pale.

Lizzie muttered, "Balderdash" in a tiny voice and the dog slumped downward. "In any event," she smiled, "you have passed the test. You are not a suspect, Miss Turpin. But I must ask you, as young as I am, I do not fail to notice that you have an erudite attitude befitting an academy girl. May I inquire where you have been schooled?"

Miss Turpin looked suspiciously at her interrogator, and then her face slackened as if flattery had melted her cheeks. "Why, I had the honor to go to the Cony Academy in Augusta. I went there for three years."

"They must have been very productive years. Concentrated study?"

"That is an understatement."

"I remember hearing from my father that you were very well versed in the classics. Did you read Horace's *Odes* in the original?"

The woman's face tightened, but she said nothing.

"Perhaps you can summon up your Latin and translate this verse for us," said Lizzie holding out the strip of vellum that had been found in the dead man's mouth. Turpin recoiled from it like it was a thing unnatural.

"How dare you?! Are you trying to trick me into confessing to this murder? I must remind you, Miss Lizzie Borden of Second Street, you translated it yourself this very afternoon with very little effort, I can imagine. It's a famous poem, indeed."

"Yes," Lizzie replied. "Famous enough to be taught in Latin class at the Cony Female Academy. You may go."

"I go because I have errands to run," said Miss Turpin. "Not because a fifteen year old girl allows me to depart." With that, she headed for the door and vanished from the room, leaving them with only a clattering of heels on the hallway marble.

"What a performance," C.B.M. said, clapping his hands together. "I do believe that only Sarah Bernhardt can outdo her in bravado. What do you make of it, Lizzie Borden?"

"I do not yet know," she said calmly.

Andrew pushed a hand to his face. "Did you hear what she said about Mr. Darling, and myself, and William! She is a liar! Dear God, did I have a murderer in my midst all those months?"

Deputy Wixon tapped his fingers on his belt. "Miss Lizzie, you accused the General Secretary of the Fall River Animal Suffrage League of murder?"

"On the contrary, Deputy Wixon, I exonerated her. And yet I can't help but wonder if she knows more than she is saying."

"Or more than she is not saying," C.B.M. added.

"I'm not so sure she is not saying what she is not saying," Lizzie concluded, staring down at Herr von Trotter, who perked up as if expecting a treat. "Very well" Lizzie said emphatically. "The next witness I would like to interrogate is Andrew Jackson Borden."

Andrew stepped back, fish-mouthed as if he were trying hard to find the air. "Lizzie," he said, "you cannot be serious."

"Very," she said, pointing at the chair. "Sit!"

Chapter 8

A Summer's Fancy

Andrew Borden sat opposite his daughter, the hairy and panting face of the canine floating between them. He lowered his head, half in shadow, as his white fingers clutched his knees nervously. Why only a few years past he had played hide-and-go-seek with her amongst the pear trees, with this trusting and dutiful daughter. Now she sat as his judge, shaming him before his own partner and men he had met no more than an hour past. His youngest daughter, once so devoted, now held a sword of Damocles over his skull.

Lizzie was not without her own conflicts. This man who once stood so tall above her, whose solitary presence signified comfort and protection, was now humbled and afraid to catch her eye. Lizzie considered her options, the extent and flavor of her interrogation, whether to hit him hard, play the tactics she had learned so well as a detective, embarrass him in front of Mr. Almy, force him to lower his pride before his own daughter, or to play soft, allowing him the chance to confess.

Confess? She asked herself. Did she dare believe the unthinkable?

"Why do you plunge me into an ordeal?" Andrew pleaded. "I feel the fool, I do."

"Father," she implored, "trust my instincts and no harm will come to you."

"No harm? You are interrogating me about a murder committed in my own shop. I should be beyond reproach."

"There are unanswered questions," Lizzie said exhaustedly. "Please, you are making this harder for me."

Andrew almost laughed. "I am not sitting here for your sense of comfort. Stop this crazed delusion that you are some sort of detective. We have a watchman in our midst who can conduct this investigation properly."

"Deputy sheriff," Wixon corrected him.

"He is a professional," Andrew added. "You are but a child, and play this game irresponsibly!"

"You have never encouraged my ambitions," Lizzie said sharply. "I find a good deal of pleasure and challenge in being a detective. I'd like to think that whatever occupation I pursue in my mature years will be more engaging than running a dress shop or preparing meals for a stuffy husband every night. I will make of my life as I wish."

"You have a lot to learn about the ways of the world," Andrew countered. "You did not have to work your way up from nothing, like I had to. You have had half the game handed to you even as you leapt into life. Go out there," he said waving a hand towards the window and the crowded street beyond. "See how far you can get on your wits alone."

Lizzie looked down, embarrassed. "I'm sorry to presume too much about your difficult start in life. But I do stand firm in my declaration that I will find my niche in this world, even if my name has to forever be associated with crime or murder. I declare this as I stand!"

"What?" Andrew said, half-rising from his chair. "Eh! What?"

"Now, Andrew," Mr. Almy said calmingly. "You need not be upset. Miss Lizzie is doing our city a good turn today. I say you respect her instincts and stand in witness before her."

Andrew grumbled, shuffling in his seat, and after much fidgeting, lifted his face to hers. "Proceed as you will," he conceded.

"Now," Lizzie began. "I must ask you precisely when Miss Turpin came into your employ."

Andrew froze, his hands clenching in his lap.

"You must answer the question, Andrew," Mr. Almy cautioned.

His partner grunted, then rubbed his jaw bristle, conjuring up memories. "Yes…well, she came to me July of three years past, for the summer cabinet sale, as you recall. It was a mere sales strategy. She struck me as…well, handsome, if you take my meaning. I thought that clients would spend more than a few customary moments looking at the furniture on display if they had a pretty and congenial face to present it to them. Yes, perhaps that was an inferior idea, and perhaps I should have protected her virtue more than I did. But there you have it, nothing less and nothing more."

Lizzie leaned forward. "Did Mr. Darling treat her in ways that compromised her virtue?"

Andrew's brow turned stormy. "If such was the case, I certainly knew nothing of it."

"I knew of it," Mr. Almy said gloomily. "I took Miss Turpin's accusations with dead seriousness, so I had words with Mr. Darling."

"And the situation was resolved," Lizzie said, "by firing the woman upon whom the outrage had been performed?"

"Now see here, Lizzie!" Andrew roared. "You would have acted in the same manner if you were in my position. Darling is a loyal employee who had lasted with me for nigh on a decade. He helped grow this concern from its humble origins, and has labored dearly, and sacrificed much. He was the more skilled and experienced, and Turpin was green and didn't even know the business, nor could she do any woodwork. I'm sure Mr. Almy considered Mr. Darling's position carefully and—"

"I do not care to see things from your position, or Darling's position, or Mr. Almy's position. I am talking here about Miss Turpin's position."

"Ouch," C.B.M. smiled. "That is a thunderbolt, indeed. What say you, Andrew?"

"Miss Turpin was not fired," Andrew strained through his teeth. "She resigned."

Mr. Almy shouted, "Andrew, you cannot be serious."

"No, I am perfectly truthful. She did quit, but not without provocation. And not due to Darling's prurience."

"This you must explain," Lizzie insisted.

"It was a mere passing fancy of mine," Andrew began. "And one you cannot tell Mrs. Borden about. I did take a fancy to her. Perhaps it was her pretty forehead. Yes, that was it. I fancied the curve of her forehead. It was very…relaxed. And one day I commented upon it. She was very forthcoming with me, telling me how the compliment about her forehead was an oasis of gentlemanly civility after the most ferocious assaults on her dignity by one she called a 'feather bed drummer' whom I now realize must have been Darling. I sensed danger approaching, for we had moved slightly together, closer than we had ever been before. Her fingers lifted themselves to my jacket buttons and began to touch them."

"Sporting old boy!" C.B.M. raised a fist.

"No, Charles. This is not something to boast upon. It was a moment of titanic shame. I went home that night all in a muddle. Perhaps Lizzie you remember that evening, when you wanted me to sit with you and help you read that Latin primer. I snarled at you, telling you that I could not abide Latin and knew not a word of it."

"I remember," Lizzie replied.

"In that book we read one bit of Latin verse: the *Memento Mori*. I shuddered when I thought of its conceit, and I was determined to remind Miss Turpin that all fleshy desires are but mere folly when placed on the mighty scales of Life and Death. Perhaps if she saw me as a mere mortal who would vanish into dust at the end of my allotted span, she could not possibly see me as an object of affection. Yes, I needed to place distance between her and myself."

"So you copied the poem from my book," Lizzie said flatly.

"Yes, I snatched the book from your room and copied the verse. I used a prime piece of vellum I did, the very one that is before you now. In the morning, I left it at her station and retired to my office. By the time I emerged, she had told Mr. Almy that she must leave her position and never talk to me again. I did not see her or the vellum with the Latin verse until this very morning when they both came back into my life quite unexpectedly."

"Andrew," Mr. Almy said. "You have resolved a mystery that has long plagued me. Miss Turpin threatened to call the police that very morning and turn Mr. Darling in for a morbid assault on her dignity. She claimed he had sent her a poem about Death and that she could not stand in the same parlor as him for one more moment."

"She knew the poem was mine," Andrew said sadly. "Her affections for me encouraged her to point a finger of guilt at another man."

"Father," Lizzie said. "What you tell me is most grievous, but you must tell me: why do you confess this now? Why so freely? And do you realize that you have cast suspicion upon yourself?"

He bolted upwards, his congress boots squeaking upon the floorboard. "Cast suspicion on me? I gave Miss Turpin the poem during that summer fancy, and I have not seen it again until today!"

Mr. Almy placed a palm on his friend's shoulder. "Andrew, you have nothing to fear. I did witness Miss Turpin holding the vellum that summer. She walked off with it. And no doubt she walked off with the keys as well. I don't recall her returning them."

"No!" Andrew's face lengthened. "She did not return the keys."

"And you who are so careful with your keys," Lizzie said. "I think not."

"I will not sit here and be accused of murder by my own daughter! Miss Turpin had possession of the poem! She had the keys to the basement! Daughter, can you not see reason? What possible motive could I have had to kill a stranger and place his body in my own basement?"

"None that I can think of," Lizzie said, stretching out her hands to calm him. "And I cannot imagine Miss Turpin's motives either. No, I don't think she committed this crime. It is the same with the clothing of Albert Duey. Why would a murderer implicate himself so blatantly?"

"You think that the killer tried to cast suspicion upon Miss Turpin as well?" Deputy Wixon asked breathlessly.

"Perhaps," Lizzie said, stroking her chin. "I do encourage everyone here to keep silent on what we have just learned. It seems as if the killer has tried to implicate more than one of us." She peered at Herr von Trotter, who raised his panting face towards hers. "More than one of us," she repeated. After a museful pause, she patted the dog and sighed.

"Are you done with me?" Andrew asked sadly.

"No, Father," Lizzie replied. "I have one last question, and one which I encourage you to answer truthfully."

He peered at her with caution, and then muttered slowly, "Activate the dog."

"Balderdash!" Lizzie shouted, and Herr von Trotter snapped to attention, his jaw quivering, his whiskers radiating outward like tiny wires. After a bated breath, Lizzie asked, "Andrew Jackson Borden, were you in love with Miss Evangeline Turpin?"

"No," he said briskly and confidently. "It was a passing fancy, soon turned sour and riddled with guilt."

Lizzie glanced down at the dog, who stood braced and unmoving. As much as she was muddled about the dog's responses, the canine silence began to purge her anxiety. She asked, "Who had commissioned the second coffin?"

"What?" Andrew asked, confused.

"What?!" Mr. Almy echoed. "The second coffin?"

"Yes," Lizzie insisted. "Mr. Jimmy Pell commissioned the first, the one in which the body of Professor Albert Duey made its dramatic appearance. But the second coffin, so like in appearance, exactly the same proportions, the same wood, the same latched cover. Who had commissioned that one, and where was it to be delivered?"

A dark hush came over the room. Andrew's face grew deeper with confusion as he searched his memory. "My God," he said plainly. "How could I not have seen this at the time?"

Lizzie reached out her hands as if attempting to retrieve an invisible object from her father. "Tell me," she said. "Who?"

Andrew stared her straight in the face. "Opportunity Borden."

C.B.M. let out a bray of laughter. "My mother?! What are you saying?"

"Yes," Andrew confirmed, his jaw jutting. "Your mother ordered the second coffin! I took the order myself, delivered by telegram from her fortress on the Hill."

"You didn't speak to her yourself?" C.B.M. pressed. "You didn't see her, or hear her voice?"

"No," Andrew said. "I didn't think of it at the time, but her husband, your father, has been dead for ten years. Has there been another death in the family?"

"Not likely," C.B.M. said incredulously. "My, do I have a bone to pick when I get home. My mother? Ordering a coffin behind my back!"

"I would not think it was her," Lizzie interrupted. "We are dealing with a killer who has implicated all of us. I have no doubt Jimmy Pell is also an assumed name, some form of prank that has been played. Either way, C.B.M., can you arrange for me to talk to your mother, just to set the story straight?"

"I can do that," C.B.M. chuckled. "But I don't think you will get much sense out of her. She is not quite in her right mind these days."

"Nonetheless, I need to talk to her. If you cannot bring her here, let me go to your home, perhaps for dinner if you can arrange that. We can take a short break, so arrangements can be made. Afterwards, we will talk to Manchester Root and learn what he knows about the Minuscule Monk."

She looked over at her father, who was grasping his beard with both hands, his eyes staring intently into the half-light of the office. Clapping her hands gently in the direction of the dog, she pronounced, "Balderdash!" after which Herr von Trotter sagged and his eyes turned listless. "Father," Lizzie announced, "we are now done."

Andrew let out an uncomfortable groan and tottered as he headed for the door. "What a fool I have been," he said under his breath, as Lizzie considered the damage she had just inflicted.

Chapter 9

The Petulant Root

The Canine was far from content. It was impossible for him to feel the degree of safety that could be labeled contentment.

All the Canine knew was that the Curious Girl needed him, and that she was more truthful than any in the room. Nothing they did improved his opinion of their species, but the Girl was different. There was an integrity and a caution in her that he had not experienced before, not even in the Fat One. She was different.

The Box Builders were slippery, confined to their self-concerns. One had just been pummeled by the Curious Girl and he appeared to be weeping as if betrayed, but it was his own fault. All the Curious Girl had done was expose the lies on her own.

The Belted Man was muddled and hard to read, but ultimately just as prone to shiftiness as any other of his species. Everything he spoke was uncertain, and the Canine hated him for it. The Canine preferred confidence, self-purpose. He did not suffer ditherers gladly.

The Tapping Woman was deceitful in her very intentions. This was a subtlety that few of the Master species understood: to lie with your body motions, with your stolen gazes, with the manner of your speech rather than the actual words. This Woman excelled at the practice and could teach all other of her kind many subtler ways to lie.

The Mannered Boy was arrogant, even lustful. The Canine saw clearly how he would take in the sight of the Curious Girl, how his face would leer and prepare itself for violence. The Canine knew this from his previous Master, the one with the whip. They all were quick to pat, to feed him hard-tack biscuits as rewards for some inane task, to take him for walks long enough for him to void his bowels, but in the end they knew they were Masters and their compassion was limited to his obedience to their will. None of his own deeper needs would ever be considered, like his need for a mate, to see his species continue in smaller versions of himself. Yes, that would be sublime, but the Mannered Boy would never consider it. Neither would the others.

The Fat One, who was now entering the room, was the worst of all. He lied not just in his words and not just in his intentions, but in his very existence. This was the hardest to test, since it took all of the Canine's instincts to sense beyond the comfort and attention he was given. There was a whole building devoted to him and he was paraded before all those who lied, asked to express his contempt for all the dishonesty and balderdash they dished out. It was mostly their rallies, when they spoke to huge crowds, where his patience came to an end. His barking would be so continuous, he would pass out from the strain and sleep in his shelter for days before allowing himself to be brought before another liar. At those rallies, even the women and children in the crowds were lying, by their very attendance.

He was afraid of what he would do if he got his fangs in any of them. He remembered the Red Bird who not only suffered gladly the lies of the humans, but repeated them back without comment, without censure. For that sin, he had to die. He did not taste good, but such was the price one paid for truth.

Yes, the Curious Girl was different. She cared. She too felt contempt for the lies, not out of any self-interest, but from the desire to make the world a better place, to stop the bad men with the whips, the dishonest chiefs with their false tongues.

Manchester Root entered the room with the gravity of a mountain, his mouth pursed and swollen cheeks tinged with red. He spied the terrier who posed attentively on the desk before Lizzie and answered its stare with a petulant scowl.

"Et tu, Hugo?" he whispered, then sighed. "Now you sit at the hand of a new master, ready to turn your truth-telling magic against me. Am I not the Manchester Root who salvaged you from the scourges of an ill-tempered owner? I cannot expect you now to lie, nor should you, since I will speak truth. But I ask you, indeed implore you, my dear Hugo whom I have known since you were but a raggedy scruff, go gentle with my fortunes. Yes, indeed, go gentle."

The dog's tongue extended as if commenting upon Root's pleas; then it swiped upwards against its wet nostrils.

"Forget the animal," Deputy Wixon cautioned. "Heed the detective."

"Yes, Mr. Root," Lizzie said. "I urge you to tell the truth, minding Herr von Trotter's abilities." She laid gentle fingers between the dog's erect ears, and said quite liltingly, "Balderdash, Hugo."

As Herr von Trotter's stance tightened and turned just a fraction more menacing, Root lowered himself into the gilded chair, which groaned under his weight. He raised his cane before him as a balancing point for his closed hands and said, "Do your worst. I have nothing to hide."

"Did you know Jack Pratt before today?" Lizzie began.

"If you mean the carpenter at the Academy Building, yes," retorted Root. Upon his answer, the dog began to casually lick one of his paws.

"In what capacity?"

"I hired him for various tasks at the League, none the least of which was the immortalizing of the previous mascot. He also helped with carpentry and painting. At times I took him on as a night janitor."

"And what was your impression of him during that time?"

"He was an odd sort, always concerned about the comfort of the animals, even when they were dead. He felt they had sensation after death, and his immortalizing was designed to make them as comfortable as possible in their journey through the afterlife."

"He believes that the dead have sensation?"

"Yes, I argued science with the man, but his beliefs were firm. I cannot judge him since the outcome of the belief, as misleading as it may be, is at the very least charitable. There are times I envied his certitude; would that my hopes for the hereafter be so optimistic."

"And what are your beliefs on the subject?"

His face sagged as he carefully constructed his answer. "I cannot put much faith in either mystical fancy or spiritual yearning. Alas, to Manchester Root, life is a short span of vapidity palliated solely by the charitable but ultimately futile deeds of a wretched few."

The dog stopped his grooming and stared up at his employer, his ears once more alert, his eyes twinkling. Root spoke softly, "I cannot speak for canine beliefs, but for their sake, I hope that animals share our one dismal chance at some meaning in life."

For a fleeting moment, Root could discern something resembling empathy in the dog's watering eyes. Perhaps he was only imagining it, but Herr Hugo von Trotter seemed to be crying at his words. The animal's dark pupils were inscrutable, yet hinted at self-pity. Root quickly withdrew his gaze. The sensation had disturbed him.

"Did you help Jack Pratt kill Albert Duey?" Lizzie blurted.

"I most certainly did not murder anyone!" Root said, his feet pressing harder against the floor boards. "I am outraged at the suggestion!"

"Please be calm, Mr. Root," Lizzie smiled. "As you can see from Herr von Trotter's contented panting he certainly cannot object to your answer, and so far I have little reason to doubt his instincts. But I must ask you: Did you have anything to gain from Albert Duey's death?"

"No! The idea is preposterous."

"Would you have anything to gain from his being alive?"

"What?"

"It is a simple question. Would you benefit from Duey being alive?"

"The answer must remain the same, since dead or alive, Albert Duey owes me nothing."

A sharp barking came from Herr von Trotter, and Root eyed him with a fearful shudder. "I suppose," he said, "you will take that as a lie. But I stand firm: I do not benefit one jot, not one tittle, from Duey being alive or dead."

The dog continued his barking, its ferocity increasing to the point where each snap lifted his body off the desk. Lizzie placed a calming hand on him, and he settled down to an angry growl.

"So you do benefit from Albert Duey being dead?" Lizzie continued.

"No, I do not!" Root roared, and the dog fell silent. The disappearance of the sharp barking created an eerie stillness. "See, there is your answer."

"But you did not benefit from him being alive," Lizzie continued.

"You are boxing me in," Root complained, slapping his thigh. "No! The answer is no!" And once more the dog started barking. "Balderdash!" shouted Root, and the dog fell silent. "That must be the end of the ordeal. There are too many insufferable questions and too many inane answers. None of this will ever stand up in a court of law."

"I find no answer inane" Lizzie said. "I merely ascertained that you had every reason to benefit from Albert Duey being alive."

"But it is a point that will be fruitless to pursue," Root said, twisting his monocle, "since the man is most decidedly dead."

"Did you see the body?" Lizzie asked quickly.

"No, I did not. But I have heard it described. The killer stole Jack Pratt's work clothes, attempting to deceive those who discovered the body. Perhaps the killer wanted us to believe that the dead man was Pratt? But Pratt still walks, he breathes, he hammers nails into floor planks. It would take an immense fool to believe him dead."

"A fool indeed," Lizzie agreed. "So why do you think the dead man was dressed in Pratt's clothing?"

"Again, these are questions I cannot answer. I'd sooner ask them of Herr Hugo here and expect him to speak in plain English. It is pointless. The fact remains that Duey is dead, and Jack Pratt walks amongst us. So our hope is to prove that he committed the crime, is it not?"

"A hard detail, I'd say, if there is no body to prove there was even a murder," C.B.M. said.

"Of course there was a murder," Root bellowed. "You all saw the body! Why do you doubt your own senses?" He glanced sneeringly at C.B.M. "Well, him I would understand, but the rest of you are wallowing in dead-end reasoning. I do not see the point of this interrogation. Do you openly accuse me of being part of this?"

"Yes," Lizzie said. "I'm afraid that you are suspected."

Root blinked. "I see. Well, activate that canine again and I will exonerate myself. Ask me direct questions."

Lizzie smiled, "Are you sure that you want direct interrogation?"

"Without doubt! As direct as an arrow! Turn your worst upon me! Balderdash!"

The dog perked up, staring eagerly at him. Lizzie said to Root calmly, "I ask you one more time: do you wish a direct examination, straight questions, no beating about the bush?"

"Yes!" said Root, a finger thrusting into the air.

"Fine," said Lizzie. "What do you know about the Minuscule Monk?"

His hand dropped and his face darkened. After a moment, he lifted his heavy chin. "What do you think I know about the Minuscule Monk?"

"Everything, I believe."

"I know he was born, he performed wicked deeds, and then was shot dead."

"Then why did you put up the financing to have the wax statue made? And why did Jack Pratt take it from your office to hide it in the stage trap? What we need to know now, Mr. Root, is exactly who Albert Duey was and why he came to Fall River, for I believe that you know all the answers."

Manchester Root's head lowered. His monocle seemed to twist on its own. He was losing weight before their eyes.

"A palpable hit!" C.B.M. roared, clapping his hands.

"You have me," Root muttered, watching Herr von Trotter's jowls tremble. "By the Prophet's Beard, you have me."

"I thought you to be a religious skeptic, Mr. Root," Lizzie said. "Why change your tune now?"

"I meant a metaphorical prophet. Balderdash!" he roared, then explained, "Spare me the indignity of Hugo's judgment. I will confess all in truth."

Lizzie nodded in agreement. "I could bring you back in time to the moment at the Academy when you and Pratt had a little exchange, a simple banter pregnant with subtle signals that only an observant ear could detect. I could walk you through the reasoning within my head, the manner in which I deduced the nature of the relationship between you, Mr. Pratt, and the effigy within that child's coffin. I could do that."

"Then why don't you?" said Root with a dispirited exhalation.

"For I gambled to hear you in judgment before the dog," Lizzie explained as Herr von Trotter bent over to bite at a flea in his pelt.

"I did not kill Albert Duey," Root replied. "Despite what you are about to hear!"

"Perhaps we should be the judge of that, Mr. Root," Deputy Wixon said.

Lizzie folded her hands contentedly in her lap as if she had all the time that the day would allow. "Please Mr. Root: we are waiting."

"I must pause first to collect myself," he groaned. "Perhaps after an intermission, for charity's sake?"

"No," Lizzie insisted. "Here and now upon this very hour, all present will hear a tale that you are holding inside of you like a boatload of unconfessed sins. Now, we will hear the untold history of the Minuscule Monk."

After a minute of desperate breathing, Manchester Root gave his monocle one last twist, cleared his throat and began his tale.

Chapter 10

The Wager

Herbert Augustus Beauchamp Caleb Dray Eff was born in mid-summer 1848. His nativity cradle was a sawed-off barrel inside a crime-ridden ruin known as the Old Brewery in New York City's Five Points, a notorious slum. The derelict building, once a place of employment for half the neighborhood, had in its abandoned state become a breeding ground for criminals and a shelter for hordes of homeless immigrants. Some of the children who were born there didn't see life beyond its walls until they were old enough to fight in the street gangs that dominated the life of their community. Into those long corridors of poverty and murder came the small boy whose body was "shorter than his name" as his father, an unemployed beef butcher, ambiguously announced upon Herbert's arrival in the world.

It happened to be true. If you wrote out the boy's full nomenclature on a strip of paper and laid it like a rule from the boy's toes towards his top, you would run out of boy while you still had a few names left. He was the tiniest creature anyone in the Old Brewery had ever witnessed, so much so that the administrating midwife went back to check that some of him hadn't gotten stuck inside his mother.

"At least most of him is alphabetized," his father proclaimed after getting drunk and before getting knifed to death. Any chance the boy had of learning the trade of beef butchering and hence a respectable life came to a truncated end in a bloody back alley not far from the Brewery. But Herbert had received a lasting legacy from the father who had failed him in every other respect: most of him was alphabetized.

His mother lingered on another year before the violence of the street took her as well. Herbert was left alone in a home (really a corridor of the brewery centered around a warming fire and a pit of garbage) populated by half-men, half-wolves (they howled at night to dissuade assailants from other gangs) who had dubbed themselves the Beaver Tops and who, needless to say, did not exercise any quality parenting skills in raising poor orphaned Herbert. There were a few women in the gang, but they hardly shared the finer attributes of their sex, and were far more proficient at garroting a victim in a dark alley than changing a diaper.

The years passed and the boy had not grown significantly closer to any ceiling, and a fear took hold that the boy might not be able to defend himself if he ever left the Beaver Top corridor. He was subjected to a regimen of training: how to cut a throat with a single blade attack, how to strangle a man with rope (practiced upon cloth dummies), how to fire a six-shooter and how to run money through the streets without getting killed (such a skill required an intimate knowledge of every building, corridor and alleyway). His height made him particularly well-suited for smuggling and for climbing under fences and through holes in dilapidated walls. Trained thus, young Herbert quickly became a valuable asset to the gang. The Bowery Boys, the True Blues, the Plug Uglies, the Dead Rabbits, the Natives and the Know Nothings all envied his unique abilities and made him various recruitment offers.

When the Beaver Tops were killed to the last man in a police raid on the Brewery, the poor boy was left alone, living in an alleyway, a pitiful target for predators. He quickly swore his allegiance to Benny Browbeat the Barber, the cruel and feared leader of the Molasses Gang, a petty corps that had earned their moniker by filling hats with molasses, which was then poured over their victim's heads before knifing them in the ribs. Browbeat was the ideal patron, well-heeled, half-way book learned (he claimed to have finished *Moby Dick* but there were skeptics), connected to all the crooked politicians at Tammany Hall (when it suited his needs he boasted a Hibernian pedigree), corrupt to the gills, and as ruthless with his enemies as he was loyal to his gang members. All the sporting boys in New York City wanted to run with Benny Browbeat, for survival if nothing else.

Herbert started as a lookout and intelligence agent for Browbeat, reporting to the Leonard Street barber shop that operated below a notorious brothel. At this establishment, run by the infamous Manhattan Madam, Herbert first gained a reputation for a shyness with the ladies that hinted a deliberate celibacy. Try as they might, the brothel inmates could not entice him to the upper floors and took to calling him by the moniker that stuck for the rest of his life: the Minuscule Monk.

Even after he had attained adulthood and a maximum height of three feet and one inch, he remained unaffected by feminine allures. According to the testimony of the Manhattan Madam, a woman who scrupulously defended her clients, but otherwise was honest to a fault, the Monk was surrounded by harlots in their undressed state but practiced the unmanly indifference of a harem eunuch. It was soon rumored amongst the Molasses Gang that the Minuscule Monk was lacking certain pieces of anatomy that would otherwise have influenced his moral choices. Such a condition may also explain his inability to grow beyond a certain height.

"I wanted to make him a lieutenant," Benny Browbeat announced during a summit meeting at the barber shop. "But a man who don't pursue women-folk like a voracious rabbit is not someone I want covering my back in a gang war. I have to fathom the secrets of this little man before entrusting him with my loyalty." He paused for an uncommon time, leaving his lieutenants in a heightened state of expectation, and then muttered, seemingly to himself, "Is there no one here who can riddle out this meddlesome midget?"

Once upon a time, such an offhand comment had changed the course of the English monarchy, but the semi-illiterate sporting boys did not know their history. They did, however, catch the subtle command and pledged to their leader to hunt the Monk and settle a wager, begun in the dimness of that Leonard Street shop, as to whether the Monk was gonadically intact.

Browbeat set the initial pot at three dollars, and various gang members tossed their own coppers into the pool, raising it to ten. Within a few weeks, it had grown to an enormous sum, the exact enumeration of which was known only to Browbeat, who kept the money in his private safe. No one tipped the Monk that such a wager was on, but he did notice that when he relieved his bladder in a back alley, there were eyes floating in the niches, and when he went to his hovel to change into his nightshirt, strange whispers leaked from the darkened corridors.

After a month, the wager was rumored to be up to hundreds of American dollars. News of the extraordinary size of the pot soon spread to areas outside the Five Points, and then, it is rumored, across the river to Brooklyn where it had doubled and tripled, depending on whose account you wish to believe. Walt Whitman, who was said to have tossed in a dime or two, wrote a poem called "When the Low Boy Last in my Courtyard Sang" for the second edition of *Leaves of Grass*, but withdrew the verse for reasons unknown. This claim is dismissed by Whitman scholars as spurious and anecdotal.

Soon, murmuring had begun that all the punters were demanding satisfaction. They no longer wanted the truth about the Minuscule Monk's nether regions, they simply wanted to end the whole business and collect their money. The hardened criminals of New York were driven to nervous distraction, needing a resolution to the mystery more than they needed the money in the barber shop's pot. There was talk of flat-out murder. If espionage wouldn't settle the wager, then a stiletto or a derringer might do the trick.

After a time, the Monk couldn't get to sleep at nights because there were always greedy folks about who would slit his throat just to get a look down his britches. He took to slinging his guns to protect himself wherever he went and grew gargantuan moustaches to obscure his identity, although he was incapable of growing a few inches in the vertical dimension to complete the disguise. Rather than hide in some hole, or escape to the wilds of New Jersey where outlaws could disappear into the backwater trails of the Pine Barrens, he stayed in the Five Points, living openly in a small hovel above a tar and leather shop, and eating *al fresco* at the fruit carts and sausage counters. The Monk thereby enjoyed a brief season of normal living, the last in his natural life.

During the second day of the Draft Riots, the streets of New York were filled with chaos and murder. The Molasses Gang felt that they had done their fair share of protecting the Monk through all the violent years, and that they had the moral and even legal right (by gang standards) to hang the Monk from a lamppost, cut away his dungarees to settle the bet and collect the money that had been accumulating. Everyone knew this, and the Monk knew it too, and the Monk knew that in such an assault not a soul would stand by his side.

As the riots plunged the city into chaos, two of Browbeat's stooges found the Monk hiding from the killing mobs in a fish barrel on Mulberry Street. Gabe the Rube and Whiney Willy proceeded to string up the small man from a lamppost with a convenient length of hemp. He cursed and bargained, even suggested to them that they spare his dignity, if not his life, and simply rob the barber shop pot of the money. They grinned at him and hurled the hanging rope skywards.

"Personally," sneered Gabe the Rube, "I'm on the side of the opinion that you are lacking in your privates. And if I turn out to be wrong, well, let's just say I'm happy glad that I brought along my bucking knife!"

This was all the Monk had to hear. He darted forward and dived between Gabe's legs, then tripped up Whiney Willy's boot heels and knocked both to the ground. The two sporting boys were now in a twee. Mere seconds earlier they had cornered the Monk and even had a noose around his neck. Now they had been pinned down and rendered helpless, steel death flashing in their faces. Even if they had managed to escape with their lives, their street credibility had been wounded to the core. The Monk showed them mercy, however, and tied them up using some extra rope from a nearby donkey cart whose operator had abandoned his cargo to escape the riots. The Monk anointed the stooges' heads with some vile commentary that the donkey had unceremoniously dumped upon the ground, a mocking reference to their molasses assaults, and then gave them a message for their gang boss.

"You tell Benny," he said pressing the tip of his blade into Gabe's temple, "that he should keep that wager going in his barber shop. In fact, he should sell shares of it across the country, extend the gamble to all who walk in crooked and evil ways. Let the price on my head be as tall as a mountain for all I care. I'll keep my one never-sleeping eye upon the door, ever ready for the assault. I'll wait for his boys and give them the same treatment I gave you after you had me stand there on that hanging barrel. And tell Benny that he's a girlie-bird if ever I saw one, and he'll never keep my wits in a twee for I fear nothing about him. You tell Benny this and make sure he increases that punter's pot! I'll even toss in a copper for charm's sake! Do you gobble-gobble me, my skenchback?!"

"You insane little monster," Gabe gasped. "You go racing, Minuscule Monk, like the coward you are! Get to scramming! If there's anything we want now, it's a cross-country midget chase!"

The Monk growled, ferocity erupting in his volcanic eyes. With all the impotent hurt that had festered inside him for years, he slashed Gabe across the face, severing one eye and taking out part of his nose. Then he vamoosed, disappearing across Paradise Square into the haunted streets of Five Points. Gabe the Rube, who shrieked and howled until his ululations had brought lawmen and a medic to the alley, from that day hence was known as Gobble-Eyed Gabe, and swore upon a Roman Catholic Bible (he converted to the Faith solely for the purpose of taking the oath—the best investment in his life, he called it) that he would mutilate the Minuscule Monk with his bucking knife before he, himself, pulled the blanket of eternity over the midget's head.

Upon the successful and popular printing of a newspaper account of the alley fight (an event that eclipsed the draft riots themselves in the eyes of some New York newsmongers), the Monk then passed from what is ordinarily perceived as the semblance of a common man, one you can meet face-to-face and engage in neighborly discourse, into the realm of legend where a flesh-and-blood encounter seemed unimaginable. Over the next decade, the Monk's criminal legend—and the pot of money in the Leonard Street barber shop—grew and grew.

Benny Browbeat, infuriated upon hearing that his two most violent and deadly henchmen, each of whom stood a good two heads taller than the Monk, had been so beaten and mauled even after wrapping their hanging rope around their bounty's neck, declared Gobble-Eyed Gabe and Whiney Willie infamous rodents, tied them up to barber chairs and threatened them with extinction if they did not pledge their lives to the hunting down and destruction of the Monk.

Upon hearing of the Monk's challenge to go national with the wager, Benny subsequently posted a notice in one hundred national newspapers, as well as on leaflets distributed in villages, towns, hamlets, crossroad taverns, libraries, post offices, mining camps, horse yards, trading posts, military bivouacs, outposts, forts, feed stores, dairy farms, cattle ranches, religious monasteries, churches, grain mills, general stores, and any place in which more than one person might be gathered for any express human purpose whatsoever. He even advertised in places where there was only guaranteed to be one person, such as hermit shacks in woods and provision huts on top of remote mountains; and sometimes even in places where there was no guarantee to be humans at all, like on a post in the midst of a dusty wilderness where there was only a whisper of a railroad passing within miles of that very spot, in anticipation that the onrush of farmers, homesteaders, land speculators, frontier women, and their literate children who would follow the railroad might contemplate the wager's harvest and seek to reap its benefits. In the end, Benny even had the wager posted in graveyards, covering his bets in both worlds, since he was open-minded to the possibility of an afterlife and the soul's ability to still read printed matter in the spiritual realm.

The wager, printed in clear type on tanned oil paper, buckled at the edges and perforated top and bottom with small nails to keep it firm against any standing post, tree or notice board that was most convenient to fix it upon, read in bold, unshrinking terms, declaring to all the known population of the North American Continent:

Oyez! Oyez! Oyez!
Be it known that Bennett Buckingham Browbeat
of Five Points, Manhattan Island
Has posted a wager questioning the anatomical state
Of one Herbert Augustus Beauchamp Caleb Dray Eff
Known hitherto as the Minuscule Monk
That a punter's pot shall be distributed to all who
Can accurately guess the condition of the Monk's
Southern Gonadic Regions
Which will determine his peculiar predilection for Abstinence
Which we the wager holder deem unnatural
If the subject be not Priest or Eunuch!

The rules of the wager are as follows:
That any one who can obtain physical proof of such
Said condition whether through tin type reproduction
Or through sketches based upon actual witnessing
Or through production of the Monk's physical body
Dead or alive
Shall receive one half of the monies collected hitherto
(summed at this time as 5,000 United States dollars,
Scoundrel Confederate Script not included)
From an undisclosed location
And the remaining portions of which shall be
Portioned out to all who wagered according to
The condition based upon the actual condition
Of his condition!

The man known as the Minuscule Monk is the only person
On this World we call the Earth that is
Excluded from being allowed to collect on the wager

Also his family!

Here are artist renditions of the Monk as portrayed by Oswald Fetch
New York Journalism's most established portrait artist

Underneath, flanked by scattered five-pointed stars depicting some constellation of patriotism as if fallen from an American flag that the Monk, presumably, had defiled, defamed, ignored or insulted, were two nearly identical portraits of the gunslinger's physiognomic likeness, the same almond-shaped head, the droopy lids, the flat cheeks and the world-weary forehead. The only difference between the two was the absence in one, and the presence in the other, of a stupefying set of facial whiskers that dominated the left-handed likeness, obliterating any view of the puckered mouth and discolored lips. To the right of both of these portraits was a crude drawing of the entire body, swathed in denim, a badly drawn caliper, larger than life, stretched into a wide angle, touching one tip to the Monk's head and one to his feet, with a few numbers plugged in for the purposes of determining his true height, indicated here as three feet and one inch. The base of the caliper seemed to be coming out of some spangled cloud, as if it were the measuring stick of Providence come to examine His own creation because He could barely believe the anomaly.

The wager sheet was indeed a masterpiece of public propaganda, designed to not only anger and thrill the citizens of the nation, but also to implant within their imaginations the Monk's unnatural and abominable nature. Benny knew well that the reduction of one's enemy to something not as human as oneself makes it far easier to commit violence, sin or even murder, against said enemy. Benny Browbeat congratulated himself upon many occasions as to the brilliance of his own proclamation and even suggested that his wager terms be submitted for some writing award amongst those folks that were wise in such craft.

Word spread like brush fire across the heated plains and gnarly mountains of the continent, and for several weeks there was only one question stuck in the breath of gunslingers, desperados, drummers, itinerant salesmen, village idiots, cowboys, ranchers, saloon proprietors, circus rubber men, bearded ladies, dime museum grinners, starvation artists, ceiling walkers, grouch bag manufacturers, unlicensed dentists, sludge shovelers, male models for orthopedic spats, defrocked priests, asylum inmates, cloth doffers, organ grinders, engine drivers and crop farmers alike: "Where is the Minuscule Monk?!"

What started as a drunken prank in a barber shop had exploded into an American phenomenon. Children in city streets jumped rope to the doggerel that described in metaphorical terms the Monk's nether properties; parlor pianos played sheet music about the Monk's exploits in New York (the most popular being *The Mighty Midget of Mulberry Street*); voracious readers devoured thirty-seven printings of the novel *The Barber And The Monk*; and preachers in houses of worship filled the ears of their congregations with morality tales centered around the Monk's sinful profession. Benny's wager had turned good American men of fine Christian upbringing into snarling ravenous bounty hunters, even sending them into gambling dens and houses of assignation, wherein they were corrupted by the temptations such establishments offer, and to which they easily succumbed once they had seen the futility of their search and the pleasures of the offerings.

Meantime, the Monk, unaware of the cultural phenomenon surrounding his bounty, was residing quite profitably in Upsidedown, Missouri, a small tent village named after the settlement's main sign, which had spun around on its nail during a windstorm, leaving folks not quite willing to bend their necks to read the proper name. Here a dirt road carnival ran its confidence tricks on the local population. The main attraction was advertised as Tornation the Terrible, a muscle man of monstrous proportions. The Minuscule Monk had acquired a running stint as Tornation's Ape, the small assistant who ran about harem-scarem like a circus clown, handing his master barbells and iron rods to bend.

The Monk was unrecognizable in his greased hair, parted in the middle, and his well-clipped moustaches, plus his red and white striped barker's suit. Little did the Missouri crowds realize that the Monk had designed his outfit after New York City barbers, an ironic salute to the profession that had put a price on his head back in Five Points.

Tornation the Terrible, whose real name is lost to history's dust, was thought to be a lumber man from the mining camps of the Dakota territories: an ugly, violent and sadistic villain escaping a past deed so terrible that were it to be printed in a town's newspaper, he would need to kill with his bare hands the entire population of the town rather than risk that periodical's dissemination.

The Monk knew this, and Tornation knew it, and Tornation knew the Monk knew it, and Tornation also knew that the Monk was escaping some past situation of his own so terrible that he would rather spend his days handing barbells to a man who would kill him in a heartbeat than lam it to a respectful town with a right-side up name and a proper legal system, an honest mayor and an elected sheriff to protect its citizenry. Hence, the two men were in a stand-off that was sustainable for the moment, but was plagued by so much tension that neither one ever went to sleep without expecting to wake up in another world, having been murdered in the night by his roommate.

One evening, during a howling dust storm that sent the entire town to the cellars for safety, Tornation got roaring drunk and started hurling the Monk around their boarding house room, aiming him like a bowling ball at a painting that hung as a useful target. When the Monk had hit the ground, he bounced up like a rubber ball and pitched forward with a sudden violence, ramming his small body directly at Tornation, driving an ice pick, previously concealed, into the man's eyes with two swift stabs. His master was so drunk that he could not put up a defense, and spent the last few moments of his life as blind as a cave bat. He roared and raged about the room, clutching his bleeding eyes with one hand, swirling the other about to catch his attacker, but the Monk, being so small, watched in amusement as the giant man's hand grasped a few feet above his head, a Cyclops in his death-throes.

"I curse you!" Tornation roared. "May your body never have peace, even after your death!" He flailed about groaning and snapping. "I see you," he declared, "dead and stuffed, and feeble-minded folk paying their dimes to laugh at your bones!"

Terrified by this prophecy, one seeming more authentic coming from a blind man, the Monk hit the stairs and ran for the edge of town just as a hell-spawned tornado touched down from the dark sky onto the boarding house, ignoring the other buildings as if targeting the strong man's rage. He looked back only once to witness the mountainous shape of Tornation the Terrible get sucked by the winds out of the second floor window, then whipped about in hawk-like circles a few dozen yards above the hard earth. The body flipped over and about like kippers in a savage griddle, then flew straight off on a tangent towards the distant hills. A split second later, the entire rooming house was shattered into splinters, which shot like thousands of bullets into the roaring black funnel. The Monk, who had never seen nature act so cruelly with a human body or any of its habitations before, grinned and reveled in the one true moment of his life when God, or the Universe, or Nature, or whatever anyone on this stinking ball of earth wanted to call it, was on his side.

"Who's laughing now?" he asked Tornation with an evil chuckle.

In the gust of his freedom, he began to run. He kept running and kept running. The sun fell and rose again, and he was still running. Then he ran until the sun fell a second time, then he collapsed in the dirt by a deserted roadside. When the sun arose he started running again, through farmers' fields, across meadows, through rocky regions and blasted cornfields, tangles of cacti, dusty dribbling streams; and when he got to rivers, he swam across them, kicking with his feet which was, in a way, a form of running. And so in the end, he ran for three days and nights.

On the afternoon of the fourth day, he was running in the wilderness, not too far from the border between Kansas and Missouri, and he could not have reached it at a more inopportune moment in history. Here stood the isolated cabins and burnt-out shells of houses that had been subjected to savage raids by Kansas jayhawkers and all the fury of the slave-free territory that dared defend the Union. The communities, or what was left of them for the Monk to run through, were as ruined and as silent as the corpses that still swung from the tree branches. The Monk, who had paid little attention to the political life of the nation (what relevance did politics have in the murderous streets of Five Points?), or the question of slavery (being enslaved to a gang boss's will was second nature to the Monk), or the battles raging against Abraham Lincoln's Federal States (the draft riots had cast New York's vote against that ridiculous parade), likewise ignored the torched homes and dead animals lying in the abandoned roads. The causes of such conflicts were invisible to him, while the carnage about him was a visceral reality. It reflected, most of all, the devastation that burned within.

Eventually, the Monk's lungs gave out, refusing to pump a single bellows more, and the small exile collapsed like a dead man. There, in the dust, under the heat of the mid-day Missouri sky, the Monk lay in his striped barber suit, barely thinking; and what little thought coursed through his mind was bent on self-destruction. Taking one last look at the indifferent sun, he reckoned, "I'll just bake to death if I lie here still enough. In fact, I want that on my tombstone: 'Here lies the Monk, who got killed by the Sun and not by any man born of woman.' That'll be my epitaph."

And so he closed his eyes, expecting not to open them again upon anything mortal or earthly. He had no premonition that all of the evil deeds and sins that would write him into the tome of history were just over the next fearful sunrise.

Chapter 11

The Burning

He awoke not from any willful act within his slumbering mind, which was baked enough, nor from the heat of the sun, which had burned for hours before he awoke, but due to a palpable presence that hovered over him, partially blocking the daylight and appearing only to his waking eyes in silhouette. As the light softened, a soured face and flaming moustaches came into view. It was a man of imposing proportions. His ragged uniform was dignified but dusty, made from patch-work that confessed participation in a furtive, perhaps illegal, war, not one fought by regular fighting men within the Union or Rebel armies, but by men who lived beyond the prescribed boundaries of civilization. They were men who lived in caves, by roadsides, within an endless series of dirty hideouts and dilapidated cabins, men who spent more time collecting grime upon their parched skin than in the act of cleaning it off, more time in the saddle hiding from the law than obeying its ordinances, and firing more bullets at hapless civilians than what one could legally call an enemy. The Monk knew this man by sight, even by scent. He could smell that outrageous and unmistakable stench that wafted off corpses whose souls had been taken by dark infamy, which emanated from men who danced under impromptu gallows erected by midnight murder mobs, and that rose from the fog of fear that billowed from an outlaw's pistol hovering quite solidly before one's eyes. Yes, this man had that stench, and the Monk knew it well.

The palpable man could only be William "Bloody Bill" Anderson, the shameless bushwhacker and rebel scout who walked a path of blood and violence, who once boasted that he had introduced more bullets into human bodies than spats of tobacco juice into spittoons, and who in all his wanderings and crazed killing sprees had never laid eyes upon a man so small as the one lying beneath him. He adjusted his eyes in the blazing sun, and then poked the lad's leather chaps with his boot.

"Why, you're like me, only shrunken!" Bloody Bill roared.

"Get your leg off me," the Monk retorted. "Or I'll bring you down to my size!"

"Stop that yapping; you don't know who you're talking to."

And the Monk, who had never reckoned much about current affairs, knew the man solely from the notoriety of his body count, recounted in the Five Points by ambitious young murderers looking for a legend to hang their future upon. "Hell I don't!" he insisted, then lifted his head from the dust. "If it isn't Bloody Bill! I recognize your death stench. Once a shootist gets that into him, there's no cleaning those stables."

Bloody Bill peered with creased eyebrows, thought for a moment, rubbed his forehead with his pistol, and then concluded, "You're the dankest and meanest low boy I've ever seen! Give me one of those mitts and I'll get you back on your heels."

And so the bushwhacking murderer lifted up the wounded vagrant in the striped carnival jacket and dusted him off and put him on a pony and took him up a Missouri road to the rebel camp where something of great import was stirring. There upwards of two hundred men were mustered, cooking their lunch in fry pans, chewing and spitting tobacco, oiling their guns and feeding their horses. They possessed all the restraint of those who travelled furtively in large numbers, talking in low murmurs so those living just outside the wood would not hear their voices. They were smelly and rumpled, coated in road dirt with blackened faces, encrusted hands, frayed coats, busted hats and rusty guns. They were varied in their dress and manner, having come from different corners of the state. Many of them had not known each other the last time the sun was in its present position in the sky, and their congregation was due to neither any conceit of entertainment nor common practical need. They were drawn to the killing lands via that indomitable ugly spirit that pervades any unquestioned ideology, a call to action that is invariably accompanied by loaded firearms and the will to use them. The Minuscule Monk, upon first eyeballing this filthy bunch, knew that they were rebels, and that their presence near the unprotected border of Kansas could only mean that by the time the sun once more reached its present position in the sky, there would be as many souls departed from this world as there were men standing in attendance in Bloody Bill's camp, mayhap more.

"Welcome to Hell," Bill announced, slapping the Monk's head, and such a welcome was never more appropriate. The bushwhackers, now noticing the newcomer, fell into silence. They put down their pans and pipes and guns and surrounded the small man, poking and pushing him to see if he was made of the same material as their own flesh. Then without any overt debate, they agreed that here was some new species of human, a strange parody of their own created being. So with a hup and a hooray they lifted him high above their shoulders and carried him about the camp, tossing him skyward in a celebratory manner.

For the Monk's unusual physical dimensions were a viable solution to a problem that the Missouri bushwhacker had in his ongoing battle with the Kansas jayhawker. The border war had begun when John Brown attacked that federal arsenal at Harper's Ferry, and, ever since, the two states had been raiding each other with increasing levels of violence. Once-calm meadows were now trampled by thundering hooves carrying mercenary men of war, killers who felt it their mission to murder anyone who opposed their chosen way of life. They raided towns, lynched men, violated women, traumatized children, and burned everything in their path. Both sides were doing it, the tide always turning, now on the side of the jayhawkers, now bent back towards the bushwhackers, the only constant being the mounting toll of bodies and burned homes. Few were able to count the number of the dead, far fewer the wounded, even fewer the number of violent surprise attacks. Most of the borderline between the two states had been reduced to charred grass, abandoned cabins, and the smoking husks of once generous estates whose only fault was to be serviced by Negro slaves, or not to be serviced by them. No man, especially one over the average height of five foot eight, could safely navigate No Man's Land, but the Minuscule Monk had that advantage. His training in the tunnels under Mulberry Street had served him well. Here were the makings of a fine bushwhack scout who could render himself invisible with nothing more than a harsh crop of saw grass.

So they sent him ahead, over the border, all by himself towards the bountiful town of Lawrence, just fifteen miles past the border, down along the Kaw River, shaded in the overhang of Mount Oread with all its Biblical allusions. Here was a town that had surpassed all other towns within the territories in civic stability and art and literature and education. These were no yokels whose daily chores kept them from the fineries of life. The men were handsome and refined; the women were nurturing and elegant, traits of which the invaders were contemptuously indifferent.

Even more unacceptable to the killers: Lawrence had invented a new way of conducting life. Here was a storefront business run exclusively off groceries, unheard of back in New York; and a large hotel in which resided statesmen and journalists who sent their dispatches back East along the telegraph to be published in big city papers. Lawrence was the Jewel of Kansas, and no bushwhacker denied it. But, in the minds of men like Bloody Bill Anderson, if it be beautiful, it must be marred; if it be elegant, it must be laid to waste; if it be proud and civilized, the citizens must be made to snarl in the streets like beasts, pleading for their lives under the governance of the Remington rifle, the knightly pike of the Bushwhacker.

By the time the sun had peeked over the edge of the earth, rising on Lawrence for the last time before it died, the Minuscule Monk had crawled back to the high ground and rejoined his rebel army. In his absence, the gang had picked up nearly two hundred more allies, including their leader, William Quantrill, the gentleman murderer who lorded it over the troops like a low-brow General Lee. The fair-haired, soft-eyed young man with the neat moustache stood dignified and steadfast next to Bloody Bill, his grimy second-in-command, and surveyed the early morning mist that floated over the city.

"Word may have gotten out," Bloody Bill suggested in a hoarse whisper. "The men are rumoring that there's a whole union army down there waiting for us."

"Those men been riding for three days and nights with hardly any sleep," Quantrill noted. "I promised them a right massacre and they'll get one. The low boy's back from scouting; he'll give us the straight."

"Not a single union gun," the Monk reported, "just townsfolk sleeping."

Quantrill nodded, then peered down at the quiet city, straining to draw in every detail he could with his naked eye. "There's Pat Hainey delivering the milk," he murmured, "and Ma Wheeler opening her barn. There's Senator Lane taking his morning stretch. And Governor Robinson contemplating his mountain as if he were about to draw down the commandments."

Bloody Bill sneered. "The governor is looking for something pious in this world, and by God, we'll reveal unto him the burning bush by dawn. Haw-haw!!"

The army moved as a unified force over the remaining mile to the same bluff from which the Monk had scouted. Down at the river's edge, reclining on the bank like a gentleman from a French painting, was a smartly dressed young man playing with a calico cat. He was blissfully unaware that just across the river, a veritable army of killers watched him with great interest. The man was child-like in appearance, and the way he grinned at the creature, it seemed to be his entire world. He was taking great pleasure in watching the feline jump up at a thin string that was being dangled from a large ball over its upturned and twitching face.

Quantrill came in close to the Monk's ear, pressed a cold rifle into his hands and said in a delicate whisper: "Give us our first kill."

"Does that man mean anything to me?" the Monk asked.

"Doesn't matter," came the reply. "His father must have jayhawked all the way to St. Louis and plundered many a Missouri home. If he had a rifle and it was pointing at you, he would not hesitate one moment to snuff out your candle. Stop your philosophizing and give him his due."

The Monk raised the weapon, steadied it over his knee, got the innocent man in his sights, and pulled his finger. He didn't think for a moment, just went through the motions like they were stage directions embedded deep enough in his mind to require no thinking for their recall. He didn't even blink when the man's body flopped backwards, dead before he hit the ground. The cat darted away, a small creature trapped in a moment that it could not comprehend, bouncing like a frantic rabbit across the level grass towards the town line.

The bushwhackers who had witnessed the spectacle let out with a spontaneous cheer, which they quickly stifled so the town across the river wouldn't hear their huzzahs. The Monk was sent down the bluff to verify the first kill of the day. He stood over the man's body and kicked thoughtlessly at the ball of string that unraveled in the dirt under his feet. Quantrill came down to counsel his newly-forged killer.

"How does it feel?" Quantrill asked the Monk.

"How does what?"

"To be a killer?"

"Doesn't feel like anything."

"Does it matter that the man had done you no harm and now the cat's got no playmate?"

"Not my problem. He's done, so I'm satisfied."

"I'm glad to hear it. Your bullet was a bloody message to a free state that we won't take any more of their jayhawking hogwash. Do you follow? Do you believe?"

"My enemy is dead. That's theology enough for me."

Quantrill smiled. "Now just hold that feeling for the next three thousand Kansans you kill, and you'll be fine. Don't let the absurdity of death get near your thoughts. And by God! No conscience! You show one shred of it and I'll take you out myself."

"Sir, yes, sir," the Minuscule Monk responded boldly, then added, "You want me to tell you what I become after killing that man?"

"I'd like to hear it, Monk."

"I'll tell you true."

And this is what the Minuscule Monk said he had become after killing the innocent man on the bluff: "I'm one nasty godless son-of-a-bitch born in a garbage can and I just shot the humanity out of me."

"Amen to that," Bloody Bill hooted. "Now let's tear down this town and get those freedom loving jayhawkers!"

And that's how the Monk lost his remaining humanity on the bloody morning that Lawrence, Kansas died.

They had raided many towns before, burned many homes, ended many lives, but those towns had been small, easily destroyed in an hour, sometimes nothing more than a traveler's inn, a general store, or an isolated farmhouse. But the city of Lawrence now spread out before them was large and regal, full of dignity and comfort, and more significantly, was civilized. The hundreds of men who roared down on horseback from out of the East like thunder had been trained by Quantrill that there was nothing more repulsive than folks who moralized about slavery and acted so highfalutin about it. Quantrill's basic teachings, his noble truths as they were known, were thus: all that was good had to be destroyed, dignity was a façade over a painful existence, and a human soul that had never known violation needed to be taught a lesson. This was the destructive ideology that had transformed Herbert Augustus Beauchamp Caleb Dray Eff from a street corner thug into his final incarnation as the Minuscule Monk. He was finally, after his baptism of gunfire, fully alphabetized.

The few citizens who were unfortunate enough to be walking about town when the riders came, those who survived at least, later claimed that Quantrill personally led the assault, and by his side was Bloody Bill, whose face they had only seen on poster drawings and had never expected to see in the flesh. But they also claimed, and it was to be another few years before the reports were confirmed, that Bloody Bill had, riding on his same mount, a tiny demon whose eyes flamed with all sorts of evil, whose twisted lip was more terrifying than the thundering hooves, the flash of the guns, and the screams of the first victims upon the ground. That tiny visage, so deathly void of any recognizable human emotion, was a fire let loose from perdition to scatter death in its path. All the rest of the men in the army were just so much window dressing for that demon.

The column of men, mounted, fierce and terrifying, carried no flag, and therefore played by no rules of civilized warfare. They fanned into separate columns that went parallel up Massachusetts Street, New Hampshire Street, and Vermont Street, covering both the fronts and rears of buildings, taking shots at anyone who tried to escape. Throughout the town came the cries of people who had woken up only moments before, who watched from their bedroom windows, all bellowing the deathly cry of "Quantrill is here! Quantrill!" Those daring enough to fire their own weapons in some pitiful hope of defense were answered with returned volleys from skilled marksmen that tore through their curtains and their bodies. Others who managed to get into the streets and to run as fast as the fear of death could propel them, did not get far before bullets took them down.

The separate columns converged before the Eldridge Hotel, firing random shots at the upper stories, hooting and roaring. A few furtive shadows appeared briefly at the windows and then faded back at the sight of the mounted militia. Presently a white sheet appeared, waving from the third floor, a concession that it would be pointless to die defending the building. There was no organized defense, no federal troops that could ride to the rescue in time. The city was doomed.

Quantrill gave a silent order with one wave of his finger, and then bushwhackers marched through the front entrance of the Eldridge, guns drawn, mouths screaming oaths and curses, and began to pillage the rooms. They smashed in doors, shot off locks, rampaged into apartments pulling frightened folks from their beds, pointing guns to heads, firing shots into ceilings, kicking open trunks, ferreting through cabinets and dresser drawers, filling their pockets with handfuls of jewelry, coins and watches. A few ascended to the roof, shot their guns and hooted at the sight of the smoke and flames that now rose from other streets. The post office, the town hall, the newspaper office, the grocery store, the livery stables, all began to burn. And all to the discordant strains of screaming victims.

It is not within the power of this narrative to itemize the atrocities of that day, although they were considerable. Indeed, they can strike terror into the heart of the reader by reminding him that men who are capable of such actions are present in any society, no matter how civilized. Such a plundering and murderous army always sees itself as doing something right and justified and never has a single thought about the human tragedy. The bushwhackers who murdered Lawrence saw themselves decidedly as heroes and nothing less.

They held the belief that life itself could not be sustained without slavery and were angered that the Kansans had the unctuous nerve to reject that belief, to even consider it an act against God. If this tale has a moral, be it thus: Shun the preacher with his hypocritical dogmas; be skeptical of the businessman with his shady investments; heed not the philosopher with his fancy lexicons. Yes, take all those precautions. But when it comes to the man who would enslave another, run my friend. Run as fast as you can for the closest border of any other country where folks don't pay such mind, and don't stop running until you get there. For the widows of Lawrence, the dead of Lawrence, the damaged and disenfranchised and orphaned and crippled of Lawrence, know full well what men are capable of doing when they are driven by such passions.

The Monk witnessed these acts. His eyes took in the bloody images. His ears heard the piteous screams. But he watched and listened with an inhuman indifference, as a mill foreman would watch his river wheel spin, caring not for the act of spinning itself, but satisfied that all was going well because the spinning has not stopped.

The Monk patrolled the back of the hotel, searching for anyone who might attempt escape, hoping to cut him down with his Colts. Behind the horse yard, a tall, thin drummer still in his nightshirt, barefoot and bare-headed, led a trio of black men dressed in the indigo cotton pants and coats of escaped slaves down the back alley and towards the safety of an unpatrolled street. It mattered little to Monk that the black men were human beings who didn't want to die, who had hearts and minds, perhaps even wives whose well-being depended upon them conquering the odds and running to a free state where they could arrange liberty for all their children. None of this mattered to the Monk, whose only thought was that no one was supposed to leave the hotel, and if they did, the act deserved the penalty of death. Dispatching these men would be as practical as a farmer plugging up a hole through which grain was escaping from his silo. Thus with a terrible and ferocious speed that could never be predicted from his truncated gait, he darted after his prey, his face blank and dark, his eyes lost in the vacant nothingness of a killer's gaze.

He tracked them through the burning streets towards the river, past the landing where a few bushwhackers were shooting at a Union flag that hung like a rag on the town's liberty pole, and finally down to the ferry landing where the men stopped to take their breath, oblivious to the presence of their predator. The Monk darted behind a stranded wagon and peered out to catch a glimpse of them. The tall thin man and the three black men huddled together, all peering back at the burning town where four hundred killers were at work ending their way of life. They engaged in quick conversation and as they talked, the Monk calculated his trajectories, gauging how he could make each of the bullets in his shooter count.

He fired when it felt right to do so. Within half a minute, all three slaves lay sprawled on the wooden planks of the landing, their lives now beyond the concerns of the mundane world, and their leader, the white man, stood shivering before the Monk, who had emerged from his concealment.

"You killed them," the man said, his voice saturated with hate.

"That I did," the Monk said. "And I got two more silvers in this here rusty, so you'd best stand still and let it all happen."

"You're going to do it," the man shouted. "Just like that? I've never done a thing to you, never met you before in my life. And you'll kill me for some damn principle that won't mean a blasted thing once this war is over."

"Not the principle," the Monk said. "Just something I got to do."

"Why don't you find something else to do?"

"Can't do anything else. I tried to find other business but it eluded me. This is my business now."

"So the whole town burns, and women and children will die, so you can be what you need to be."

"You called it," the Monk said. "But I want to know your name before I take it away from you."

"Albert Duey," replied the man. "And I suppose it isn't too soon for me to join the choir. I saved the lives of hundreds already, mostly the same color as these gentlemen you just murdered. When the accounts are all reckoned, I'll do all right. Here's my breast, take your best."

"Gobble-gobble!" the Monk clucked and fired, and the man fell down.

After the shot, the Monk spent no more than a second ascertaining the palpability of his hit, and then fled back towards Lawrence to do more killing. From that moment on, for the rest of his life, right up until he took a bullet during his last game of Faro in Black Bone, Dakota Territory eight years later, he would never spend a single second of his existence thinking about Albert Duey.

And the Monk didn't just forget his victim's name, but also what he had said before he died, despite its eloquence and truthfulness, despite the humanity and the profundity of it, despite the fact that they were the last words of a dying man who deserved at least that much respect. They had made absolutely no impression whatsoever on the Minuscule Monk, who had listened to the words, then pushed them from his ears. He walked away from the his victim as blankly as he would after swatting a fly. He had more souls to dispatch in the bleeding streets of Kansas.

Chapter Twelve

The Hunting

But Albert Duey was not dead, or else he would not have been capable of assassinating the Monk in that Faro game in Black Bone eight years later, and it certainly would not have been possible for him to turn up as a corpse in Fall River several years after that. Defying the advanced laws of probability, he survived the single bullet that the Minuscule Monk had fired into his chest. It had glided past all the critical internal organs, damaging only certain pieces that could afford to be damaged, and exited from his back in a way that left no bullet to fester within his torso. When he awoke, his head was splitting with pain and his chest felt as if it had been mauled by a bear, but he was still capable of moving his limbs and blinking his eyes and his brain still entertained coherent thoughts. Few men shot in the chest by a savage killer could boast as much.

Duey looked about to see that the things that had been in the world, like rocks and trees and the sun in the sky, were all back in their rightful place, just where they had been before he left. By poking his torso with his fingers, he determined that he had been shot and it would behoove him to get to some sort of surgeon before he bled to death. With such a conviction in mind, he crawled on his belly back towards town, painfully and slowly, for over an hour, until he reached a lonesome house where a fellow Kansan was hiding from the bushwhackers. By that hour, the massacre was over, but from the man's back porch, they could see the smoke pillars rising from the ruined city.

"Lawrence is murdered," the man said with solemnity.

The man, who introduced himself as Jimmy Pell, explained that he had been a doctor at the First Battle of Bull Run, had in fact deserted the Union Army and fled to Kansas where he figured the fighting wouldn't reach him ("Dangdest nonsense I ever let into my head!" he commented in retrospect). He was a good man, not a demon like the Monk or Quantrill or any of that killing bunch, and set about inspecting Duey's wounds, then cleaned and dressed them, promising all the while that when the carnage was over, Pell would go to town and poke about the ruins looking for anyone who was a certified surgeon and who wasn't dead. Anyone who fell short of those two qualifications would be summarily dismissed.

"Who were they?" Duey asked, staring at the smoke.

"'Quantrill'", I heard them screaming. "'Quantrill is coming', they screamed. "And he must have had that mad dog Anderson by his side."

"Didn't Quantrill used to be the school teacher here?"

Pell sighed. "You get Quantrill by himself and you'd be seduced by his smile. He'll have you convinced you can trust him to hold your new born baby over a cliff. But then that façade falls fast, and monsters like Anderson come out from behind him to back up his currency."

"Is this Quantrill knee-high to a buckboard's wheel?"

"No, that skunk who shot you wasn't the Captain. But I never heard of a midget bushwhacker."

"Wasn't no bushwhacker," Duey said. "It was a demon."

"You'd best explain that business," Pell said.

"Imagine that the ground opens, and after some fumes and fire belch forth, this creature with a face like a shrunken head with eyes lacking in anything recognizably human emerges and fires a gun straight at you. Then you go dark and wake up hours later and the whole town you've been living in for the past three years is burned to the ground. So don't run on about Quantrill and Bill Anderson because I didn't see any of that action. All I know is that a demon came to Lawrence, and with one look from his greasy face, the whole town is murdered."

"Well, whether it was Quantrill or a demon doesn't make much difference now. A lot of folk who were sitting down to supper at this time yesterday are now ready to be buried."

"Then let's go bury them!" Duey struggled to his feet and stumbled towards the door, against the protests of his amateur surgeon. They headed out, guided by the pillars of smoke and fire that burst upwards, merging together into a canopy that obliterated the sky. Everywhere houses and buildings were aflame, and even in the homes in which the fires had danced out, hot coals still burned in the cellars, casting strange lights against the smoke, turning basements that had been exposed to the open air into fiery furnaces. All about were the screams and lamentations of the living and the half-living, all stumbling like shadows in the mist, searching for their loved ones in the rubble and the collapsed walls of what were once their homes. Many stood stunned in the streets, unable to recognize each other, gaped-mouthed and vacant-eyed as if the atrocity had not yet imprinted itself on their minds.

On every street, the bodies had been laid, many unclaimed, many unrecognizable after being pulled from their burning homes. A small coterie of women had organized a brigade to pull the bodies to a common ground for identification, and another team had been dispatched to gather wood for the coffins. Duey, for all his pain from the shooting, quickly volunteered to direct one of the teams. For hours he labored, roaming the buildings, locating bodies buried under rubble, directing the efforts to establish their identities, calming down the wounded and giving them stale words of comfort. His savior, Jimmy Pell, was assigned the task of searching for carpenters, and then leading the effort to build the coffins. The fires had not yet gone out, but if they waited too long to bury the corpses, the residue and stench of death would soon overwhelm the living.

Duey acted out of compassion, but his mind was only half dedicated to his life saving tasks. No matter who he aided, male or female, adult or child, black man or white, he asked them the same question: "Did you see the face of the demon?" The answers he received were various, depending upon the level of dementia, shock and physical pain that clouded the victim's judgment and memory. Some said they had seen a child in the form of a bushwhacker, raging through the town killing for what seemed to be the sake of it, as if he had been given license after years of self-restraint. Others did not believe their senses, insisting that they had only imagined a midget killer. It was a hallucination, one wounded man said right before expiring, thereby adding to the demon's death count.

While digging out the ruins of the dry goods store, Duey found what he was looking for. A half-unconscious man had been pulled from beneath the collapsed timbers and brought back to sensibility with some careful nursing. Struggling against his pain and what later turned out to be a collapsed lung, the unfortunate man responded to Duey's question with a cogent answer. "I saw your demon," he said. "And I know his name."

"Do you now?" Duey said with surprise.

"I can see it wrote in hell-smoke."

"Are you some sort of conjurer?"

"No," choked the man. "Just a skenchback from New York."

"What does New York have to do with it?"

The man slowly raised his head, oblivious to his near fatal condition. He had a ragged patch on his left eye and a scar that ran down his face, taking out a piece of his nose. The disfigurement was an old battle wound, perhaps a knife. "Your demon wasn't born in Hell," he snarled, "unless you consider the Five Points a suburb of that realm."

Duey fell silent for a pace, and then asked carefully, "You said you know his name. What is it?"

"A nice long one. Longer than his body. And it's mostly alphabetized. I'll tell it to you straight, but I ask one thing in return."

"What may that be?"

"When you find him, and you kill him, you make sure you collect on the Browbeat Wager. And once you get that princely sum, you find old Gobble-Eyed Gabe, and you share it with him. For I'll be danged hanged if any Kansan two-bit abolitionist is going to get the pot drop on me!"

Albert Duey sat on the floor before the man's pallet and crossed his arms over his chest.

"I got some time," he said. "You'd best start from the beginning and fill in the missing pieces as you go along."

The path taken by the Minuscule Monk after the war between the states is well documented in both yellow-back press and history tomes, including *A Common History of Bloodletters and Bad Men* by Giles Matheson (Arcanum & Strange, New York, 1873). Armed with such a scholarly work, one could trace the trail of bodies across the

Great Plains and the Northwestern states and territories. From the end of the Confederate rebellion to the height of the great industrial expansion, the decade belonged famously to the Monk. Children were put to bed at night afraid of the demon gunslinger of legend. Lawmen dreamed of making history by being the hunter who plugged him into finality. Newspapers delighted in all the tales and tallies of the dead that arrived with every stagecoach, regardless of the source's veracity. The name of the Monk, descriptions of his appearance, and elaborate reckonings of his infamy became common fare, even in such far flung regions as North Carolina, the only state, as it was told, that did not have any citizens who were killed by him (one prevalent theory held that the Monk had relations there and didn't want to displease a dyspeptic aunt). A total reckoning of his exploits would be exhaustively lengthy as well as endlessly repetitive, there being only a handful of ways to describe cold-blooded murder; and in the end, many of the stories would no doubt be false, or exaggerations, or hybrids of real incidents in which petty details could be endlessly squabbled over by folk who weren't even there when they happened. But the total truth is this: the Minuscule Monk eventually became an illegal version of what he had been during the war: a killer who knew no conscience and no remorse, and as rumor has it, no humanity.

All in all, there were several thousand tales to choose from, the Monk being accused of everything from taking out a whole town because he had lost a poker hand, to gunning down a priest who dared to suggest that he had redemptive powers within him ("Heaven's got no grappling hooks in me!" was the Monk's cynical reply). There was even a dark rumor, one discussed at great length in Matheson's tome, that the Monk had been the real assassin of Abraham Lincoln, John Wilkes Booth's only role in the affair having been to smuggle the Monk into Ford's Theater inside a surgeon's bag.

There was no infamy too depraved not to be attributed to the Monk, and Albert Duey, Jimmy Pell and Gobble-Eyed Gabe collected them all. They called themselves the Terrible Trio, and gossip had it that these survivors of the Lawrence Massacre were the most vicious gang of vigilantes the West had ever known, and that the Monk had best be looking over his shoulder even when he was surrounded by funhouse mirrors. After swearing to a pact that they would live together, eat together, sleep together and, if necessary, die together as long as their trail ended with the capture of the Minuscule Monk, the Terrible Trio grappled with the dilemma of money that dogged their daily meal, stage coach fare and hotel bill.

"How do we fund this venture?" Duey asked. "My aborted career as an abolitionist didn't bring in any coppers. We're flat broke."

"Maybe we can get an advance on the punter's pot," Pell said naively. His two partners looked at him with crumpled brows. "It just may work," he added. "Gabe here used to run with the Barber; perhaps he can play upon old allegiances."

"Used to run from him," Gabe corrected. "On the anniversary of the riots, he tied me to a chair and beat the devil out of me because I once had a hanging rope round the Monk and still managed to lose him along with my eye."

"Yes," Pell announced, "but Benny beat you in that chair simply because it wasn't the Monk sitting there. You were just a surrogate. Imagine what accolades he would bestow on you if he thought you were bringing him the real deal."

Gabe rubbed his chin and mused. "Seems like sound reckoning."

"Indeed it does," said Duey. "That would be sweet if we can get a pay-off in advance. Money folk at the Bourse couldn't have thought up such a scam. Let's to it!"

Gobble-Eyed Gabe wrote the letter, saluting Benny Browbeat, his old friend and comrade-in-crime, confessing that he had never stopped thinking of Mulberry Street and the grand old times they had knifing Irish people to death in the Old Brewery. Happily, he announced that he had sniffed out the trail of the Minuscule Monk and needed only some money to live upon until they reached the conclusion. In fact, there were two rangers with him, men trained in the art of tracking through the Western wilderness, whether it be a forest undergrowth or a series of saloons through which a gunslinger would typically blaze. Results would be expeditious if not immediate.

They mailed the letter, and a week later, much to their surprise, they received a hundred dollars in paper bills and a directive in the handwriting of Benny Browbeat himself, to "do this right or else there will be no place on earth where you can hide from me!"

"Once we spend the first penny of this money," Gabe told his companions, "we are bound to the devil. Fully committed."

But results were neither expeditious nor immediate. For the next several years the Terrible Trio travelled the West on Benny Browbeat's dime, sleeping in flophouses, haunting gambling dens and saloons, interviewing victims of the Monk's crimes and survivors of his violence, mapping a path of atrocities that cut across the continent like a harvest scythe. Trails turned hot and cold on them, and there were times that they sensed defeat, a prospect made all the more despairing since they were living off Browbeat's money. Every night they had a bed to sleep upon and every mealtime they had food before them, they were reminded that their benefactor would be extremely unhappy if they did not succeed in their mission. Every month, they telegraphed their location back to New York, always with the promise of a conclusion to the affair just around the next bend, in the next saloon, over the next crooked horizon. One week after each dispatch, no matter where they resided, a banker's note would follow, always with an attached letter explaining that patience was wearing thin and results were needed immediately, followed by some vivid description of what would be done to their physical bodies should they fail. Each time they telegraphed back: "Got a lead that's impeccable. Town full of cowards and scoundrels. One may squawk. Two more weeks will suffice."

After stalling thus for nearly five years, the Trio got bogged down in Cracked Field, Nebraska, where they worked at a standing carnival performing jobs beneath their dignities, most of which had to do with the animal tents and the latrines. Pell got a hankering for carny games and learned a few swindle tricks from the resident barker. These included creating a monster by sewing together body parts from a cow, a baby chicken, and a moose. The creature had fooled not a single customer but succeeded in stinking up the fairway. Pell, Duey and Gabe were subsequently ridden out of town by rowdy co-workers who reminded them, as they were beaten down the road, that had a pot of tar and a heap of feathers been within convenient reach at the time of their humiliation, their eviction from the town would have been much more complicated.

Weeks later, in a town called Nut House, Missouri, the Terrible Trio, getting drunk on cheap beer in a saloon filled with drummers and shootists, heard the name of the Minuscule Monk from a piano player who was trying out some new sheet music. Word had it that the punter's pot of Benny Browbeat was currently up to half a million dollars. Thus, a new wave of ebullient songwriting had swept the nation to celebrate the landmark.

"A Dude So True / Can Settle in Seattle / With that Minuscule Monkish Pot," the pianist wailed, improvising the rest of the lyrics as he proceeded.

"That's torn it," Gabe announced. "We got to catch the bastard or start spending Browbeat's money on false whiskers and one-way tickets to Mexico."

Pell shrugged. "We've followed every lead and turned over every stone. Maybe the guy doesn't even exist. Have you ever thought of that? Those newspaper hacks have wild imaginations."

"There are times *I* doubt his existence," said Duey, strangely. "I saw him only for a minute, and then I was dead. Doesn't exactly scream of certainty."

"Well," replied Gabe. "We've already swindled Browbeat for several thousand dollars. We either have to bring him the Monk, or go for the whole hog."

"And what is the whole hog?" Duey asked.

"The carny swipe."

"I don't get you."

"Let me read you verbatim from the wager," Gabe snickered, producing a torn sheet of newspaper from his pocket. He read in a dry voice:

The rules of the wager are as follows:
That any one who can obtain physical proof of such
Said condition whether through tin type reproduction
Or through sketches based upon actual witnessing
Or through production of the Monk's physical body
Dead or alive
Shall receive one half of the monies collected hitherto
From an undisclosed location

Duey's eyes brightened as his mind flooded with possibilities. "I believe I am beginning to see your reasoning."

Gabe slammed the table with a fist. "Carnival's got a few of them low boys! We can sneak back over the border and kill us one, dude him up like Monk and—"

"No!" Duey snapped. "There'll be no killing of anyone besides the Monk. I am not a murderer. We'll do this right. First, we flush out an old goof-ball addict, as artistic as any we can find. I hear tell the local opium den is full of aspiring Michelangelos just desperate for some lucrative commissions. Then we'll fix him up in a bohemian studio and supply him with sketches. We'll make a wax spoof of that demon and then get some tintypist to take an image of it for the Barber."

"He won't tell the difference," Gabe agreed. "Benny never could snuff out an artist from a lawman's lineup!"

So they went to the Chinese flophouse and found who they were looking for, an old, gnarled and disillusioned wretch who had taken to a small bunk in a back room as the ideal spot where he could smoke his way into opium oblivion. They took him round to a tonsorial parlor and had his gray whiskers shaved, which revealed underneath the quiet eyes and slanted smile of a once-optimistic sculptor. To secure his loyalty, they told him that they represented a venerable Philadelphia art museum and that one sure bet you could make on an Eastern crowd of art lovers was that they would pay a fortune for images of gunslingers from the West. And not just any gunslinger, but real short ones, like they were children dolled up in holsters and ten-gallons. The junky fell for it, and wrote out for them a list of the materials he needed.

They rented a broken-down room in a flea-bag hotel and dubbed it his studio, and then brought him all the wax they could muster, as well as human hair from the barber shop, and as much paint and ragged clothing as they could find. The last gift they gave him was a few sketches of the Monk, decked in all his regalia, along with the directive to make the wax dummy seem as life-like as possible, as if the varmint were physically present in the room.

"We want a murdered man," Duey added. "But make him look as if he were shot to pieces, as if the bullets that killed him did away with his nether familiars. Do you get my meaning?"

And so they retired to their own carousing and drinking on Benny Browbeat's bill and waited for the artist to complete his work. The old man came through, for in his fogged mind, he perceived his current commission to be the one that would cast him into Philadelphia society, perhaps even to launch his own art gallery, to live on Market Street like a fabulously well-to-do aristocrat, and to have all the money in the world with which to buy his junk. With enthusiasm and single-mindedness worthy of the great Leonardo, the artist produced the humanoid figure to the Trio's precise specifications, making sure of two measurements more meaningful than all others: the figure lay three-foot one-inch from head to toe, and lacked any reasonable representation of his nethers. The forehead was decorated with a jagged wound suggesting the little man had ended his days in an act of gunslinging violence; he was dressed in the cowhide vest and holsters of an authentic Western shootist, and topped with hair both on his skull and beneath his nose.

When Albert Duey saw the figure unveiled, he felt a deep shudder penetrate his torso as violently as the bullet that once almost ended his life. "It's as if he were standing before me," he muttered. "Take it from my sight boys; I can barely look at it."

They brought the creation to a back alley and propped him up against a leaning board as if he were on exhibit at a cheap carnival, and hired a tintypist who, for a rather significant sum, gave them a photograph of the waxen Monk, both clothed and unclothed, and a promise that he would never reveal to a soul alive what his commission had been. The tintype, once processed and framed, was shipped off to the Five Points Barber Shop in New York City on the next stagecoach along with a letter describing their accomplishments and some bluster about why they couldn't bring the body back to the East because it had been ripped apart by a crowd of angry widows whose husbands had died at the hands of the Monk.

They held their breath waiting for Browbeat's response.

A week later it was gloriously announced across the country that the five-year-old wager had finally been satisfied and the incredibly large amount of cash that had been stewing under Browbeat's floor-boards for all that time was finally going to be dispersed to active punters, the largest portion going to an undisclosed party in the West who had finally managed to bring the Minuscule Monk to justice. Newspapers from San Francisco to Bangor printed the banner, causing the tidal wave of Monk-Mania that had held the nation's concern hostage for years to finally abate. In short, folks felt they could return to their normal lives and stop obsessing from this point hence about the Minuscule Monk and the Five Points Barber and the half-million-dollar-pot.

All was well for one week. The goofball artist was returned to his flophouse, still believing he would be dining with the elite of Philadelphia by the end of the summer, and disappeared back into his opium haze. The Trio packed their bags, checked out of their digs and booked passage on an Eastern-bound stage to go collect their money in person. While engaged in one last round of drinks in the local saloon, the report hit the streets. Telegraphs had brought the news that Benny Browbeat had received a personal hand-written letter from none other than the Minuscule Monk.

In the letter (the only known sample of the Monk's writing that is known to be extant) the writer stated emphatically, "The rumors of my demise are tall tales generated by men who have put the sting on Benny Browbeat. If the Molasses Gang had any stones in their pants, they would revive the wager and demand the bleeding heads of the men who claimed the money. Thus speaks the Monk!"

The letter was accompanied by a tintype of the Monk, his face dark with rage, holding up a newspaper dated five days after the claim had been filed by the Terrible Trio. It is said that Benny Browbeat went into such a fury when he heard of the deception that he bit off the ear of the man standing next to him and swallowed it whole without chewing.

A new wager went out by way of thousands of printed posters on the next stagecoach to the Western States and territories:

Scilicet, Videlicet, and Viz my Brothers
Be it known that Bennett Buckingham Browbeat
of Five Points, Manahattan Island
Has posted a wanted reward for three
Pestilent creatures
Known hitherto as the Rat Fink Swindlers
That a punter's pot of half a million Dollars
Shall be distributed to any man
Who can bring me these men

(Albert Duey, Jimmy Pell and Gabriel Pike
The last one missing an eyeball and left nostril)
Dead or Alive
with or without their
Southern Gonadic Regions

A triple crown and throne shall be advanced
To the man who can drag before me personally
Both the Rat Fink Swindlers and the Minuscule Monk
Otherwise known as
Herbert Augustus Beauchamp Caleb Dray Eff

Photographs of the remains of either are not acceptable
Since they have proven their lack of dependency
And a curious ability to swindle on their own
Exploiting the fact that such artifacts
Can be tampered with and deceive the Human Eye
like "hellos" trapped within a canyon

Here are artist renditions of the Rat Fink Swindlers
as portrayed by Harry Dade
New York Journalism's most excellent spoof artist

For this bit of doggerel, the Barber claimed no literary elegance. His mind was monomaniacally bent upon the destruction of Jimmy Pell, Albert Duey and Gobble-Eyed Gabe.

The Terrible Trio, once so proud and fierce, was now living as three scared and insecure renegades. Subsequent flyers from the Barber presented their spoofs, accurate down to the last facial blemish, and all the public's fascination and predatory ambitions with the Monk now turned on them. Walking down the street with their faces exposed became a non-trivial matter, especially for Gabe who could not hide his deformity. Before fleeing the small town they had used as their home base for so long, they were forced to don floppy beards and goggle-like eyepieces. Gabe fitted himself with a golden nose and pretended to be a prospector who felt such a nasal guard would help him sniff out the nuggets.

They flitted from town to town, not even following any plan other than to stay alive, but couldn't escape the flood of flyers that came pouring out of Five Points on every stage coach. Before long, they were reduced to feral beasts, hiding in their flophouse rooms and fearing the light of day. Their patience with one another, long strained by living together and eating together and sleeping together for many years, now became a tattered thread that was in danger every day of snapping.

In fact, it wasn't long before each of them began to accuse the others of trying to kill the other two and collecting at least two-thirds of the punter's pot on their own. The paranoia between them grew so bad, that they finally split, feeling that anyone looking for a trio of Rat Fink Swindlers would be keeping an eye out for a gang of three and not a single gent no matter how suspicious he may be acting.

Albert Duey fled to Tar Pit, Arizona where he got a job raking latrines and taking care of a blind bartender who had the uncanny ability to mix any man's drink upon demand, but couldn't even feed himself when it came time for victuals. For two years, he labored in this degraded existence, suffering such fear of being caught, tortured, mutilated and murdered (in that precise order), that he eventually suspected the blind bartender of spying for Browbeat and fled to an even filthier town to became a recluse, hiding in a bug-infested room above a funeral home.

Then one afternoon, as he lay in his own swill on a decayed mattress, he realized that there was only one path that would rescue him from his prison, avenge his own attempted murder, resolve all disturbances, satisfy all claims, redress the damage done to several hundred victims who had suffered in the wake of the killing that had started its bloody trail in the Old Brewery of Five Points seven years before and had subsequently spread to all corners of the country: Duey would hunt down the Monk, wherever he was in this whirligig of a world, and kill him with no more compassion than he would have for swatting a fly. Then he would drag the broken and bleeding body back to New York and deposit it personally at the feet of Benny the Barber in his Leonard Street establishment, demanding the copious coppers in the punter's pot, hoping that the Barber would consider the monies forwarded to the Terrible Trio through the years to have been an advance on a corpse now delivered. Such an act of charity, Duey prayed, would prove him to be a man of honesty, and liberate him from the curse of the revised wager.

He would do this, even if it meant his death. And even that wouldn't stop him. For if an afterlife did exist, and Duey had no reason to believe it did, he would somehow find a way that his ectoplasmic equivalent in that other world would coalesce into physical matter and complete the hunt, drawing it to a terrible conclusion.

Thus he swore.

Chapter Thirteen

The Detective Who Wasn't There

Long after Kansas had stopped bleeding, after the South had been subdued and forced to give up its slaves, after the states were once more united, a passenger sloop docked at a landing in Mount Hope Bay, Fall River, Bristol County in the Commonwealth of Massachusetts. From it, a tall, thin man with a wispy moustache and a dusty travelling suit alighted onto shore. After dispatching his bags and a rather large steamer trunk to the hotel at which he planned to reside, he stared up at the range of houses, churches, banks and factories that together gave the city its distinct scrambled skyline. With a heaving sigh, he advanced up the hill towards the highlands, pausing every few streets to ask directions from an accommodating stranger. Soon, he was stationed before an imposing gabled and turreted house on Rock Street which squatted under the clouded skies with peeling paint and drapery-obscured windows.

The bell was answered by a grim valet and after some formalities, the visitor was ushered upstairs to a dark, shadowed bedroom where a massive man lay dying under a canopy in a four-poster bed carved from mahogany. The invalid's face was beaded with sweat, his eyes bulging as if trying to get closer to something he saw only inside his head. The last remaining white strands of hair lay on the pillow as if attempting to escape from the scalp that had tormented them for decades. His speckled fingers reached for the visitor's hands and clung tightly.

He was barely able to breathe the words. "Is it true?"

"Yes," the visitor said. "He is dead."

The invalid's eyes pressed closed and he whispered a prayer of exaltation. "The Minuscule Monk is dead," he smiled, then opened his eyes, gurgled in his throat, attempted to reach for his mouth with his bloated fingers, slumped sideways and then lay very still. At the last second of his life, his mouth had a small curve of a smile.

The visitor lowered his face for a moment of respect, then turned to the valet and nodded.

He was guided to an outer hallway and started his approach to the grand stairs. A shadow passed along the wall and a wide man appeared on the landing, supporting himself with a thick silver-headed cane. Despite his bulk, he was a smaller version of the invalid who had just died, unmistakably of the same stock. In one eye he had plugged a monocle which he looked through ferociously trying to bring the entire world closer to his pupil. Nestled in one of his ample arms was a small dog with a large black and white head who was panting goofily as if the entire world were one giant field in which to chase a stick.

"I heard what he said to you," the man holding the dog snapped. "Who is sending word about the Minuscule Monk, then?"

The visitor was quite stoic. "None of your business."

"No, it is my business." The man's monocle appeared to steam with displeasure. "My father was on his death-bed and the only thought on his mind was whether this Monk was dead; I deserve an explanation."

"So he was your father?"

"Yes, my name is Manchester Root. Now you know my name, but I know you only as the Taxidermist. That's what my father called you as he babbled in his delirium. He was thinking more about you than his own son. I demand to know why."

"My name is Jack Pratt, if such information would serve you. And to be clear about the matter, I prefer the title Immortalist."

"That means nothing to me."

"Nor should it. I'm a humble practitioner of the immortalization of animal souls, and I have been tasked with delivering a message to your father before he died. It appears he kept himself alive long enough to hear it, and when its content seemed to satisfy him, he let go of life. I don't believe my identity was of any interest to him. Why the Minuscule Monk meant so much to him, I cannot say."

Manchester moved his head back and forth, trying to focus Pratt's image in his monocle while mentally digesting the man's explanation. Finally, he buzzed dismissively. "Fah! That's all well and good, but I have to put it to the test." He peered down at the terrier crouched in his arm and tickled its forehead. "Balderdash!" he exclaimed, and the dog stopped its panting and stared obsessively forward with two marble black eyes.

"What is that beast going to do?" asked the visitor, stepping back a pace.

"Never you mind, just answer my question. Who hired you to deliver this message to my father?"

"A man by the name of Browbeat from New York. He paid me to go to your father and give him the news."

To Pratt's alarm, the dog burst forth with a carnal wailing so seismic as to almost split the beast in two. A calm pat from Manchester who also whispered the cryptic word, "Balderdash" settled the animal back into its calm, goofy state of gentle tongue-panting. "Clearly, you lie," the large man said with a pained smile.

"This beast can tell that I'm lying?" Pratt asked, a glimmer of astonishment coming over his face. "That is remarkable."

"There is much about this dog that is remarkable. I advise you to answer all my questions truthfully."

Jack Pratt stared blankly and said, "Then I'd best tell you all about it. The barber shop, the wager, the punter's pot, the Terrible Trio."

"Yes, I am a man with a penchant for tales, and your tale sounds intriguing. You mention a wager? How much money is in this punter's pot? And what can you do to help me win it!"

Pratt eyed the trembling dog. There was much mystery there.

"Can I bother you for a drink?" Pratt asked. "My throat is dry and we have much to discuss."

"Why, yes," Manchester laughed. "Come into my study, and we will have a singular discourse."

The office air hung heavy as Manchester Root's words faded to silence. The sunlight, once so warm and inviting, had mellowed to a dim amber across the desk. Herr von Trotter, nestled under Lizzie's trembling hand, turned up his watery eyes, as if he had endured a canine melancholy to hear the violent and tragic tale.

Mr. Almy broke the silence. "Herbert must have been a long suffering soul indeed, to have lived such bitterness and to have turned so black within his heart."

"It is true," Root sighed, his wind spent. "He was a bushwhacker, murderer of innocent folk, shameless rapscallion and gun-toting vermin. His deeds were dark. But somewhere in the dim past, he was a mother's child and suckled at the fount of compassion." He peered quickly at the small coffin tilted on the window ledge and then withdrew his gaze, his arms crossing the curve of his belly and his face falling downward.

"So," asked Lizzie, briskly altering the subject, "you and Jack Pratt created a waxen Monk in order to collect the punter's pot? And you colluded with him to hide the counterfeit in the Academy Building until a representative from Five Points could collect it?"

Root's cheek twitched. "In a manner of speaking, within the parameters of so many words, paraphrased and condensed into phonemes of inestimable use and value: Yes."

"And why was Jack Pratt sent to your father and by whom?"

"That I never learned. The man, as you may recall, is wickedly taciturn, and all subsequent attempts by Herr von Trotter to ferret out his truth were to no avail. It is as if after that first round, Pratt learned how to control that very vibration within his voice that Hugo is so sensitive to. No other man on this earth has done as much."

"What was your father's interest in the Monk?"

"For reasons I never discovered, he was obsessed with the Browbeat wager. Perhaps he had a stake in it himself, I cannot tell."

Lizzie broke out into a fluster. "Why did you not tell us this from the very beginning? You could have saved us time!"

Root's eyes watered. "If I have not been straight out, I beg your indulgence. I played loose with the facts, for knowledge can be a dangerous thing, and under certain circumstances, it must be hidden from those who can do harm to it."

"In other words," Deputy Wixon huffed, "you flat-out lied."

"And to an officer of the law," Mr. Almy added.

"Oh," Root wailed, "your phrasing makes such a trivial matter of my moral choices."

"It sounded like a lie to me," Andrew confirmed. "And I don't need any slobbering dog to tell me so! Wixon, drag this man in irons to the jail for withholding evidence."

"But I led you to the man!" Root pleaded. "I had C.B.M. show you the effigy!"

As Wixon took a few steps in the crying man's direction, Lizzie shouted, "No! I think I have an understanding of Root's motives. He was seated in his office, this very room in fact, lorded over by the portrait of his paternal conscience…" She tipped a hand towards the painting of the elder Root, his fiery brows raging like lofty magistrates at a moment of terrible judgment. "…and confronted by a party of strangers, led by a policeman of the city, all shouting about a murder, a dead body, and a trail of evidence that has led back to his very door. What is such a man to think at such a moment? That the poor moral choices of his past can, in one careful confession, cast unwarranted suspicion on his actions, perhaps even to be accused of the murder? And this after two years of building an institution based on a belief in the very heinousness of falsehoods of which we now accuse him? Why, here stands Manchester Root, a pillar of this community, a man who believes that his fellow humans should not tell lies to elevate themselves into political power. His entire mission is to defend the truth! I say that Manchester Root is forgiven his false testimony, for it was not the vandalism of truth, but a simple withholding of the facts. And his purpose was to gather more information, to scope out within the privacy of his own mind the strange trail of evidence and circumstances that put Albert Duey in that coffin. And in the end, it is Manchester Root who is handing us the very murderer and motive that we seek. Because of him, we are poised upon a conclusion to our mystery. We must congratulate Mr. Root for bursting forth the dam of his own turbulent conscience."

"Do you hear?" nodded Root, his reanimated face flushing crimson. "Listen to the lady. She is wise beyond her years, what say you all?"

"I say my feelings are bruised," confessed C.B.M., his body slumping against the wood-paneled wall. "Manchester, why didn't you tell me all this when you employed me to spy on Pratt?"

"If I did not tell you," Root snapped, "then it did not exist; and if it did not exist, then there was nothing to tell."

C.B.M. screwed up his eyes and blinked. "Sounds logical to me," he concluded.

"Besides," Root roared, "I did not know Pratt's endgame! I had no idea that he was leading Albert Duey into a trap. I truly believed in my heart that Pratt came to my father's side as part of some confidence game to collect on the Browbeat wager. We made that wax effigy together and sent the photographs to New York and never received an answer. Now Duey shows up in Fall River with his own wax midget in a coffin and gets himself killed. What is happening? Where's the real Monk? We still don't know!"

"Duey didn't have the Monk when he came here," Wixon added. "I inspected that casket myself and there was nothing in it but a dummy."

"How did you know it was a dummy?" Lizzie asked.

"What?" Wixon gulped. "I touched it; I picked up its arms and found them to be as limp as if stuffed with knotted rags, as were the legs. The hands were colored rubber. The shoes were stitched to the bottom of the trouser legs and were completely empty. The face was as hard as wax."

"Did you take it from the coffin?" C.B.M. asked. "Undress it? Cut into its nose with a knife?"

"Of course not," Wixon blushed. "I saw no need to desecrate the man's property. It was a dummy, like they use in a pantomime act."

"It is not the contents of the casket that is of importance," said Root solemnly, "but the casket itself that you should be concerned about."

"Are you saying," Lizzie flashed, "that there was a false bottom? Or a sliding panel?"

"No," Root said. "Not necessarily. But a man coming into town with a casket that is inspected inside and out by the law is bound to leave town unexamined, is he not?"

Deputy Wixon paused and scratched his whiskers. "How-dee-do!" he chortled. "Yes, if I saw him leaving town tomorrow with the same casket, I would be twice less inclined to inspect it. He would enter into Fall River with a dummy of rags and rubber, and leave with a mummified midget gunslinger."

"This is assuming the Monk was in Fall River when he arrived," grunted Root.

"God's lids, it all makes sense," shouted Mr. Almy. "Albert Duey was in town not to bring the Monk, but to fetch him. But from whom? And what went wrong?"

"Pratt," Root thundered. "Interrogate him once more. I care not a fig for his alibi; someone is lying."

"I still do not believe that Jack Pratt is the murderer," Lizzie said pointedly. "The man would not be so careless about the clothing, as well as the vellum in the mouth."

"The clothing I cannot explain," Root confessed.

Andrew slapped his hands together, producing a loud report that drew all attention. "I've had enough of this!" He gestured towards Herr von Trotter and shouted, "Balderdash!" after which the dog braced himself. "I have a question for Root! Do you know where the body of the Minuscule Monk is held?"

Root's flabby cheeks quivered, and then he said, "I know not where the Monk resides, but as sure as I am Manchester Root, I will help you find out."

Andrew lowered his long torso and twisted his face towards the dog, who began to lick his chops, puffed his cheeks, but let go with a slight whimper. "Sufficiently ambiguous," Andrew announced, "but I'll buy it for now." He muttered a quick "Balderdash," and Herr von Trotter lowered his heavy chin into his paws.

C.B.M. Borden thumped his chest. "I don't suppose all the minds within this room can compete with my own conclusions."

"Why don't you enlighten us," Lizzie sighed.

"To me, it is as simple as an ox, a house and a camel. For those of us in the know, that is code for A, B and C—for every letter has its corresponding image. A for example is an Ox, B is a House."

"The man is insane," said Andrew, jerking a thumb. "What does this alphabet have to do with—"

"No, I assure you, Mr. Borden, that I am quite sane. For if you would allow me to elaborate: the letters are associated with numbers, and each number added together gives us a sum that represents the message that the killer was trying to give us. And if you take the letters of the Minuscule Monk's name, the H being anomalous, but appended onto the beginning when it truly belongs on the end, we have a message that the ending is appended to the beginning; at the head of things, in the beginning, a Biblical reference. I have come to the conclusion, which is indeed the beginning, since the stream of time seems to be moving backwards in this case, that the ending has already passed us by, while in our midst we are seeing the progression of the middle."

Andrew placed his straw hat on his head. "I don't know about all of you, but I am certainly going to make it home for supper."

Mr. Almy held up a hand and motioned for him to be still. "No, Andrew, I don't believe the man is as much a blinking idiot as you may think. His words may be revelatory."

"Of course," said C.B.M. with a smirk. "I have given you the answer already. For if the ending is in the beginning, then the murder has not yet taken place, which is why the body is not extant, for the murder and the murderer are moving backwards in time while we are moving forward. Therefore, we can stop the murder before it even happens."

The room fell silent, broken only by the shuffling of feet and a few bored sniffles. Finally, Mr. Almy raised his stentorian voice. "I owe you an apology Andrew; you'd best take off for supper. This man is a blinking idiot."

"No!" came an unexpected cry from Lizzie. "C.B.M., you may be wrong in the details, but correct in the spirit. Go on."

C.B.M. took a slight bow towards his champion and continued. "If indeed I am correct, the murderer only now is planning the death of Albert Duey, and if we do not find him with enough time, we will miss the moment when he conceives of the murder. And if we catch him after the moment he conceives of the murder, we have no case against him, for only after that particular moment will he be completely innocent. He will be guilty in the past, but innocent in the future."

Lizzie tilted her head as if C.B.M.'s words would convey some meaning that would be missing in a more up-tilted position. "What about the clothing?" she asked. "The clothing?"

"Why, Duey's clothing of tomorrow may not be the clothing of yesterday. Hence, it is possible that he bought the clothing before his murder, which was in the past for him but not for us, so even now they do not belong to him, but may belong to him in the future."

"But his clothes are not his own?" Lizzie said, as if begging for the validation of her own as yet unspoken theory.

"Nay, and if indeed I am correct, there is the possibility that they never did belong to him, nor will they ever, but forever be on a time track of their own, outside the confines of the *a priori* space and time that our minds are, at this very moment, creating about us."

"So the clothes only existed for the point in time at which we found the body, and then they disappeared into a different dimension of time. Am I correct?"

"That is my theory. So while my reasoning may be convoluted, such is the nature of time and space. Why I dare not stop even there. I would go further to say that the dead body never even existed."

"What?" Deputy Wixon cried out. "I touched the man's cold hands with my own!"

"Ah, indeed he may have existed as a corporeal entity. But as a continuous body in time and space, he may be as vaporous as the ether that stirs through the universal, invisible and undetected by anything but the most delicate of instruments."

Andrew stomped across the room towards C.B.M., getting larger as he approached. The young millionaire crouched down and sat upon a chair, raising his arms as if to protect himself.

"Charles," howled Andrew, thrusting his fingers at the boy. "You are making a muddle out of my head and I need you to be quiet."

"One more question, Father," Lizzie said. "I need to ask C.B.M. if he is suggesting that the dead body was a ghost."

"Why that's exactly what I'm saying," C.B.M. said to Lizzie, keeping one eye on Andrew. "After all, why cannot a ghost come back as a dead body? Why do we perceive ghosts as only being animated souls walking about in white shrouds and speaking gloomy soliloquies about their fate? Cannot a ghost manifest as a dead body? And if I am correct about the victim moving backwards in time, then the man who was murdered is as of this moment very much alive, and the killer who killed him is planning the foul deed. Or perhaps they are switched in some invisible nook of time and space, swapping identities. Indeed, we may very well find out that the killer is the murdered man, and the murdered man is right now planning his own murder."

"My God!" Lizzie said with a startled jump. "I can hardly believe it! Father! Deputy Wixon! Mr. Root! We let C.B.M. ramble on with a theory that can be described as dementia at best, but despite the absurdity of his theory, despite his complete lack of reality and his deluded viewpoint of the way that everything in the universe behaves, I think he has a point."

"Well," C.B.M. said, pulling at his cuffs, "I take that as a compliment,"

"We are all looking at this from the wrong direction," Lizzie mused, placing a finger on her lip. "Yes, perhaps we have it all backwards." Her thoughts wandered for a moment and her forehead crinkled; then she brightened and raised her hands with pleasure towards C.B.M. "You old mystic, you," she announced, and then said gloomily, "But I must wait and collect more data. This is only a flash of imagination on my behalf; no, not yet, not yet!"

There was an abrupt clearing of a throat, and all eyes turned towards the doorway, where a strange man advanced, swathed in a dark greatcoat and a tanned and feathered bowler, his side-whiskers obscuring his cheeks and his lips pursed in the tight formation of devoted service.

"Benkin," C.B.M. said, showing no surprise. "I suppose Mother has ordered you to chase me down."

"*Chase you down* was not the exact phrase," the servant said grimly.

"Supper?" the young man asked.

"Indeed. She keeps insisting that you are endangering your health for the sake of your mental pursuits."

"But the old woman is mad. She never serves supper, just presents us with empty plates."

"I am aware of that condition, sir. But she insists, nonetheless." After a moment of tense silence, Benkin added, "We have a mutual agreement to indulge her faltering mind, do we not, Master Charles?"

"Yes, we do. Well, I have a twist to throw into this silly game she plays. Tell her I am inviting two people for dinner, the most delightful guests she would ever be quite pleasured to meet: Lizzie Borden the Girl Detective of Fall River, and her father, Andrew Jackson Borden of the concern of Borden & Almy's. She once told me that if I wanted to become a detective, I should seek the company of detectives. So tell the old, mad badger that she should take the nothingness she serves upon empty plates and triple the portions, if such a thing is philosophically possible."

"I shall," Benkin said, as if such paradoxical speech was common-place to his ears. He dipped his torso slightly forward, and then withdrew from the room like receding fog.

"There," said C.B.M. "I hope you don't mind meeting Mother, if you could ignore her mania."

"She serves empty trays?" Lizzie asked.

"Yes, quite mad in that respect, but perfectly sane in all else. Well, excepting her epistemological views which we clash upon quite often. I think it may be amusing for you to prove to her that I am keeping good company. And we can also discuss the case. Putting all our minds together may be beneficial."

"Do we have time for this?" Andrew asked his daughter. "That widow woman is very queer. I have seen her at the shops trying to pay for empty boxes with invisible money."

"Father," she replied. "Do not forget that it is the Widow Mrs. Borden who ordered the second coffin. We cannot afford to let her go unexamined."

"I need have to run back home and tell Mrs. Borden," Andrew said. "Empty plates?" he puzzled. "Lizzie, I'll make sure there is something hot waiting for us when we return."

His daughter nodded. "There is not much more we can do here for the rest of the evening. The City Marshal will interrogate Pratt in the morning and we will be present, yes."

"Fine," said C.B.M. "I'll take charge of Hugo." He leaned down and patted the panting dog on the head. "One hour?" he asked. "Providing that Mother's nothingness doesn't go cold in the interval. My, yes, that's rich! Ha!" And he exited the room with the dog nestled in his arm, both disappearing after his valet.

"Mr. Root," Lizzie said. "I will be at your offices at six o'clock and we will discuss this matter at greater length. There is much more that we need to discover."

"Most decidedly," Root returned. "And don't think I will miss the interrogation of Pratt. The man has led me into a trap, and one far deeper than the stage at the Academy. Now if you will excuse me, I will console Miss Turpin. She must be beside herself."

He turned to exit, but stopped abruptly upon seeing the coffin propped eerily against the window. "That is my property. I paid my father's money for it."

"The statue will be safe," Deputy Wixon boasted. "I'll stay here and keep guard."

Root gazed deeply at the wooden cover. "My demon," he whispered, and then his bulk was gone.

"Miss Lizzie," C.B.M. said, bowing slightly. "I honor our tete-a-tete. It was most invigorating."

"Most," Lizzie answered. "Do you really believe all that philosophy about existence and non-existence?"

"It is not a matter of belief," C.B.M. explained. "The world is, or is not, and therefore it is how I think."

"A most delightful non-answer," Lizzie chuckled, and patted Herr von Trotter on the white patch between his ears. "Perhaps Herr Hugo's beastial mind hides a greater instinct than ours summed together."

The dog licked his paw and then stared quizzically upwards, his whiskers braced and tingling.

"Then again," C.B.M. said, "perhaps not." And he took Lizzie's arm to escort her to the street.

Mr. Almy nodded to Wixon who saluted back and then placed a palm on his partner's shoulder. "My friend, we have seen many strange days together."

"Yes, William," Andrew sighed. "This is the indeed the strangest."

"I'm sorry about the coffin."

"You had no way of knowing, William. It was business."

"We've come a long way since we pushed our barrow through the streets."

"Time has a way of vanishing," Andrew quipped. "Old Fall River is gone. It has all gotten so complicated. Perhaps the past was only an illusion, William." His lips curled into a smile. "But here I am sounding like that Charles Borden fellow. I'll go to my dinner of lunacy, and then perhaps we'll return to the solid world where things stay put and don't have a way of becoming nothing."

"Amen to that," his partner said solemnly.

The two men, accompanied by the lawman, strolled to the lobby and then out into the late afternoon streets, saying little and minding the aftermath of the horse traffic.

Chapter Fourteen

The Horse That Wasn't There

Andrew Jackson Borden lived on Second Street, just a short walk from his furniture concern, in a modest home on a tree-lined street populated by other homes of similar shape and size. His had been built in the Greek Revival style, a noble pre-war architecture that had befitted a man of Andrew's then prosperous standing within the community. He had bought the home from a man named Trafton for a modest sum, although it had been built to accommodate two families, one on each floor; and Andrew, in his desire to provide the maximum amount of comfort for his wife and two daughters, had redone the interior. A kitchen emptied to become a bedroom, a bedroom folded into a closet, and two more bedrooms expanded to be a dining room. Fireplaces were closed and communicating doors sealed. The whole exterior, once a calming tan color, was now painted a drab green; a small placard reading AJ Borden in plain block letters had been nailed to the front, announcing to Fall River, from the city boundaries at Mount Hope Bay in the west to the great ponds of Watuppa in the east, that Andrew Jackson Borden, a man of means, pedigree and dignity, had arrived.

His people, the Bordens, had been living on the banks of the falling river for more than two hundred years, hoarding its water, harvesting its flood plain, tapping its strength with wheels and engines. They cleared trees, killed Indians, raised enormous families, sent sons off to wars, and financed the mills. The Bordens had been proud stewards of their fortunes, as nurturing of their dividends as they were of the crops that grew in their top soil. To their enemies they were a virulent strain, impossible to put into remission. Richard and Jefferson, the two titan brothers of milling and shipping, had reached the pinnacle of success, as far towards the Babel top as an aspirant can go before his Calvinist nature anchored him to the ground. The brothers were men of industry, of real estate, of water rights and enormous houses. They lorded it over the extended family like minor deities. To be nodded at by a man such as Jefferson Borden at a board meeting or across the lobby of a bank was to be handed on a golden plate a singular certainty of identity. You were not somebody until an elect Borden made you so. After that moment, you were always in danger of becoming nothing again.

Andrew knew this, and from the days of his first wife and the birth of his two daughters, he planned to rescue them from the house of his fish-mongering father and migrate up into the commerce classes. If they couldn't get a mansion in the Highlands where the likes of Richard and Jefferson dwelled, they would settle just a short two blocks from City Hall and the Quequechan, the river now under-ground, which once had boasted Bordens as its masters.

His wife, Abby, had taken one look at the Second Street house on the day of the mortgage closing and muttered, "Good enough." She hoisted up her skirts, and proceeded to move her hat boxes from the furniture wagon to her new dressing room. For several years after entering the house, she hardly left it. She cooked in the kitchen, scrubbed the floors in the hallways, pounded laundry in the basement, and endlessly chased after whatever Irish Maggie was currently in their employ. It was difficult to tell if Abby was content or not. From a purely physical viewpoint, she smiled a few times a day, held Andrew's hand when she wanted to feel affection, and was occasionally known to say something like, "A piano and a few sheets of Mr. Foster's ditties would make the perfect finishing touch, don't you think?" indicating that in some inner way, she had resigned herself to the notion that Second Street was her home and would be for the rest of her life. No, it was not Abby who concerned Andrew, but the girls.

The older, Emma, had painfully vivid memories of that evening on Ferry Street when Sarah Borden, her mother, had succumbed to her internal malady. Andrew played the scene over in his imagination, often bringing himself to weeping from the sheer sadness of the memory. Emma had been brave, but clearly what she lost that night was irreplaceable. Lizzie was too young to remember, but no one could forget how the two-year old touched her mother's arm and then began to cry. Emma took her into the other room and calmed her, and for the remainder of Lizzie's childhood, Sarah was never mentioned again. When Andrew remarried, there was little explanation.

The courtship had been hidden from the girls. Abby showed up one evening with a few geegaws and a bag full of stockings, a placating symbol of the peace and good will that neither Emma nor Lizzie would ever return, although they subsequently wore out the stockings. Since that time, Emma was ever sulking, ever on the verge of anger, always turbulent. Lizzie, the small girl who Emma's mother had, on her death bed, charged with protecting, was often the target of that anger. Many a time Abby had to separate the sisters in fear they would harm each other. As the years unfolded, Lizzie responded to Emma's attitude with amusement, casting wry smiles and ironic glances, sending Emma into deeper frustration.

Lizzie's damned intellect, Andrew thought with a shudder. If only she were feeble-minded, or mentally disturbed, so Emma could feel appreciated. Lizzie was always stealing the limelight, proving to be more competent, educated, and mature in years than her sister, and this caused no end of grief within the house. This problem was beyond Andrew's capacity to fix. It could not be mended like a broken nail in a cabinet. No science yet existed in the medical realm, not even in the nervous hospitals, to heal the emotional rifts between sister and sister, or daughters and parents. There was no cure for what clouds had formed over their family the evening that Sarah Borden had closed her eyes forever on her own daughters.

Andrew hashed over these thoughts as he walked with Lizzie up the side path to the kitchen entrance. His interrogation and the subsequent revelations had put a wobble in his step. He held Lizzie's hand as if his senile years had prematurely arrived. Sensing the disquiet, she gave him a small smile and pointed towards the screen door. Behind the mesh was a familiar sight: the wide, weary form of Abby Borden.

"When were you going to tell me," she said blisteringly, "that you were not coming home for supper?"

Andrew shook the memories from his head and focused on his wife. "We had some hub-bub at the store."

"The store?" Abby said, raising her hands. "Are you going to look me in the eye, Mr. Borden, and tell me a bold fib? Half of Fall River saw you and Lizzie there crissing and crossing the town half the day accompanied by a constable! And carrying a coffin!"

"I thought there was a burglary," Andrew improvised. "But everything is all correct, now."

"Pash!" Abby hissed. "I want to know the truth! If you are going into the horse thieving business, you'd best tell me right now."

Andrew froze. "God, woman, what did you say?"

"I suffered your schemes during the war," she continued, "especially when you had that plan to sell caskets to the Confederates!"

"That was one month before Fort Sumter!" Andrew protested. "You can hardly—"

Abby shouted louder. "At least there you were encouraging the enemy to lay still in their graves. But this…this is a right shame on our family name."

Before Lizzie could follow her father up the side steps, he had flung open the screen door with a mighty swath of his large arm, and had pushed his wife back into the house. There was a prolonged series of loud voices out-vying each other for domination, then a thunderous crack as if a piece of wood had split under the presidency of a descending axe. Lizzie raced to the kitchen and found her father grabbing at his head while his wife, armed with a cast iron frying pan, threatened to beat him again.

"Before God, Abby—" he swore, holding out one hand into the pain-induced fog cloud around him.

"Before God," came an unexpected voice, calm and reasoned, but somewhat angered. "Andrew, you know better than to invoke Providence while the Judgment would surely be against you."

A beefy, ham-faced man in a worker's shirt and heavy denims had come up behind his wife from the sitting room. His words ushered forth from under a prodigious moustache, but were laced with the intensity of his accusatory eyes. This was McDermott, the stable master, and his mien was formidable.

"Mr. McDermott," Andrew said, twitching. "I did not see you.

Forgive my domestic anarchy."

"If I had the resource of such a pan," McDermott replied, "I would have done no less." He tilted his attention towards Lizzie and flipped a finger to his cap brim. "Begging young Miss Lizzie's pardon."

"What do you need here, Mr. McDermott," Lizzie said, yanking the pan from her step-mother's startled grasp. "And what could you have possibly told Mrs. Borden about my father and horse thieving?"

"I'll tell you," Abby said, lowering the pan. "Mr. McDermott's stables have been burgled. One of his finest saddle horses stolen. And lo and behold: the creature turns up in our barn!"

Lizzie watched her father gesture pleadingly with his hands. "Is there something else you have been holding back on me?" she boldly asked. She had half a mind to grab the frying pan and do his pate more grief.

"Suffering splinters!" Andrew bellowed. "A man comes home to his own house, a place that should be a sanctuary from the cares of the woeful world, and before he can even place his hat on its rack, he's attacked by his wife, and accused of thievery by the entire household!"

McDermott loured at Andrew. "I'm willing to hold court and judge you against the evidence," McDermott said. "But you've got some up-front explaining to do while the Jewel is in your barn. Don't believe me? Go take a look, or if you stop cursing long enough you may hear the whinnying from apace. Listen! Who do you think is making that racket?"

"I believe you enough," Andrew said, touching his head with a careful palm. "It's not the first time today a rabbit appeared from a hat."

Abby frowned. "Did you say—"

"I don't care about rabbits," McDermott said, his voice losing its composure. "I just want my horse back, and I want damages from the lost rentals. Not to mention an explanation of how you did it and how you expected to get away with it."

"I know as much about a horse in my barn as I know about…" Andrew paused for a moment, trying to finish his comparison. "…Egyptian mummification!"

"Well," pondered McDermott. "I've had enough of this. I'm going to fetch a police officer."

"No!" Andrew cried, gesturing for McDermott to stay his ground.

"I just need you to know that I'm completely innocent, despite your horse in my barn." He blinked towards Lizzie. "But I haven't seen this horse yet, yes, that's right. How do I know it even exists if I haven't seen it? Go fetch that Charles fellow; he may be able to reason the whole creature out of existence. Every time he's around, something that was, turns out to be a wasn't. I tell you McDermott, I know a way to make the horse un-exist."

"Have you gone mad?" Abby asked, her eyes dancing wildly on her husband. "You *have* gone mad."

"No matter," McDermott slapped his hands together. "The facts are that at six in the morning I came to my stables and found my best saddle horse gone. Yes, the Jewel was gone, and was nowhere to be seen. I found the night watchman passed out on the floor. He was sleeping off a horrific drunk so it took several boot kicks to get him back on his stool, and he remembered nothing. I naturally assumed that the horse's instinct for freedom caused him to leave the stables of his own accord and never suspected thievery until a half hour ago. Right here, outside your house, at the head of your side path, I saw a pile of equine droppings that led me right to your barn."

"You suspect me a thief because of some horse dung?" Andrew said, baffled.

"Not just any horse dung," McDermott smiled. "But a pile from which wafted a scent of the spiced oats that I took great liberty to attain for my finest horse. I boldly strode up the path and opened your barn myself. There was the Jewel, staring at me like a lost child, traumatized by your treachery."

"You entered my barn?" Andrew squawked. "Trespassing! I shall call the police!"

"Father," Lizzie said with caution, "I would hold that off for the time being, considering our…" She raised her eyebrows, "…other situation."

"Trespassing?" McDermott sneered. "I'd like to see that fly by the constables. On the one hand I have my right as a citizen to investigate with probable cause, and on the other hand I have you kidnapping a horse from my stable while my night watchman snored on the floorboards. Who do you think the Marshal is going to sympathize with, especially with the evidence in your very barn?"

"You could have put it there yourself!" Andrew pointed out. "You have had it in for me ever since that time I rented you that room."

McDermott's cheeks flinched imperceptibly. "Don't remind me," he warned. "We have many unspoken words about that incident." He grabbed Andrew by his string tie, forcing his arms up over his face. "Come," he said, dragging the dazzled man towards the door. "See for yourself."

Abby, who had been wringing her hands, nodded at Lizzie. "You and your father have been up to something, disappearing all day, wandering the streets with a constable and some strange folk. What do you have to say for yourself, Lizzie?"

"We'd best go see the horse," the young girl said with a smirk and followed the men into the yard.

The barn door was pulled open, and sunlight flooded the inner stable where, indeed, a large chestnut roan was standing in one of the dank cubicles. His long head and expressionless eyes squinted down to adjust to the sudden light; then he came to a stillness, one giant pupil fixed on the humans who stood in the doorway. His interior feelings were impenetrable.

"What do you say to that?" McDermott asked sadly. He pointed towards Borden's well-worn draft horse who cowered in another cubicle. "And there's your ragged creature," he spat. "He's not good enough for you?"

"It's good enough to pull my Stanhope, McDermott," Andrew hissed. "Besides, how do we know this beast here is yours?"

"Look at that white diamond on its forehead. That's distinct; no other horse in my stable has such a mark."

"Is that why you named it Jewel?"

"None of your business. What matters is that he's standing here…" McDermott pointed towards the earthy floor of the barn, "…instead of back there…" His arm twisted and stiffened in the general direction of his stables. "What gives, Borden? You needed another horse, you could have just asked."

"But I didn't take it," Andrew said, his voice flat and defeated. "I'm not surprised to see it, however. Today's been a strange one for disappearances, reappearances, and other apparitions. No doubt this horse will be gone as soon as I've turned from it." He shook a fist above his brow. "I can no longer speak for the veracity of reality."

McDermott frowned. "I just want my horse back! Just because you say you didn't take it, doesn't mean it isn't here."

Andrew's face folded at McDermott's words. He reached forward towards the roan's muzzle. "But I see it," he said. The horse reciprocated with a snort and a sniff. "I can touch it." His fingertips stroked the white diamond, and then withdrew. "I'm not entirely sure that it is there. If I close my eyes, I will not see it, so how can it exist?"

"If you think jabber-talk will give you a free ticket out of jail, think again. The Marshal will be standing right here looking at the horse. Whatever he sees, exists, believe you me."

"Then I am a doomed man. I'd best give up the midget."

"Damned right," McDermott agreed. "I would…yes..but…what? Midget? What say you Borden?"

"I have seen many strange things this day."

"And this is not one of them," Lizzie announced. "Father, you are the victim of a hoax."

"Of course, she would think so," McDermott spat.

"But it's true!" Lizzie insisted, pressing her gloved fingers to the horse's forehead and pressed downward; the whiteness of the diamond smeared down onto the nostrils. Now the Jewel's forehead decoration resembled melting wax in a tallow candle.

"What's this?" McDermott barked. "The jewel is vanishing!"

"It's chalk," Lizzie explained. "Someone marked him to look like the Jewel. But note the fringe along the mane and the peculiar ovoid shape of the hooves; this is clearly another horse altogether."

McDermott peered closely, touched the diamond and smeared it some more, held some of the chalk near his nose. "She may be right. Of course, she's right. This is quite some scandal! Borden, what's your game? You steal a horse and mark him up to look like a horse that was stolen from my stable? Did you expect to sell him back to me? How long would you believe such a confidence game to last? Is there no bottom to the pit of your wretched greed?"

"I've done neither," Andrew groaned. "I know not whose horse this is, and I suspect you don't either. Lizzie may have a clue, but she won't talk until all the pieces fall into place. Can this have something to do with the dead midget? Or the man with the poetry in his mouth? Or the hat without hair? Or the dog who knows when you lie? Can it?"

"You're asking me?" McDermott cried. "I don't care about midgets and hats and dogs; I just found out that the horse stolen from my stables is not the horse stolen from my stables." His brow crumpled and he wiggled his fingers over his cheeks. "Wait, I mean…"

Andrew's face brightened. "If this is not your horse, you can't prosecute me!"

McDermott smirked. "Either the horse that had been in my stables is not the Jewel, and when he was stolen, he was painted to look like the Jewel. Or, equally compelling, the horse had been the Jewel, but when he was stolen, Borden stole a horse from another stable and painted him to look like the Jewel, for reasons unknown."

"Or perhaps," Lizzie suggested, "there is a third way. Perhaps there never was a Jewel, and the horse you thought was the Jewel was an imposter. The diamond forehead would have served little purpose since the original Jewel, who does not exist, only exists as a horse who is not himself, painted up to look like what the Jewel should look like in the eyes of those who believe in him. Then one day, the horse gets free and wanders to the Borden barn. There, he is stolen by someone who believes that he is stealing a fine roan from Andrew Borden and replaces him with a lesser constituted beast who does not have the distinctive diamond forehead. A few slaps of paint and an escape into the streets and now we have a horse who is not the Jewel standing in for a horse who was a replacement for another horse who never even existed."

McDermott started counting on his fingers and muttered softly. "Give me a second," he implored, then lifted his face. "No, that doesn't add up. The Jewel kind of just drops out the picture altogether, doesn't he?"

"Perhaps," Lizzie continued. "Either way, we have a horse painted up to look like the Jewel, or a horse who was made up to look like the second horse, who in turn was made up to look like the original horse. At such a distance in the chain of identities, the original horse vanishes and becomes nothing."

McDermott turned sideways as if he had been punched in one shoulder, then almost fell off his feet. "Borden, between you and Miss Lizzie, you did make the horse un-exist!"

"McDermott," Andrew said, drunk with confusion. "Take your

damned horse back. Painted head and all. At least it looks like the horse you *thought* you had. And *your* horse may originally have looked like a horse you *never* had, so this one would do just as well. I never got to use it, and I certainly didn't steal it, so my only harm is failure to pay your stable fee, although it was my own damned stable the beast was stabling in. So why don't we call it a draw, like gentlemen."

"All right, Borden," McDermott sighed. "But I'm going to keep an eye on you. You are not in your right mind. A moment ago you were raising hell about midgets and talking dogs. Go calm your nerves somewhere, or by jingo you'll wind up down at Taunton with the nervous doctors."

"I feel I am there already," Andrew grumbled.

Lizzie helped McDermott remount the horse's saddle and tugged at the bridle to get the beast out the barn and onto the path. "Thank you, Miss Lizzie," McDermott said, tipping his bowler. "You ever want to go buggy riding into Providence, just let me know. I have plenty of buggies to spare."

"I'm sure you do, Mr. McDermott."

"Delighted, Miss Lizzie." And he turned and strolled off with his fake Jewel, its long drooping nose smeared with white chalk, like a melting diamond.

After horse and man had disappeared into the Second Street traffic, Andrew raised his fists to his temples. "I don't know what just happened but I won't stand for it anymore!" he roared. "To be so accused, so many times in one day!"

"I'm not sure what that was about," Lizzie said, watching the man and the horse disappear into the traffic of Second Street. "It could have been an honest mistake."

"But the diamond? The paint? Who would do such a thing? Steal a horse and then paint up another horse to plant on my property? Do you think this is connected to that other affair?"

"It's possible," Lizzie replied, stroking her chin. "If nothing else unusual had happened today, I would have thought—"

Her musings were interrupted by Abby Borden, her face layered with shades of impatience. "McDermott's not a man in this neighborhood to enrage, you know that. Unless we get a team of our own, we need that man. Now I fear we'll never have his business again."

"Quiet, Mrs. Borden," Andrew said. "There are things that you know nothing of, and before you wield your frying pan against my skull a second time, take a moment to ask me what the deuce is going on."

"Fine. What is going on?" she asked. "I've been waiting to hear!"

"I don't even know myself!" Andrew said, holding a palm to his sore head. "Lizzie and I are going to supper; we've been invited by the Widow Mrs. Borden."

Abby's forehead crinkled. "You mean the Widow Mrs. Borden of Weybosset Street?"

"No!" Andrew scowled. "That's the other Widow Mrs. Borden."

"Mrs. C.E.B. Borden?"

"Not quite, she's the Widow Mrs. Borden on Pleasant Street. I mean the Widow Mrs. Borden who was your cousin's third husband's aunt."

Abby's face scrunched as she tried to calculate the tangle branches in Andrew's explanation. "That would be the fifth Mrs. Borden from the Highland Bordens on the mother's side."

"Perhaps, all I know is that she eats non-existent food. Don't ask me anything about that, I'm not even sure what I just said. So leave us be. You and Emma are on your own."

"When did you plan to tell me this?" she crowed. "I went all over town collecting tonight's supper! Now you want to go off and waggle your eyebrows at some widow."

"My eyebrows?" Andrew said. He fumbled for a response, then headed off for the house mumbling nonsense. Abby trailed after him, shouting exclamations and derisions.

Lizzie strayed into the barn and inspected the interior, trying to piece together some fractured puzzle. How many mysteries in one day? How many crimes? Did any of those crimes even exist? If she had not seen the grotesque corpse in her father's coffin, its mouth hideously stitched, its knotted hands grabbing as if convulsed with some painful poison, she would have thought everything a hoax. So far, everything could have been a hoax, except for the reality of the corpse. And the corpse was far enough in the past, too much of a memory, to even have a claim to reality any more. Once a moment, an event, a person, a thing, was in memory and out of sensual perception, did it even exist? And if it only existed for a moment in time, what made it appear out of the nothing, and what made it go back to the nothing?

Such thinking was anathema to Lizzie. A proper investigation needed facts, evidence that didn't shift into unreality, things that stayed put and could be measured multiple times without any change in the sum. Once it became acceptable to think in terms of tentative existence, the whole art of the detective was obviated. To build an investigation on such philosophical principles would be to plant the foundation of your house on sinking sand.

Confound that Bishop Berkeley, Lizzie thought, almost out loud, and whirled about to face the house and a very severe looking Emma Borden, who stood on the path before her. Emma was tall and thin, dour and chinless, decorated in a simple periwinkle blue calico dress that Lizzie would never even think of wearing in public, since it lacked the frills and small bustle and waistband that so dignified the persona. Such an unadorned apparel made Emma look ordinary, mundane even.

"I did not think you would even make an appearance today," Emma chided. "Your lecture ended hours ago, and I have not seen you since."

"I was detained," Lizzie answered. "There was much going on."

"Too much to trust your own family? Do you realize how many people have come calling today, asking what you and Father were doing in the streets with a deputy and that Root fellow?"

"What do you know about Root?" Lizzie asked.

"Nothing, except that he's insane and thinks his dog can talk. What is happening, Lizzie? Tell me? You used to tell me all sorts of things."

Lizzie rubbed her cheek and stared at the grass lawn of the yard. She did not answer. After a few moments, Emma wrung her hands. "So be it," she said dejectedly. "If you will not tell me what you have been up to, then I will not tell you the secret of the horse."

Lizzie's face rose sharply. "What horse? The Jewel? Do you know something about this?"

"Perhaps," Emma said. "Doesn't that feel horrible? That I have the upper hand? Not a very nice feeling, is it, dear sister?"

"You must tell me all you know," Lizzie implored.

"Ah! Yes, but of course. You will not tell me likewise, but I am in a giving vein today, and since our family's reputation is on the line, perhaps I will be the gunman who blinks. I'm sure that will tickle your vanity that you have won me over in your clever game."

"I am not trying to be clever, Emma," Lizzie said, musing over her sister's use of the gunfight metaphor. "I'm doing this to help Father."

"Help Father?" Emma asked. "Very well, I'll give you your ammunition. Earlier today, I was in the yard pulling some pears from the trees for supper, when I noticed something odd on the path. There was a trail of barley oats leading from the street into the yard and up to the very door of our barn. Peculiar, I thought, but I left it on the ground, hoping that some explanation would reveal itself. As I went about my daily affairs, I kept glancing out the screen door and seeing the same trail of oats, undisturbed."

"What time was this?"

"I first saw the trail about one o'clock. And at three o'clock sharp, I heard a clomping of a horse, closer than the street. Before I could apprehend what was happening, I was at the screen door watching the horse with the diamond patch walking slowly up the path eating the oats. When it got to the barn door, it looked up and stared at the obstruction. It was my Christian charity that obliged me to open the barn and give the horse shelter."

"Then the horse coming to the house was orchestrated by persons unknown?"

"Perhaps," Emma said. "But it was I who let it in the barn."

"Why did you not tell this to Mr. McDermott? Or to Mrs. Borden? Or Father for that matter?"

"Because I was not in the giving vein. There's a certain power to knowing facts that elude others. I'm sure you are familiar with that feeling."

"That was dreadful," Lizzie said. "You should not have withheld that information."

"What difference would it have made? Father would have been accused of laying out the oat trail. I suppose…" She halted, her voice choking. With a hand to her throat, she cleared it and continued. "I suppose I wanted to give the information to someone who knew what to do with it."

Lizzie's eyes softened, and she smiled gently. "Why Emma, that is a fine compliment. I appreciate the gesture. I thank you for your information."

Emma's face dipped in acknowledgement. "Yes," she said. "But don't forget, I have provided a clue for your investigation."

"Duly noted and agreed."

"Perhaps there's hope for me yet," Emma said, and then turned suddenly and bolted for the house. From her trembling voice to her hurried gait, it was clear she was hiding any overt emotion that had stirred her.

Lizzie stood motionless, surrounded by the Borden yard, the open barn, and the house on Second Street, Fall River—her entire world. She did not exist apart from it all. If she closed her eyes, it would all disappear, and only faith would give her the confidence that it would all still be there when she opened her eyes. Yet, even with her gaze fixed upon the solid reality about her, it all seemed so transient, as if it could disappear in an eye blink. Like a sculling boat of her youth, sunk to the bottom of memory, at a desperately unguarded moment.

Chapter Fifteen

The Widow's Son

As Andrew climbed Rock Street with his daughter to the Widow Mrs. Borden's house in the Highlands, pedestrians tipped their hats and parted before his funereal stride, as if they feared a grim undertaker's passing might cast an evil omen on their daily affairs. Lizzie held his hand gently, a little bit out of a family affection for the man who had given her life, but also as a public display, imparting some bit of humanity to his dark presence. She fingered the ring that she had given him just weeks before, feeling pleased that he saw fit to wear it and display his own affections for her.

"Daughter," Andrew said after a long silence. "You have thrown me to the wolves."

"I assure you," she gripped his hand, "you are not suspected in this murder. If you had committed the act, you would not have disposed of the body in your own store."

He halted in his tracks and stared at her, his palm going cold. "You tell me that as an assurance? Do you think me capable of that?"

She grinned and tightened her grip. "Of course not," she said. "I merely meant you would not have pointed suspicion at yourself."

"I would prefer to hear you say," Andrew said solemnly, "that you would not think me capable of such an act."

Lizzie nodded. "It occurs to me that Miss Turpin would not do anything to cast suspicion on herself, either. Likewise for Manchester Root, and Jack Pratt. And Mrs. Borden, C.B.M.'s mother, if I am not mistaken. The killer had some reason to cast suspicion on all of them; however, it makes no sense to be so patently obvious about it."

"I would prefer," Andrew repeated, "that you would not think me

157

capable of such an act."

She interrupted her deep thought, then grunted and tugged her father forward. With an eye fixed on the luxurious houses about them, she asked, "Father, do you think we can ever improve our lot in life?"

Andrew noted a Queen Anne mansion cascading upwards with its flowery color pattern and tall gables. "You mean get fleeced by an estate agent in exchange for one of these ostentatious indulgences?" he snapped.

Feeling a cold shiver up her arm, she withdrew her hand. "Well, I did not think of it like that. I was merely speculating as to whether we can expand the room in which we live so we do not have to be piled on top of one another as we are. Forgive me, Father, if you find that impertinent."

"Lizzie," said Andrew, in a measured tone, "I can provide for you and Mrs. Borden and Emma, and even retain a servant, but I'll be damned if my dividends will go towards increasing the wealth of some builder. What we have is sufficient."

Her temple boiled, her fingers tightened. "I apologize if I mentioned it," she said bluntly. And then they arrived at the front door of the Widow Mrs. Borden.

The pilasters and colonnades that festooned the façade were pleasing and harmonious, and Lizzie made a mental notation to study the fabulous house at her leisure. The large wooden front door was beveled and embossed with flowery designs. They knocked hard with the iron ring that sprouted from a lion head's mouth. The visage of the valet, Benkin, replaced the door panels and they were ushered into the front hallway. A gangling C.B.M., in a smart cloth coat and dapper pants, came limping down the front staircase.

"Brilliant," he announced, smacking his hands. "Mother is just about ready to receive you. I'm sorry there's no food, but we pay that price to keep her happy."

"We will eat at home this evening," Andrew assured him.

"Excellent, follow me!"

The entrance to the dining room was a large, elaborately paneled door that bulged outward. Once inside, Lizzie could make out that the entire room was in a sort of oval shape, and the four curved entrances, which all opened at the cardinal points, were contoured to continue the impression of the oval.

"Mother," C.B.M. said wistfully. "May I introduce Mr. Andrew Jackson Borden and his delightful daughter, Lizzie. And they are ever so famished!"

Lizzie's eyesight adjusted to the dimness, and out from the other end of a rectangular dining table emerged the image of the seated Widow Mrs. Borden. She appeared as a solid column of black silk with velvet trimmings, capped with a clutch of white lace at her throat. Her face was a pale moon in an inky night sky, the eyes glistening and the lips trembling. Her crown was a mass of braided raven hair and a flaring hair comb of splendid Whitby Jet.

"Come," she said, her voice a throaty escape of air. "Join me at my table. I have been waiting so long."

"Mrs. Borden," Andrew said, taking a hasty bow.

"Don't stand on ceremony," the Widow said, raising a bony finger. "There is much to discuss. We have lost so many years." Her eyes drifted to a corner of the room. "So many years," she repeated.

They took their seats around the table's sparkling armada of heavy silver-plated serving pieces at anchor on the snow lace tablecloth. The crusted man-servant had glided across the carpet with a white soup tureen on a service tray, which he held before him as a priest would a communion wafer.

"Carrot stew," the Widow Mrs. Borden announced. "A fine introduction to a most excellent repast."

The old servant deftly dipped the tureen spoon and came up with a flourish, helping it down towards Andrew's bowl. "I'll take two scoops," Andrew requested. Nothing came out of the spoon; it was inherently empty.

C.B.M. coughed, and pointed towards the tureen. "That is all you are going to get by way of carrot stew. Best enjoy what you can." He gestured with two fingers towards his mother and made a strange swaying motion towards his head, while the servant continued his rounds about the table.

"I'll take a double portion," Lizzie said, forcing some cheer. "Yes, that seems fine; what delightful steam, so rich in scent. I can feel the carrots being yanked from the soil in which they have formed."

"They are from my garden," Mrs. Borden said, her face creasing into a smile. "It takes a long time to grow each one."

"Yes," Andrew hastened. "Well, if it's good enough for Lizzie, it's good enough for me." And he took up his soup spoon and dipped it into the bowl, swaying his hand over the expanse of the china. He then raised it towards his lips, which he pursed. "Cheers," he announced, and blew air at the empty spoon's lip.

"Cheers," C.B.M. said, doing likewise. Then he motioned for Lizzie to follow suit. The Widow Borden grinned and raised a hand to the servant, whose serving spoon was hovering over the bowl.

"I will partake tonight only of the peccary," she said. "I am trying to reduce my waistline!"

"Mrs. Borden," Lizzie said, resting her hands together beneath her chin. "I'm honored to be your guest and I thank you for having the courtesy to invite my father. We do have a matter of urgency which we must discuss."

"Yes," said the Widow, gazing rapturously at Lizzie, as if seeing her for the first time. "I have heard about you, and the service you have done some members of our community. The apprehension of the monstrous man Livermore. Such perfidy has not been known in this town, and it is to my delighted ears to hear of one who is so bold as to take on such men without consideration for one's own personal safety."

"It was nothing," Lizzie said broadly. "I had help from my friends, as well as my father. Livermore was quite careless in his crimes."

"And yet," the Widow continued, "our community is that much fairer as a result of your deed. It inspired my own son, Charles, to pursue a career in detection. He is so clever with observation. Why, only the other afternoon he remarked that I had not moved for hours from my day chair in the parlor. He had deduced this from the manner in which my dress hem lay upon the floor. Such remarkable powers do not come often in life."

"Although I believe," C.B.M. said, "that I detected your inactivity by the angle of your slippers to one another upon the floor, not the manner of your hem."

"Ah," the Widow said, her head lilting backwards. "Yes, well, you have often noticed my lazy moments from the manner of my hem."

"I have never," her son persisted, "noted the manner of your hem.

You are sadly mistaken."

"No matter," the Widow barked sharply. "I'll look back in my diary to an entry dated sometime last year when I wrote emphatically that I was deeply impressed by an observation my son made on the manner of my dress hem. Yes, I'll find that date and hurl it into your face."

"Fine," C.B.M. said, turning his attention to his empty bowl of carrot stew.

"No doubt," Lizzie intervened, "C.B.M. does indeed have extraordinary powers of observation. In fact, we have already worked together on a mystery this very afternoon. He is possessed of a particularly fine gift for detective work."

The Widow raised a finger towards her jet comb. "He's not quite right in the head, you know. Sometimes he believes I do not exist."

C.B.M. dropped his spoon with a clang. "I did not say that you do not exist. I merely commented that my essential apprehension of your existence is a tenuous affair at best, and impossible to verify and elusive to describe. Those were my exact words."

"Do you see what I mean?" she retorted, turning back towards Lizzie. "Imagine listening to that all day. I just don't know how we manage to get things done!"

Andrew patted a silk napkin against his lips and coughed to clear his throat. "Mrs. Borden," he said. "I do take delight in your most excellent carrots."

"My graces, thank you," the Widow said, her white skin betraying a slight trace of a blush. "The garnishment comes from the garden as well, as does the faint trace of turnip that surely you must perceive."

"I did not perceive a faint trace of turnip," Andrew said. "But it was a fine soup nonetheless."

"I take pride in the variety of my garden's yield. Each carrot, each turnip and radish, each distinct fruit from the tree, is a miracle of nature and does indeed cause Eternity to fall in love with the productions of Time."

"Mother," C.B.M. said dolefully. "We have discussed this quite often. There is no such thing as Eternity."

Her eyes closed and her fingers curled slightly, as if possessed with the growing need to become fists. "Yes, yes, we have indeed discussed this many times, and you always counter-challenge my poetries about

Eternity with talk of Infinity."

"That is because Eternity is a mad dream of philosophy, but Infinity is a hard fact of Science. I have explained over and over again!"

Lizzie caught a glimpse of her father raising another spoon of carrot stew to his grinning face. If only, she thought, such intellectual discourse could occur at 92 Second Street, instead of the dreary discussion of Father's real estate investments, which certainly did not evoke any romantic notions of Eternity. In a solemn way, she envied these Bordens their philosophical prowess.

"Do such distinctions matter?" Lizzie asked. "We can only speculate about such abstracts as Eternity and Infinity, which are beyond our mental capacity to resolve. Perhaps it is best to abandon all argument and consider both mere creative fictions. Then we can enjoy their musical resonance and delight in the Poet's appreciation of their beauties."

"Why there is a girl after my own heart," Mrs. Borden sighed. "I should have used that argument against you years ago, Charles."

"Fine," her son repeated, and ate more of his non-existent stew.

"I remember distinctly," came Andrew's thin voice, "a moment in my childhood when my father took me upon his knee, and made me look out upon the Taunton River. 'Look how it rolls,' he said, 'endlessly on and on. Like the flow of life. But with each cycle and season, everything around it changes, slowly, ever so slowly. Why a thousand years from now this river may not even exist. It may dry up and become a curious rock formation. And the mills that we have built will fall, as the Kingdoms of the Bible fell, and all shall be dust once more. But the river,' he said, 'flows on and on, and will stand witness to how we once walked this earth and what we did while we had our time upon it.'"

A silence fell over the table. Lizzie, startled at her father's sudden verbal flourish, blushed and announced, "So true. I did not know that Grandfather Abraham ever had such thoughts." In her mind's eye, she thought of her grandfather as that garrulous and playful survivor of the Jacksonian Age living in Spartan simplicity and self-contented peace on Ferry Street, that genial giant who used to bring her candy and dolls, and taught her all the jokes she knew, never a philosopher by any means.

"He is a reflective man," Andrew said. "I have never forgotten that moment of curious wisdom."

"Curious indeed," C.B.M. said. "And that is a reflection upon Infinity. Eternity would never allow for endless change. Eternity is beyond change, outside of the cycles of Time, which is why my intellect cannot abide it. I see it as a stained concept."

"Being born into life," Mrs. Borden said, her eyes darkening, "is a stained concept."

C.B.M. blinked. "Coming from one's mother, that is a rather dismal statement, don't you think? Wasn't there any joy upon my birthing?"

"There was some sport at your conception," Mrs. Borden said, nearly in a whisper, "no more or less than the beasts of the field in their obscene copulations. But since then you have been nothing but a memory of a sinful miscalculation."

"A rather pessimistic way of looking at children," Lizzie said, flapping her hands as if trying to distract everyone's mood. "The birth of a child is not necessarily an omen for the parent's death."

"I am still alive," Andrew beamed. "Lizzie hasn't killed me yet."

"No one is suggesting that C.B.M. will kill his mother," Lizzie explained. "I believe she is implying that his birth was a prelude to her husband's departure. But one cannot follow from the other. Mr. Borden died in a hunting accident."

"Gored by an elk," C.B.M. said, taking some delight in his mother's visible wince. "Hardly a dignified end for a banker, don't you think?"

"I am not suggesting that Charles killed his father," Mrs. Borden loudly brayed. "Of course he didn't. But his father took him on that hunting trip to Vermont with great disturbance of mind. It was to help him make a decision on whether Charles was mentally provisioned enough to take over the family banking concern."

"Ah," Andrew said, leaning in towards C.B.M. with renewed interest. "You were to inherit the First Pocasset Bank?"

"No," C.B.M. answered. "During the hunting trip I announced to my father I would not be taking interest in the family's concern. I also made a confession that rendered him witless and destroyed his hunting instincts. We were both attacked by a raging elk. I suffered damage to my leg; my father was no so lucky."

"What did you confess to him," Andrew asked, "that caused such chaos of mind? Surely you—"

C.B.M. lifted his chin with pride and declared. "My endorsement of the economic philosophy of Pierre Proudhon!"

Lizzie shifted uncomfortably in her seat. To mention the name of that French Mutualist in her father's presence seemed risky. "No, C.B.M.," she said calmly. "Proudhon?"

"Eh? What?" Andrew said, lowering his spoon, the reverie disappearing from his eyes.

"And why not?" he shouted. "I translated his books from the original French. *What is Property? War and Peace.* All of them, as many as I can get from my European contacts."

"He is a Mutualist!" Mrs. Borden barked loudly. "The offspring of my own loins subscribing to Mutualism! Can you fathom this? How I endured his blasphemous mind all these years!"

"Mother, it is hardly blasphemy. Monsieur Proudhon is quite a reasonable man, basing his economic politics on sound principles."

"You mean to overthrow the entire system," she continued, "this community that suffered to carve a civilization out of this wilderness. It was not you or your kind at all, for men such as you, Charles, cannot appreciate the hard working endurance of your grandfather's generation. They fought cruel Indians, and chased the British out. They took this bounteous land by the stream and gave birth to industry. They created all these mills and all that cloth out of nothing, out of a wood and a river, with their own bare hands!"

"Out of nothing?" C.B.M. laughed. "You really believe that Father and Grandfather created something out of nothing?"

"Yes, I do," she said, with defiance. "And all your generation has created is new and novel ways to get drunk in your family wine cellar. You have turned your back on a life of working with your bare hands and embraced one of destructive, self-indulgent philosophy."

"Destructive?"

"Property is theft…how can such a man declare such a thing?"

"Well Mother, that phrase 'Property is Theft' is clearly referring to exploitation of labor, the way in which we all grew rich off the toil of the workers. Don't you believe that such an act was lacking in mutual concern for all mankind? Imagine, an entire class of people, once proud artisans, reduced to wage slavery. You say that Father and

Grandfather created something out of nothing, but it was really the work of the common mill worker that produced the wealth. Father perceived them as nothing and took all the credit!"

"I will not sit here and listen to this," said Mrs. Borden, rising to her feet. The valet had slipped into the room, sensing the turmoil and tension, an empty tray in his hand. Mrs. Borden settled her eyes on the service tray and its large field of silver and said plainly, "Cancel the peccary; I am retiring to my room. See that my guests are escorted properly to their carriage."

"Mrs. Borden!" Andrew said, getting to his feet and pressing his bangs back with his palms. "Ah, Mrs. Borden. Please do not take offense at Charles's importunity. He is but a child, one unschooled in the ways of the world. He never had to work and he has an incomplete understanding of what it means to work. So his adoption of any sort of labor philosophy cannot be based upon any life experience. He is a romantic, a child trapped in an angry mood. Without the presence of his dear father, he lacks direction; he is poorly diverted onto a course of which he will soon tire. It is the clumsy and groping agitation of his age, nothing more, nothing less."

The Widow stared at Andrew with a softness reclaiming her face. "I have often pondered," she said, "how Charles grew into such a world view. I have considered every option, but not until now has any of it made sense. 'Clumsy and groping agitation of his age...' Why, that is beautiful, Mr. Borden."

"My boy," Andrew said, sitting down and addressing C.B.M., "you were not there when the wilderness was being cleared, when the mills were being built."

"My mind is above this sickly thing called money," C.B.M. said sourly. "My father wanted me to go into banking, but that would have meant a lifetime of materialism."

"So you reject the entire system," Lizzie said. "If so, how do you justify staying in this opulent house? Why not work with the destitute, feed the hungry, volunteer at the almshouse?"

"Because poverty is as much a trap as wealth. The poor are likewise condemned to bondage to the material world."

Andrew stroked his jaw bristle. "Well, let me tell you a story," he said. "A few years ago, I asked a skilled carpenter to make me a new front door for my business. He came and inspected the present door figuring out what it would take to replace it. After some consideration, he said to me, 'There's something about this door that doesn't add up. I need to think about this for a while,' and he went back to his home, only to return a day later. 'The sole purpose of your door,' he said, "is to get people from the street into the building. There's something not quite right about that. Let me think about this for a while.' And he went away for another day, only to return. This time he said to me, 'You only need to get people through the door because there are walls around the door that are keeping them from stealing your business product. Let me think about this for a while.' So a day later he said to me, 'You only want people in the store because you need them to buy furniture. They only need to buy furniture because we live in a society where we have to pay other people to create things that we cannot create ourselves. So instead of building you a new door for your business, I should teach every one of your customers how to build furniture, and then you'll have no need for the four walls of the building, and even less need for the door.'"

"What did you say in return?" asked an astonished C.B.M.

"I told him where he could put the *hang-blasted* doorknob after building me my damned door!" Andrew wailed. "And it is such an attitude that I sense in you, Charles. You are looking so closely at the whole picture, that you cannot pay more attention to the details."

"The carpenter," C.B.M. added, "sounds like a man after my own heart."

"I would have thought so," Andrew said, then shoved some fingers at his empty bowl. "Where's the peccary? The carrot stew gave me a hankering for more!"

"Mrs. Borden," Lizzie called to the Widow, who had been staring blankly at the table cloth. The old woman snapped upwards at the sound of her name. "I apologize if this conversation has strayed into meaninglessness. We came here to ask you a very particular question."

"It is all correct," said Mrs. Borden. "When Charles begins such debates with my guests, I drift away to a far-off place. Ask away, my young girl."

"Did you," Lizzie asked carefully, "order a coffin from my father yesterday afternoon?"

Her eyes brightened. "Of course, I did!" she said. "I had forgotten about it until this moment."

Andrew made a strange huffing noise. "You…ordered…a coffin from me?"

"Most assuredly," the Widow repeated. "But I didn't do so on my own. I spoke to the Monkey Man."

"Uh," C.B.M. said, "yes, Mother. Well, we must not be talking about the Monkey Man, now, must we?"

"And why not?" she said defiantly. "I cannot help it if a monkey can speak."

Lizzie smiled weakly. "I'm losing your meaning. A monkey who can speak ordered the coffin?"

"Yes," the Widow said, incredulous that her guests did not take her meaning. "He came to me at night, and told me that I needed to order the coffin. Standing at the foot of my bed, he was." She squinted, as if forcing herself to think. "Except he was standing *on* the foot of the bed. If he had stood on the floor, I would not be able to see him, for he is the smallest thing with whom I had ever held conversation."

"Did he speak English?" Lizzie asked.

"No, of course not. Monkey men don't speak English. He spoke French, in which I am quite fluent."

Lizzie, Andrew and C.B.M. stared wildly at one another until the young man spoke wistfully, "Mother often sees her carrot stew, if you know what I mean. Although, I am tempted to think that if she perceived this apparition in her head, then it is indeed real."

"You believe that the French speaking Monkey Man in your mother's bedroom is real," Andrew said, "but the dead body in my basement wasn't?"

"There is a distinction," C.B.M. chuckled. "The Monkey Man was never perceived at all by any of us outside my mother's head, while the dead body manifested first in the physical realm and subsequently vanished. One stayed completely within the realm of nothing, while the other came from nothing and returned to nothing."

"You see a distinction in *that*?" Andrew asked, shaking his cheeks.

"*Creatio ex nihilo*," C.B.M. intoned dramatically. "The stock-in-trade of the magician. Did you ever witness an act of magic, Miss Lizzie?"

A broad smile expanded Lizzie's face. "You mean the ancient arts of thaumaturgy? The Kabalistic art of the ancient Hebrews? The invocations of the Chaldean Oracles?"

"Eh, well, no. I'm referring to pulling rabbits out of hats."

"I have seen such an act at a carnival," Andrew said. "His name was the Great Mondo, and he made a lion appear on stage. Years later, he died from a snake bite."

"These men are great artists," C.B.M. continued, "and they perform miracles. Can you imagine making a lion appear, to conjure such a beast out of nothing but your own persistent Will? That is truly a creation from nothing."

"Rabbits, you say?" Andrew said distractedly. "The Great Mondo also had a rabbit, but it was a mere trifle after the Lion trick. Its whiskers were bent."

C.B.M. rocked on his heels, his face tightened, and then he withdrew towards the dining room entrance. "Just a moment," he said, holding up a finger. "I have something to show you." He vanished behind the cedar door.

Lizzie and her father remained with the Widow Mrs. Borden whose gaze was drifting as if her conversations with her son were now dim memory. "I am sorry about the peccary," she said. "I don't know what is keeping my servant. He is usually prompt."

"The stew was wonderful and quite sufficient," Lizzie said, touching her forearm. "You serve a delightful plate, Mrs. Borden."

The old woman's face brightened. "Oh that is good, yes, very good. I like pleasing my guests."

C.B.M. burst back into the room with a rather large hardwood box embossed on all sides with astrological symbols, scatterings of stars and planets,. He dropped it on the table, making the silverware rattle, and held out his palms with a dramatic flourish.

"This is my creation box," he announced. "For as you can see…" He flipped open a hinged lid on top and a similar lid on the side facing Lizzie and her father. The inside of the box was dim but visible: there was nothing in it. Just an empty box.

"You do witness that there is nothing," C.B.M. stated, then thrust one of his hands in through the top opening, and at the exact same time he reached around and put a hand through the front. He moved his fingers on both hands and Lizzie peered forward to see all the waggling. He withdrew his hands and slammed the two openings shut.

"In the beginning," he intoned, "the universe was without form, and void. And the Magician said: 'Let there be something!'"

With a dramatic flourish, he yanked open the top lid and thrust in his hand. There was a yelp and a squeak and a scuttling of nails against wood. Then C.B.M. pulled his arm from the box, holding in his clutching fingers the pinched skin of a furred creature. For a flickering moment, Lizzie tried to see the rabbit, but it seemed too large, too heavy. And the fur was dark and smooth, the wriggling of the beast too strange. No, it was a dog, a medium sized Boston terrier.

Herr Hugo von Trotter.

"Behold!" C.B.M. cried out. "I have reached into the Void and created life."

"Very good," said the dry voice of Mrs. Borden. "Now that you've created him, you can take him for a walk. I don't want him fouling my rug."

Lizzie raced forward to take Herr Hugo von Trotter from C.B.M.'s pinching hand. He scurried into her arms with plaintive eyes and a tiny whimper, and then nestled himself against her bosom, his frame trembling. She stroked his head to calm his nerves.

"It's a trick," Lizzie said. "It can't be real magic. There must be a trick."

"Surely there is a trick," he grinned. "There is a rational explanation for everything, but the mind makes the magic real. You perceived an empty box, and then there was a dog in it, so your mind did the magic, not me. If you learn the trick, you would be sorely disappointed. People desperately want to know the trick, but once they do learn it, all the magic vanishes, and they are left with a strange feeling of having been exploited. They revolt against me as if the trick were some act of violence. But previous to that revelation, they absolutely thought I was full of supernatural wonder."

"So what is the trick?" Lizzie said. "You have no fear of such resentment from me?"

"Ah, I bought this box and its secret at a great price. I wouldn't want to spoil it now. I merely wanted to demonstrate that Fall River and all its industry appeared from a very large box on the stage of a great magician. That magician wants you to believe it was all created from nothing. But the box has its secret, and *it* wants you to believe that it was not purchased from a novelty store, that the box was manufactured by Homer Thesinger the Boy Inventor, and there are no supernatural agencies at work. The box wants you to believe in its miracles. That's magic! That's entertainment!"

Lizzie scratched Herr von Trotter's head and found him to be comfortably contented. "But Herr Hugo knows the secret of the box," she said, pressing her pursed lips to his forehead. "For he was inside it. If only he could speak."

"Magic boxes and mentalist dogs," Andrew huffed. "This brings us no closer to the solution of our mystery, and it brings us no closer to actually eating dinner. I'm famished and I'm going home to get a proper meal. I'm sure Emma and Mrs. Borden are belching their afters as we speak."

"No, Father," Lizzie said, her forehead creasing with consternation. "You had a wonderful dinner."

"Balderdash!" Andrew shouted, and Lizzie felt Herr von Trotter's body stiffen; his breathing grew more agitated, and puffs of nostril breath blasted from his hairy face. Then Andrew took a look at the wistful hurt in the Widow's eyes and softened. "Oh, well," he said, shifting into a more graceful mode. "I did enjoy the stew, it was most filling."

The terrier immediately went into a frenzy, clawing frantically at Lizzie's forearms, and kicking his back legs in an attempt to escape her embrace. She lost the pitched battle and hurled the dog at the hardwood floors, where he scrambled and scampered and caught his footing and shot like a rocket out through the rounded doorway through which the butler was entering with another service tray of empty dishes.

"Balderdash!" Lizzie cried after the canine, and got to her feet. "You have to be more careful," she said to her father. "There is a time to lie and a time to tell the truth, and you must be wise enough to know the difference!"

Leaving her father fish-mouthed, she raced from the room and chased the scrambling dog up the front staircase and into a hallway. She whisked past several doors that were all closed, large paneled tributes to secrets dark and mildewed, holed up in the past like strange memories barely forgotten. The door at the end of the corridor was getting closer very quickly, so Lizzie broke her run, convinced that Herr von Trotter, at the pace he was going, would crash straight into the hard surface. But as the dog hit the door, he seemed to vanish right into the wood. She was astonished at first, but then spied a section above the floor wavering in the dim light. It was swinging on a hinge, just a patch of it, and upon closer inspection revealed itself to be a small opening in the panel, about one foot across by one foot tall, a tiny, rotating dog door on which was carved with great artistry the embossed image of a Boston terrier in silhouette. From the other side of the door, she could hear Herr Hugo von Trotter scuttling over hard wood floors.

The doorknob turned in her hand, so she entered, bounding into a bedroom that was lit only by the glow of a single lamp on a table by a settee. A four-poster bed dominated the room, but an entire wall was taken up with a very large desk pressed against it, the table top crowded with columns of leather-bound books interspersed with various sheaves of foolscap. Above the desk, on the wall, was a framed and dusty portrait of Bishop Berkeley, his skullcap hugging his head, his eyes glaring out with some inner luminosity, as if they were rec- ognizing that all before them existed only by the goodly grace of their liquid orbs. The painting could only mean one thing: she had entered into the private bedchamber of Charles Borden Mutability Borden, the Subjective Mutualist.

"Balderdash," Lizzie barked, and then spoke loudly, "I am not Lizzie Borden." From behind the bed came the rapid growls, snaps and yelps of the Truth Telling animal in the throes of discovery. She rounded the bed and saw the terrier spread out on a large pile of papers on which were scribbled frantic handwriting. A terrible odor rose from under the dog's flanks, indicating what opinion it had held of C.B.M.'s writing.

"Oh, you naughty thing!" she shouted, and brushed the dog off the papers with a strong sweep of her leg. Herr von Trotter accelerated sideways towards the wall, hit it with a thud and a yelp, and darted off to the safety of the other side of the room.

Lizzie bent down to retrieve the papers, and then flashed a smile at the cowering dog. She tapped the ground, assuring his attention, and said in a mannered tone, "I am Emma Andrew Borden, the Girl

Detective of Fall River." Herr von Trotter dipped his face curiously, flicked his tongue, and whimpered. "Hmm," she said, pondering the strange reaction, then gave a sharp "Balderdash!" to ensure the dog's silence for a time.

Lizzie took the papers from the ground, ignoring the stench of the dog's water. As she lifted them towards the light, she read a few of the words on the top sheet. It was a mad scramble of French words and their English equivalent, interspersed with long elegant sentences on the benefits of mutual aid and a people's bank.

"Anything interesting?" came a hushed voice from the doorway. C.B.M. was standing there, his eyes dark, glaring at her with an uncomfortable trembling. "I did not think you took an interest in Proudhon."

"This is your translation of *What Is Property?*" Lizzie announced, "I am afraid that you have gained the disapproval of your first critic."

He limped forward, his hands reaching out for the papers that she handed to him hastily. The dog's micturition drained down the sides of the slanted sheets and made droplets on his pant leg. He shouted incoherently and ran for his desk, depositing the papers in a waste basket. "All that work; now it has to be recopied."

"You could have avoided this misfortune," Lizzie commented, "if you had not put in a swing door." She jerked a thumb towards the doorway.

"That?" he said absentmindedly. "Hugo lives here."

"You are his owner?" Lizzie asked, startled.

"That is no secret," he said, staring down at his crumpled pages. "When I met Manchester, he was disconsolate over his father's death. With his parents and brother all passed on, he was challenged to find any zest in live and could not be trusted to take care of Hugo. Since then, Herr von Trotter has been in the League's employ, but his chambers are here."

"Root's brother is dead? I'm sorry to hear..."

"Lancaster Root was the true lover of animals, all sentient life in fact. He was known to walk carefully down the road least he step on ants or worms. He went out West seeking his fortune, but returned in a coffin, killed in a random act of violence during the war. Manchester found meaning in creating the League in his brother's honor, and petitioned our family to invest."

"You and your mother," Lizzie asked, "helped to finance the League?"

"I do not see why that would come as a surprise. It is a matter of public record. Mother does care for the beasts; she just doesn't like it when she feels they are reading her mind. A year living with Hugo forces one by necessity to always speak the truth. Sometimes she announces that she is about to tell a lie, just so she can remember what it feels like."

"C.B.M., I have to ask you a serious question. What is the secret of Herr von Trotter? I cannot fully fathom his responses. He has responded in inconsistent ways to statements that are opposite to each other, but my instincts tell me that he is following a pattern. He is a dog: he cannot be lying himself, he must be incapable of it."

"I have asked Manchester several times what he thinks of Hugo's abilities, and together we cannot come to a combined conclusion. We toyed with the notion that he is a new breed, and such genetic happenstance has created not just a new fringe of hair or a more pronounced forehead, but a new faculty of the mind. We considered corresponding with Charles Darwin himself to get his assessment, but ultimately the dog has been proven in many a political debate to detect falsehoods with complete accuracy. It always works."

Lizzie bent down and held out her hand for Herr von Trotter to sniff, and then scooped him up in her arms, bringing him towards her face.

"Balderdash," she said, and his face stiffened to serious attention. "I am Lizzie Borden of Fall River," she said stiffly, and the dog stared at her with trembling nostrils. "The sky is purple," she said, and he began to snap and bark. She stroked his nose and calmed him down. "Balderdash," she said, to end the session.

"Quite consistent," C.B.M. said.

"Balderdash," she said again, and stared into the dog wide eyes. "You ruined C.B.M.'s translation of Proudhon," she stated, and the dog went wild with barking. She stroked his nose.

"You ruined my translation of Proudhon," C.B.M. said, directing his words at the canine. He was rewarded with a blank stare.

"Impossible," Lizzie said, biting her lip. "There is obvious inconsistency. The dog gives contradictory responses to the same statement."

"But posed by two different people," C.B.M. stated.

"Yes," Lizzie said, her thoughts wandering. She handed the dog to C.B.M., who reluctantly took him with his open hands, peering downward to see if there was any residue threatening his trousers. "We have left your mother alone too long," Lizzie proclaimed. "Perhaps she is pining for our company."

"Yes," C.B.M. said. He leaned in close so he could feel the dog's breath on his cheek. "The dog is still active."

"What of it?" she asked.

"C.B.M. fancies the girl detective," he said abruptly.

The dog remained silent.

"Well," Lizzie said, straightening her jacket. "I can't yet say if I preferred one response or the other, but perhaps it is a sentiment best left unexpressed at this point in time."

C.B.M.'s stare was broken by a flush of red across his cheeks and a wide smile. "How can one not fancy you, Lizzie Borden? You are gifted, pretty, and intellectual, and filled with charming glamour that could spell-bind any intelligent male. Before I first laid eyes on you, I would not think such a one as you would even exist."

"Close your eyes," Lizzie said sharply. C.B.M. smiled nervously, and then lowered his lids. "Nice and tight" she ordered. "Can't see anything? Can't see me at all?"

He nodded with a gleeful giggle. "Not a single ray of light from your body is registering anywhere in my vision."

"All right, then," Lizzie said, stepping away from him. "If you do not see me, then I do not exist."

When he opened his eyes, she was mysteriously gone, leaving him alone to hold Herr Hugo von Trotter, whose fleshy nose and mouth turned with a hot blast of breath towards his owner's startled face.

Chapter Sixteen

The Night Watch

"Monkey men! Eternity! Mutualism!" Andrew was huffing and grumbling as they stumbled down Rock Street towards the town center. Twilight was descending, the streets were nearly emptied, and a church bell was ringing the hour. Lizzie trailed behind him, distressed, wringing her hands. From clear certainty, she had fallen into absolute confusion. While her father was awash in a mental sea of disconnected bits and artifacts and seemed willing enough to hand the entire affair over to the police, she wished only that she possessed the lynchpin that would create a solution out of all the chaos of evidence.

"I never want to meet with that man again," Andrew announced. "His ideas are not only wrong, they are dangerous."

"I'm not so sure they are wrong," Lizzie said, in a near whisper that almost escaped Andrew's attention. "But dangerous, yes. Perhaps for our time."

"We have enough trouble in the mills," he continued. "We don't need more crazed philosophers putting strange ideas into the workers' heads. I am sorry that I ever opened my doors this morning. Perhaps if I had never been in the shop, I never would have seen that body, and this whole affair never would have happened." He stopped, crossed his eyes, and then waggled his head. "Dear God, I'm thinking like him now!"

"But there may be some value in it," Lizzie said, following her own train of thought. "I can't shake the feeling that C.B.M.'s crazed methodology may yet yield something tangible."

"Balderdash!" Andrew spat out, and then stared madly down towards the ground. "I cannot use that word any more in fear it will raise hell."

Up ahead, in the dimly lit street, before the facade of Borden &
Almy's, something indistinct was happening. As they got closer, they
could see, before the darkened windows, Deputy Wixon and two other
figures: a shabbily-dressed factory worker, short and stocky, buried
under a cloth cap and a drooped moustache, and a small boy, equally
dirty, and threadbare in his appearance. The boy looked up first and
then pointed at Andrew, drawing the attention of the deputy sheriff
and the factory worker.

"Mr. Borden," shouted Deputy Wixon. "Speak of the Devil."

"Why this late night gathering?" Andrew huffed. "Who is this man?"

The worker took off his cap, revealing a thoroughly greased head.
"Begging your pardon, sir. Begging your pardon." His accent was not
native, perhaps Birmingham or Manchester, England. Such radicals
stirring up all that trouble!

"Pardon for what?" Andrew said, astonished.

"I only brought them here for verification," Deputy Wixon explained.
"They came to me not one hour ago, just as I was capping off for the
night, and told me about…well, perhaps little Oliver here should
fill you in."

As the boy's head swiveled upwards, he twitched and froze, his neck
muscles tightening so he could not quite lift his face. Then he blinked
uncontrollably as he spoke. "It was not my fault," he said, "that I saw
the wagon. I had never seen it before, but there it was."

"There what was?" Lizzie said. "What wagon?"

"The circus wagon, it was right back there, behind the building."

"When was this, boy?" Andrew said, stepping forward. At his
approach, the small waif tottered backwards against his father's leg.

The worker put his hands onto his son's chest and drew him in.
"Mr. Borden, sir, this happened this very afternoon, and it shook my
boy up quite right. He said it was behind the furniture store, by your
leave. A circus wagon and it had a coffin on it."

Andrew stepped back, stunned and open-mouthed. "Here?" he said,
pointing his finger to his own business. "You saw a circus wagon at
my store?"

"How do you know it was a circus wagon?" Lizzie asked. "Was it
painted bright colors? Were there animals in tow behind?"

"No," the boy said. "But it did have a little ape."

"Now that's where the story seems a little ragged…" Deputy Wixon began.

"Ragged?" Lizzie said with bated breath. "I would say it rounds things out. A monkey, yes. Dear boy, what is your name?"

The boy looked upwards as if asking permission from his father to speak. "Oliver Cromwell," he finally answered. After a difficult pause, he added, "That's really my name, and it's not my fault!"

"No, Oliver," Lizzie said. "It's not your fault," and she glanced briefly up at the boy's father. "However, it's a lovely name and an easy one to remember. But getting back to this ape, or monkey, if you will. Was this little creature dressed up in any way?"

"How does a monkey dress?" Deputy Wixon puzzled.

"Well, perhaps in a tiny Ring Master's jacket," Andrew suggested.

The boy shook his head. "He had a hat, and a big moustache."

"Curious," Lizzie said. "Was it possible this was just a little man? Perhaps a small version of a man, shall we say?" Oliver seemed to swallow silence, receding into himself. "Was there anyone else on the wagon?" Lizzie asked.

"No," the boy said. "Yes," he added.

"What is it, Oliver?" Deputy Wixon asked. "Speak freely, you will not be harmed."

"It was the crazy lady from the animal house," he said. "The woman who talks to herself, and thinks that her dog can read people's minds."

"Evangeline," Andrew whispered. "I am a doomed man. Daughter, you may as well kill me now."

"Quiet, Father," Lizzie snapped. "Oliver, what does this woman say when she talks to herself?"

"I don't know, I don't know."

"Then how do you know she talks to herself?"

"Because I see her through her window, and she is talking to the floor. I don't know what she says."

"Is it possible she's talking to the monkey?" Lizzie asked. "And he's standing on the floor where you can't see him?"

"I don't know," Oliver said, and hurled himself into his father's legs. The elder Cromwell stared downward, his face shamed and tinged with red. A silence crept over the street, making the dim lamp light feel darker.

"Are you saying," Andrew asked his daughter, "that the Minuscule Monk is still alive? And he has colluded with Evangeline Turpin to throw me in jail for murder?"

"That part is unclear," Lizzie admitted. "I think we need to get a team together. Deputy Wixon, would you be so kind as to gather all our friends from the Animal Suffrage League, as well as Mr. Almy, if he desires to be present at the resolution of our little mystery."

"Resolution?" the deputy said. "You mean, you know what's behind all this?"

"I have an incomplete theory," she confessed. "The rest I can guess at and possibly draw forth from certain individuals. But, yes, all the puzzle pieces are coming to surround one another. Gather those people I have mentioned and we will meet in one hour at the gate of Oak Grove Cemetery."

"Oak Grove," Andrew said. "I would not think we would go there so late."

"Perhaps it is best to do it under darkness," Lizzie said. "There is some moonlight to guide our way on the paths, and lanterns to reveal the inner truths of the Widow Mrs. Borden's family mausoleum." She knelt down close to Oliver Cromwell's frightened eyes. "Don't be afraid," she said calmly, and then she drew her hand along Oliver's protruding right ear. When her fingers snapped before his face, there was a silver dollar all for his grasping.

"Where did that come from?" he asked.

"I created it from nothing," she explained. "Haven't you ever heard of magic?"

"Magic doesn't exist," the boy said, grasping his father's knuckles.

"Don't put such ideas in the boy's head," the father said, protectively. "He has to get up at the five o'clock bell and now he'll be up scared half the night."

"Who said magic doesn't exist?" Lizzie purred, and put the dollar into the boy's other hand. "Without magic, nothing would exist. Isn't that right, Father?"

"I suppose," Andrew answered. "But you'd have that dollar back in your pocket!"

Chapter Seventeen

Lizzie in Nighttown

The Canine was exhausted and didn't understand why they would not let him sleep. He had been carried from the Marble House to the Wizened Woman who gave him an empty bowl, and now he was being led through the streets under the arm of the Belted Man, not his favorite of their kind. The Man had come to fetch him and told some lies to the Woman with the Empty Bowls, and then forced him to leave the house. Where was the Mannered Boy? He had not seen that one since he was yelled at for relieving himself on those worthless papers. He knew they were worthless because no one wanted to read them except for the Mannered Boy, and he spent entire nights bent over them, scratching away, writing those squiggles that no one else wanted to read, and when they did read them they got mad.

The Belted Man was now bringing him to the place where their kind are brought when they die. He didn't like that yard; there were none of his own kind there. During life, they cling to you, tell you lies to get you to love them, sing you to sleep with songs that are full of falsehoods, and force you to sit at their feet all evening while they tell each other stories that are full of balderdash. If you are lucky, they do not beat you. If you are lucky, they tell you some truths every now and again. The delusion they live with is that they love you, but when they die, they do not want to be buried with you. They want to go into the earth without their faithful companions, their lies finally revealed.

Yes, they were all full of balderdash, and he would ruin his bark if he told them all the time. Now he only told them so when they asked, when they said the word. The rest of the time, he played the fool, dancing at their demand, chasing sticks, panting and begging for head pats.

His silence was his survival and their lies their very doom.

Andrew Borden and his daughter proceeded through the streets of the Hill, past the darkened homes where dim shapes flickered behind window shutters and discordant snoring wafted on the invisible breezes. Fall River was in acquiescence, enjoying the rest that only the hours before the first bells could afford. The sun was aimed at the other side of the earth—there millions were toiling for their daily bread—but at this place and at this time, all was at peace.

Father and daughter were silent within the sphere of light from the lantern that Lizzie held aloft. Andrew pushed the handles of the wheelbarrow in which reclined the child's coffin of the waxen Monk. Only the slight tapping of some loose bolt in the front wheel disrupted the melancholic silence.

They knew the way to Oak Grove without needing to converse, having pilgrimaged there many times before. On past journeys, they had said little, even less upon their arrival, and often travelled home conversing only on the petty detailing of the remains of the day. What they had done there needed no words.

The lantern at last illuminated the main gate of the cemetery, dispersing the dark around its creeping vines and wrought iron. Almost by habit, Lizzie swept the light across the inscription in the stone arch above:

The shadows have fallen and they wait for the Day

"We should not be here at this hour," Andrew said. "There is no peace in a graveyard at night."

"But Father," Lizzie said, "if you believe there is nothing beyond this life, then this is just an old dumping ground for tired bones."

"Now is not the time for theology," Andrew shuddered.

Another lantern flickered and a metal shutter clicked open, revealing in its light the face of William Almy. "Andrew," he said. "Deputy Wixon said that you would come, but I did not expect…" He looked down at the barrow and sighed. "Have you lost your senses? What is *he* doing here?"

"I'm not here for him!" Andrew snapped. "Did you think that of me?"

Another lantern snapped in the dark, and two figures meandered from the shadows by the cemetery gate, one large and glooming, the other thin and tree-like. Manchester Root and Evangeline Turpin stepped into the triangulation of lantern light that haloed the gathering. "I do not think that Deputy Wixon will come," Manchester said amusedly. "He was practically soiling his trousers."

"I am here," came a thin voice from the side of the road. "My lantern broke," he explained. The deputy's shadow moved forward, and the familiar cloth cap and belted coat came into view. In the crook of one arm, sniveling and staring angrily about, was the small form of Herr Hugo von Trotter. "He bit my hand and I dropped it. I don't know what's got into him."

"Where's C.B.M.?" Lizzie asked.

Deputy Wixon shrugged. "I left word at his house, but his mother seemed to stare past me as if I weren't there."

"Maybe you weren't," Andrew said thinly. "I'm not sure of anything anymore."

"Gentlemen," Lizzie said, angling her light beam. "And lady," she added. "I dare say this is a grim place to gather, but I have determined there be an ending to our mystery. I cannot say with great certainty that I am correct in my assumption, but I believe I know the location of the Minuscule Monk. We must not wait. Follow me."

"In there?" Deputy Wixon asked. "I have never been in there at night."

"They cannot harm you," Lizzie said. "They only want peace. It is the living that we should fear."

A great hush embraced them, and the tinkling chatter of insects in the foliage rose to the fore. "Come," Lizzie said, and began the trek past the front gate of Oak Grove and into the walkways beyond.

They progressed along the winding path towards the interior. The sycamores and elms formed the walls of their tunnel through the dark necropolis. Beyond the canopy of branches and leaves could be seen the faint cloudy moonlight, barely raising the luminosity of their slowly moving globe of light. As they rounded a tall outcropping of rock, Andrew stopped in his tracks, the tapping wheel that had accompanied their march suddenly stopping. The silence was ominous.

"Father?" Lizzie asked in a whisper. "Do you hear something?"

Andrew raised a single finger towards the hillock. "Your mother," he said, and Lizzie went numb. A bird cried out from his hidden place in a remote tree, and the wind swirled about them as they stood.

Her father had never spoken those words on all their visits until now, and they had never visited Oak Grove with such thoughtless neglect of her grave. "Regardless," Lizzie shrugged, her lips drawn downward, "our destination is ahead."

She guided them onwards towards a mausoleum that shone out of the darkness with its own dull illumination, its white-gray sandstone glowing somewhat between the lanterns and the moon. It nestled on the front of a hillock, which buried its top and sides, providing the crypt a seamless union with the landscape into which it was built. Lizzie stopped at the rusted gate before it that slanted broken and ineffectual off its hinges. She moved her lantern about the front to reveal the etched letters in the lintel stone: Borden.

"Which Borden is this?" Mr. Almy said, holding up his lantern.

"The final resting place of Richard Durfee Brayton Jefferson Borden," Lizzie announced. "C.B.M.'s family crypt."

"What do you see?" Mr. Almy asked, peering. "There is not a lock on the door, unless I am mistaken."

"No," Lizzie said, peering about the heavy wooden barrier. "There is no lock, for that is not the entrance. Here we have a Thesinger box the size of a house, and our job is to discover what creature we can pull from its empty interior."

"Are you serious?" Miss Turpin said, laughing. "We've come here tonight to break into a tomb?"

"Perhaps you can explain how to enter it," Lizzie said grimly, tilting the lantern light towards the woman. "Did the monkey man tell you the secret?" Miss Turpin crept back, shadowing herself beyond Root's dark bulk.

"Evangeline!" Root said huskily. "You have spoken…to *him*?"

"Well," Miss Turpin whispered. "A little."

Lizzie lowered her lantern, guiding it along the door, searching it inch-by-inch, before she spotted what she was looking for: a tiny crack towards the very bottom that ran along a one-foot section of the wall in a rectangular pattern, its base touching the very bottom.

"Abracadabra!" Lizzie shouted, and tapped the wood inside the rectangle. A panel swiveled and turned, revealing a small opening. An audible collective gasp came from their simultaneous sense of wonderment and dread, an uncanny fear that caused the hairs on their necks to stiffen and their hearts to pump faster. Lizzie kicked the small door with her foot to close it shut again.

"We are disturbing the dead," said Deputy Wixon nervously. "I suggest we leave as soon as possible."

"Why?" Lizzie said. "When we are so close? I suggest we now put Herr Hugo von Trotter to the task for which he was trained. Come, Hugo." Lizzie lifted the creature from the deputy's arm, planted a small kiss on his brow and, as he whimpered softly, lowered him to the ground. Once set loose, he sniffed cautiously at the crack, and then pushed with his nose, pivoting the small panel; he darted forward, his entire body squeezing through the opening in the wood. When he had vanished, Lizzie kicked against the wood with her foot.

"I suspect we will hear some progress in a matter of seconds," she said, and then, as if an actor had been cued by a staged line, there was a crack of metal, and then a creaking noise. The hinges in the tomb's door shook their dust and the larger panel swung forward just an inch, revealing a willingness to be opened.

"Only the dog can release the bolt!" Andrew shuddered. "How macabre!"

Lizzie placed a delicate hand on the door where it was cracking and pulled the entire structure forward. Both lanterns were moved upwards and into the mausoleum. As their lanterns lit the interior, they could see, in the exact center of the musty and dank interior, the large marble indulgence of R.D.B.J. Borden's stone sarcophagus. Before it rested two pine wood coffins, flat on the dirt floor, angled towards each other and touching at the top like some weird set of twins joined at the skull.

Behind the sarcophagus was a shabby wagon, bucket-shaped with curved side-paneling atop four large wheels. Lizzie recognized it immediately as the vehicle that had been parked outside City Hall after the lecture on Egyptology that very morning, which did not surprise her. There were the rolling dunes, the pyramid on its slanted angle towards the sun, and the mummy rising from the earth with his arms crossed before him. But what she had not noticed that morning, and which she now saw in the lantern light, was that the side panels were riddled with what looked like bullet marks and sword slashes. Everyone present raced forward, surrounding the wagon, puzzled and amazed.

"What a relic," Mr. Almy said. "I have not seen such style since the year that Barrow and Dunhap's came to Boston."

"What is it doing in the Borden crypt?" Manchester Root said gloomily.

"We have the coffins," chirped Andrew. "We can take them back to the shop! That is a lot of wood to have been lost!"

"I did not think he would be able to get both," Miss Turpin said resignedly. She turned to Lizzie. "I suppose you think me capable of murder."

"No," she said. "But I do think that you know more than you are telling."

"All correct," Mr. Almy shouted, "but let us see what we have before we start accusing anyone of wrong doing," and he lifted one of the coffin lids. Inside was the stiffened and crumbled corpse of Albert Duey, the man who had appeared so unexpectedly and had disappeared so ingeniously from the basement of the furniture store not ten hours earlier. His mouth was more extended and his lips more torn, his face blackened by decay, and his hands stretched along his thighs like resting logs, but it was clearly Duey.

"Whoever populated this tomb with these fresh coffins," marveled Deputy Wixon, "must have had access to Herr von Trotter. Who else is small enough to go through the dog panel?"

"It is he!" Manchester Root shouted.

"The Mite!" Miss Turpin hissed.

"The Mite indeed," Lizzie said. "The phantom in the box begins to emerge."

"The Mite?" Andrew said. "The coward who shot the Monk? I thought that to be Albert Duey himself! What is this? Someone speak, I am perplexed."

"If Albert Duey is not the Mite," Deputy Wixon said, "and the Mite is the coward who shot the Monk..." His eyes crossed towards his nose, and he waggled his head as if attempting to rejoin his eyes, which had somehow spiraled apart from each other. "Who is in the second coffin?"

Their faces turned grim in the yellowish beams, and then they all stepped back, as if trying to find some cover in the darkness. The silence did not last long, for it was broken by the sharp snap of a firearm discharging. A shadow had fallen from the rear of the wagon and was scampering across the top of the sarcophagus. Its path was sparkling with the explosions of the gunfire. Something was shooting at them as it escaped from the tomb.

The bullets pelted about, rocketing off the walls, igniting brief flashes of flame. Snapping lights danced about crazily as the lanterns were thrown down in a mad attempt to extinguish them. Lizzie tumbled to the ground between the coffins, where she watched bullets drive into their wood.

"Crapulous creeds!" cried Manchester Root, who drove forward, his enormous bulk moving like a wall towards the doorway and the shallow promises of moonlight. Some sickening thuds reached their ears as his body took blow after blow.

With a yelp, Andrew leapt to his feet and pushed forward the wheelbarrow, driving it before Root, taking meager shelter in the obstruction he provided.

"Father!" Lizzie cried.

"You shall not kill my daughter!" Andrew bellowed. He darted out into the open, plunging from the mausoleum and heading towards the lightless paths. A bullet whizzed over his head as he ran a crazy zig-zag with the barrow over dirt, gravel, graves and stones.

"I have the Monk!" he screamed as he raced. "I have your precious Monk!"

"Andrew," Mr. Almy said, raising a hand towards the moonlight. "Don't be a fool!"

"There you are!" Manchester Root cried, and thundered forward, lashing about, grunting and cursing before lowering himself towards the ground. He clutched furiously at something invisible to all else before raising it to be silhouetted against the moonlight. It flopped like a small rag doll in the hands of Root who was spitting ugly invectives into its face. "I will squeeze the truth from you, you scoundrel!" Another crack of light and a sickening sound broke out like an explosion of dynamite, and Root fell backwards, the tiny wriggling form in his hand cascading outwards, cart-wheeling towards the ground. Root collapsed like a falling rock down a cliff face, hitting the grass with a great expulsion of breath, and then the Mite was off across the lawn, shouting in some unfamilar language, tossing aside a smoking revolver and drawing forth a new one to match the gun still clutched in his other tiny hand.

Andrew raced with the tottering barrow, revealing his position by the angry thwack from the faulty wheel. Instinctively, he was heading for his family plot. The child's coffin within bounced upwards and careened off to thud against the gravel, its lid dislodging and ejecting its grotesque cargo onto the grass. Andrew abandoned the barrow at the first sign of the path so familiar to his tearful memory, and raced up the hillock, his finger clutching desperately at empty air. "Sarah," he said, then fell across the small stone, touching its contours as his tears splashed upon the letters. "I am joining you, my beloved! Just one moment of pain and it shall be done for all Eternity!"

As a bullet darted across his scalp, burning the skin and singeing his hair, he screamed and tossed his body sideways along the ground, rolling and cursing as his limbs crashed against the hard cold ground.

"Do your worst!" he commanded, lifting himself boldly upwards. As he stood tall, mustering all the strength of his limbs and his courage, he was baffled by a loud clanking noise, and a clattering and then a muffled screaming. A strange calmness came over the scene, and by deep instinct Andrew knew that somehow, beyond reason, he was safe.

One lantern that had not been extinguished in the melee lifted upwards and shone below the cherubic face of C.B.M. Borden, revealing his expression of befuddled amusement. He stood in the path next to the wheelbarrow, which had been flipped entirely over. Something was struggling within its cavity, trapped between the metal shelf and the dirt ground of the cemetery path.

"Now you see him," the young man said boastfully. "Now you don't."

A loud strangled burst erupted like a muted cannon shot, and the wheelbarrow bounced upwards, before settling in the dust, immediately and fatally still. C.B.M. bent over it, inspecting the surface, and then tapped it gently with his foot.

"He may have shot himself," he announced. "Saves us a heap of trouble."

"William," Andrew panted. "Help me down. I am not as spry as I was in my prime."

The entourage came up the path, Deputy Wixon leading the way and Lizzie trailing behind, limping from fear, her limbs trembling. "Father," she said, and ran to his side.

"No fear," Andrew said calmly, his dignity restored. "Charles has caught the Mite. We only hope we can keep him planted there long enough to get the police."

Lizzie grabbed her father's hands and struggled to find the words. "I thought you dead for sure," she said. "I do not think what I would have done."

Manchester Root staggered onto the path. "Terrible," he was muttering. "Terrible."

C.B.M. cast his lantern light at his employer and noticed the blood stains on his shirt and coat, the back of his hands dripping. "Manchester, do we have a problem?"

Root looked down at his torso, struggling to see his shirt in the dim light. "Why, Charles, I took a few iron balls, but no matter. I have plenty of padding to protect me."

"Help me with this then," C.B.M. said, placing the lantern upon the ground and struggling downward to lift the upturned arms of the barrow. Manchester put his bulk into it, and the two men groaned as they lifted the capsized transport. After a slight pause, a small shadow inched forward and crept limply along the ground.

Mr. Almy and Deputy Wixon fell upon it and collectively lifted into the air a strange and listless body emitting tiny groans. The limbs shuffled without purpose or resistance. "There's life in him yet," Mr. Almy announced. "He is senseless, but I suggest we bind him anyway."

Manchester fished into his coat and pulled out a length of rope, holding it outwards for Mr. Almy, who stared at him blankly. "I knew we would have this encounter," Root explained. "I saw fit to come prepared." And within a moment, the Monongahela Mite, his face small and egg-shaped, his walrus moustache drooped with toil, and his limbs passive and harmless, lay prone on the ground, his feet facing west, his small fists clutched against his chest where the rope held them in check. A trickle of blood came down from his scalp, which had been grazed by a bullet.

Andrew had fished for the remaining revolver upon the ground and was inspecting it in the lantern light. "I have never heard the sound of such a thing," he marveled. "Like a whistling in my ears. I could have…" Then his face went deathly pale and his cheeks trembled. He gaped fish-mouthed for a moment, then thrust the weapon downward, sank to his knees upon a stone step, and felt outward for the comfort of his daughter's skirts.

"My daughter," he said meekly. Then he closed his eyes, drew his fists towards his chest and began to rock, muttering in a thin and whispery voice. Those who were close to him could make out the words of a strange ditty in a broken rhythm:

"No matter what may be your age…you always may cut a fine dash… if you've only got a moustache…"

"Father," Lizzie said, tears dropping on her cheek.

"Moustache," he sang, pulling his palms to his face. "If you've only got a moustache…"

His daughter knelt forward, placed her palms upon his locks, and summoning her strength to find the words that would comfort him, words that never came, she felt him tremble as he wept.

Chapter Eighteen

The First Chamber

The mummy wagon creaked ponderously down the Hill, a grim specter with wheels grinding. Those who guided it, in deference to the sleeping residents of the houses about them, slowed the pace to dampen the noise. Pulling its bulk were three men, clutching the hitches and mindful of their steps in the darkness. Before the procession walked a larger man, his shirt and coat stained with blood, holding aloft a lantern angled into the night.

On the wagon's summit were the two coffins built by Borden & Almy's, closed and latched, shifting with the movement. Walking behind the vehicle were two women and a deputy sheriff, all shuffling in a silent trance that dismissed all language. Behind them, on a length of rope pilfered from the wagon, was a small creature, plodding solidly and reluctantly, pulled forward by the indifferent and arbitrary tugs of the deputy. His mouth, muffled with a lady's handkerchief, gave off incomprehensible outbursts whose exact meaning remained obscure to all who heard them.

The funereal entourage turned onto Bedford Street, invisible to any living person at such an hour. Soon they had arrived before the towering façade of the Fall River Animal Suffrage League. The coffins were lowered by Borden and Almy, and each in turn were carried up the stone steps to the front door. Manchester Root motioned to the driveway off to the side. "Around back, the horse yard," he ordered, and the three men moved the wagon creakily away.

When they had all gathered in the front lobby, the coffins were laid down before the immortalized Labrador, whose panting visage Herr Hugo von Trotter eyed with a curious nostalgic glimmer. Manchester

Root collapsed onto a guest sofa, his pained face revealing a gradual awareness of his grim situation. C.B.M. Borden carefully examined the man's wounds with rolled-up sleeves.

"As far as I can tell," C.B.M. said, lifting his arms and wiping some blood on a towel, "the bullets just…well, just swam around inside of him and didn't hit any internal organs."

"You're not a physician," Miss Turpin said harshly. "We must bring a real doctor."

"I am fine, Evangeline," Root whispered. "I feel no pain, only a strong ennui and a profound loss of purpose." His hands covered his flabby cheeks, and he groaned. "Oh, what have I done?"

Miss Turpin blinked. "Has it been you all along?"

"I am no more responsible than everyone else in this room," Root declared. "But a man is dead, and I have spent my entire fortune on the novelty of a canine mentalist. Who can say that I am not a pathetic creature?"

"No, Manchester," Miss Turpin said. "You have done a wonderful thing for this city. We have trapped many politicians in their deceptive schemes and changed the way the public views their elected officials."

"That is merely what we tell ourselves to sleep at night," Root said mournfully.

"Now is not the time for ethical philosophy," Andrew said. "We have a mystery to resolve, and Lizzie has promised us a conclusion."

"We are waiting on one last person," Lizzie said, nodding towards Deputy Wixon. "I trust you have sent word to the Widow Borden and…"

The deputy nodded. "Arrive at midnight, I told them."

"My mother!" shouted C.B.M. "Here? If you expect her to get here by herself, you are sadly mistaken. She has no sense in her head to navigate the streets at night. We may as well—"

He stopped short in deference to the clomping of feet. Then into the lobby strolled two individuals, one a short and black-clad woman, her Whitby Jet comb flaring from her rolled plaits. In her white hands she clutched the brightly colored box that had so amused them at dinner.

The Thesinger Box.

But that was not the only surprise. Supporting her was a thin, weedy man in overalls. His weary face bespoke a desire to have done with his woes and to fall into a painless silence.

"Pratt," Deputy Wixon said. "You actually followed my directions."

"I have nothing to fear in joining this cast of clowns," Jack Pratt said. "I am innocent of all deeds except neglecting to stand guard over my clothes."

"And I believe you," Lizzie said. "In a sense."

"What do you mean by that?" Pratt scowled.

"My dear Mrs. Borden," Lizzie said, taking the old woman's frail hands and gazing in her watery eyes, which beamed with child-like expectation. "I apologize for abandoning your dinner and then taking you from your home at such a late hour."

"It is nothing," she said, holding up the box. "I always laugh when I see Charles using this thing; I don't mind another performance."

"I am delighted for that," Lizzie said. "Will you all excuse me for a moment?" and she lifted the box from the widow's hands and began walking towards the darkness of the back offices. She turned and stared down at Herr von Trotter. "Come," she said, politely, and the dog danced after her, the two disappearing around the turn in the hallway.

"That's my trick," C.B.M. said helplessly. "I paid a lot of money for that trick."

"I always wondered how it worked," Mrs. Borden said. "But seeing something appear from nothing is not my preference. It delights me more to see nothing appear to be something when all along it really wasn't anything at all."

"I almost understood that," Deputy Wixon said bemusedly.

Presently, Lizzie reappeared, unaccompanied by the dog, holding the Thesinger Box aloft in her upraised palms. She walked it to the marble table, on which rested business cards and pamphlets, and thudded it down as if relieved of a heaviness.

"Within this cube of wood," she began, "resides Herr Hugo von Trotter, the Truth Telling Dog, perhaps a bit disturbed over his imprisonment, for it was not his own willful act to enter the box. He was tricked into it by a handful of confections that I found in Mr. Root's ashtray. No doubt Hugo is puzzled and alarmed, and maybe even experiencing a bit of anxiety, but I will release him out shortly."

"Does he have air?" Miss Turpin said, clutching her neck. "I cannot abide an animal suffering."

"The box was made to host rabbits," Lizzie announced. "The air holes are in the back."

"Lizzie," Mr. Almy said, "what do you hope to prove by this?"

"Simply that a mystery with two solutions can have two possibilities. Either one is true, or the other is true. But both cannot be true at the same time. And yet in this mystery we have two truths that both appear to be false—quite an alarming paradox. Behold the Thesinger Box. It has two openings. Which opening will bring us to the dog?"

"Either one," Andrew said dismissively. "They both lead to the same chamber."

"But we cannot know until we try them," Lizzie said. "That is the beauty of a Thesinger Box. Until the box is opened, you cannot be certain."

Dramatically, with two coordinated hands, she thrust open both the front and top lid to reveal the chamber within. All present peered forward to see the cross hatched pattern of the lining inside. A bit of light shone where the top lid was laid bare, but there was no dog, no Herr Hugo von Trotter. The interior was empty.

"But even when the chamber is open," she said, "you still cannot be certain." She slammed the lids shut and waved a hand over the box.

"Voilá!" she yelled, and then dramatically flipped open the top. As she stepped back, a black-nosed snout peered out, its wet surface glistening, trembling whiskers and two sad eyes following. Herr Hugo von Trotter darted from the top, scrambling on his haunches to catch hold of the box top, and then thrust upwards. His stocky body arched through the air and landed with a thud on the table. Once composed, he sat down on his rump and thrust his two front legs downward to raise his large head and his dignity to the crowd. He ended the performance with a tiny swipe of his tongue across his nostrils.

"Where did he come from?" Andrew said in a haunted tone. "I saw the box empty myself. You all did."

Lizzie gave a hearty chuckle and patted Herr von Trotter on the head. He angled his neck to sniff her fingers. "There is a perfectly rational explanation," she said. "But I must now choose between explaining the mystery of the Thesinger Box and protecting C.B.M.'s investment as a stage magician. For once I have explained its secret, the trick will have no re-sale value."

"I would rather you not," C.B.M. cautioned. "Homer Thesinger bound me to an oath."

Lizzie made a small fizzle with her mouth. "Oh, double fudge on Homer Thesinger! I know that boy, and he will only make another trick box with a more clever mechanism."

"But I still cannot fathom how…" Mr. Almy said, his voice shortening. "Where was Herr von Trotter when you opened that box the first time?"

"I will reveal all," Lizzie said, "and herein solve several mysteries at once. As you can see," she said, flipping open both box lids, "the box is empty. But Father, would you be so kind as to lean forward and stare deeply into the box's interior."

"Would you have me stare at empty space?" Andrew replied. "I will humor you, no less." He peered into the front lid and focused his eyes. "I see something," he muttered. "There appears to be…" His back stiffened, and he fell back as if being pulled by ropes. "I see a face! A man! He has a beard!"

"Look closer," Lizzie commanded.

"I cannot look again! There is a head without a body, a monstrosity!"

Mr. Almy came forward, pushing Andrew aside. "It would be a true mystery box," he said, "if a human head could survive inside of it." He tapped his thighs and knelt over to take a look, then froze in his bent pose, before breaking out into a hearty chuckle. "Why Andrew, I'm staring into a damned mirror."

"Certainly," Lizzie confirmed. "A slanted mirror that cuts the box into two chambers: a bottom chamber that you see from the front, and a top chamber that you can access through the top lid. It was the top chamber in which Herr von Trotter was trapped."

"But we saw light coming in from the top!" Andrew sputtered.

"The light you saw coming from the top was merely a reflection of the light entering from the front. That is why I angled the box between the two lamps on either side of the room, so you would get this illusion. You saw the light and merely inferred that it was coming in from the top."

"So again," asked Mr. Almy impatiently, "what is the point of this?

That Albert Duey's body was behind a slanted mirror in our basement? Preposterous!"

She thrust the two lids shut, and then settled herself. "Just as this magic box has two chambers, this mystery has two solutions. Both are probable, but both cannot co-exist. But I will propose both. Two solutions to one mystery, like two halves of a Thesinger Box."

"Like two coffins, one unopened," Mr. Almy said, his gaze drifting.

"And two midget gunslingers: one visible and one invisible," Lizzie added. "Shall we begin?"

"Please," Manchester Root said, holding his gut with both hands. "Reveal all; let them know. And then perhaps we will have some peace."

They stood in a circular formation around the coffins and before the pedestal of the Labrador. As Lizzie spoke, she circulated, drifting from person to person. She began with a summary of the tale of the Minuscule Monk, as related earlier by Manchester Root, extracting merely the salient points for the benefit of those who were not present at the telling.

Jack Pratt seemed particularly disturbed. "If I had known," he said, staring at Root, "what a scoundrel you had been..." which tossed the large wounded man into another swoon of flushed melancholy.

"I produced your damned wax dummy!" Root snarled.

"And I helped build your shrine to canine mentalism! For one moment do you think..." Pratt then restrained himself, forcing his lips shut.

"So much for known facts," Lizzie continued. "Now we are confronted by a mystery of which there are two possible solutions, just as there are two chambers in the Thesinger Box. I will now walk you through the first chamber: an infamous gunslinger is shot to death in Dakota territory four years ago, his body mummified with arsenic into a hardened likeness of his living self, and paraded throughout the Western States by Albert Duey making money off the very man whom he had murdered."

"Duey didn't kill the Monk," Pratt said gruffly. "It was the dirty coward of the doggeral, the Mite."

"No doubt," Lizzie said. "But the Mite was a hired gun, a weapon used to surprise the Monk. Duey was very clever and knew that if he sent the real Monk's body to New York City he would never collect on the wager. The barber of Five Points who had posted it would never give up the punter's pot, and would try to find some trickery to get the Monk's body and kill Duey in the process. So there was only one thing that Duey could possibly do to resolve the situation: kill Benny Browbeat."

"Yes!" Deputy Wixon said. "Miss Lizzie, that is brilliant. That's what I would have done." He glanced about the room at the silent faces. "Of course, in actuality I would have called the police!"

"A clever plan," Lizzie said. "But he could not just walk into the barber shop on Leonard Street and take down Browbeat the way he did the Monk. No, something more clever and fool proof would have to be worked out. And it would preferably be done in a way that would also collect the reward money. It was risky, but worth a gamble."

"So Duey came to Fall River to pull a confidence game on Browbeat," Mr. Almy said, his brow furrowed, "and to steal his money."

"Would that be why he appeared at the station with a…" Deputy Wixon said, then halted. "How-dee-do!" he ejaculated. "That wasn't a dummy in the coffin at the train station. That was the Minuscule Monk in a…in a big man suit?!"

"Perhaps," Lizzie said, "in this first chamber of the mystery, we have a mummified gunslinger, a three-foot tall corpse, encased in wax, and fleshed out, so to speak, in a big man's suit. The coat arms and trouser legs that were too long for the Monk were stuffed with knotted rags. Between the waxen face and the floppy limbs, you did not see the man inside the dummy."

"And so the Monk came to Fall River," Jack Pratt sighed. "If I had known…."

"You would have done what?" Lizzie asked, clapping her hands. "Murder Duey? Take the body for yourself?"

"No," he said, stepping back, "I…" Then he glanced nervously at Herr Hugo von Trotter, who stared up at him from the floor, his nose twitching. "Get him away from me."

"Afraid of revealing secrets," Lizzie observed. "As we all are, and that is our worst fear, that the secret of our magic box may be revealed. But in this chamber of the box, Mr. Pratt, we have a plot hatched by the Fall River Animal Suffrage League, one designed to not only obtain the Monk, but to get Benny Browbeat out of the way, forever.

This would require a combination of skills. The strategy can be pieced together by the existing physical evidence.

"At first, it was difficult for me to see it, but we had a common thread that brought together the random objects. There was the clothing upon the dead man's body, admittedly belonging to Jack Pratt, the immortalist at the League and carpenter at the Academy Building. Then there was the vellum in the dead man's mouth, a piece of evidence that implicated both Miss Turpin and my father. Next was the fact that the man had been murdered and coffined in the basement of Borden & Almy's, implicating everyone present, including Mr. Darling. Finally, there was the felt hat, which caused me great puzzlement, and which I could only assume was another attempt to implicate the innocent. But it was a hat that belonged to a bald man, and no one involved in this case is bald. So who can this be?"

She paused dramatically and then glanced at Manchester Root. "Short of wearing a head of false hair," she said, pointing, "I suspect the hat has some deeper meaning for you."

"Yes," Manchester Root said grimly. "I would rather you not reveal it. It is enough that you know it was meant to accuse me of the crime."

"For now, I will honor your request," Lizzie said. "But not for long, since the owner of that hat will, I suspect, bring the final piece of the puzzle into place."

"I would appreciate that you preserve my dignity," Root sighed, "by leaving that until the end of your performance."

"Granted," Lizzie said. "But the drawing of innocent people into suspicion did not stop with the felt hat. There was the mysterious Mr. Jimmy Pell, survivor of the Lawrence Massacre and a member of Albert Duey's Terrible Trio, who gave precise instructions to build a coffin in the same dimensions as one ordered by the Widow Mrs. Borden of Rock Street, thereby casting suspicion on the poor old woman."

"I don't need a coffin," the Widow said. "I still have a few more breaths in me, thank you much."

"The coffin was not meant for you," Lizzie explained. "Neither was it ever meant to be delivered to you. But the body of Albert Duey *was* meant to be found. The killer certainly would have expected us to call the police after the discovery. It would have been a public sensation, revealed to all. Albert Duey dead! The man who killed the Minuscule Monk! The newspapers would have sold many copies, and the eyes of the nation would have come down upon us. But no, each of us would have had every reason to avoid the attention, because we each had either something to hide or we would have been scandalized by the discovery. Certainly neither my father nor Mr. Almy would have wanted their business to be associated with a foul murder. And Miss Turpin would not have wanted her adventure at Borden & Almy's so publicly scrutinized. Jack Pratt would have been ruined by the murdered man wearing his clothes, and he would have been exiled to an itinerant life in other mill towns. Mr. Root would not have survived the scandal if the true identity of the hat's owner would had been revealed."

"Utterly ruined," Root said, as his body sagged deeper into the couch.

"Certainly," Lizzie continued. "You all wanted to keep it a secret, either for fear of public embarrassment, or hiding something from your past. So you had encouraged Deputy Wixon to keep this to himself and to hide it from his superiors who, to this moment, still do not know that a murder has been committed."

"That was beginning to trouble me," Deputy Wixon confessed. "I have a lot of explaining to do."

"And I will be there by your side when we finally go to the Marshal!" Lizzie announced. "And I will explain that the killer planted all this evidence in an attempt to keep the murder secret. He knew we would not know how to handle the situation, that we would somehow try to keep the body concealed. That is the reason the coffins were stolen back, so we would all fear being arrested for a crime we didn't commit."

"You really believe this?" C.B.M. said, his eyes darting in wonder. "You think that Albert Duey was murdered so we would be afraid of being arrested? You said it yourself; he brought the Monk to Fall River. He was murdered to snatch away the Monk."

"Yes," Lizzie said. "In this chamber of the mystery box, the killer wanted to possess the Monk and to get rid of Albert Duey simultaneously. That would upset the balance of things, set into motion waves of paranoia amongst the very people who would have been able to decipher his crime."

"It is certainly possible," Andrew said, wringing his hands.

"So Benny Browbeat comes to Fall River to intercept Albert Duey, orders the coffins to be built in a way that implicates the Widow Mrs. Borden and Pell of the Terrible Trio, steals from each of us some secret possession, lures his victim into my basement, murders him and steals the Monk. He is certain that he will not get caught because the crime will never be reported. Then the murdered man is stolen back and hidden in Oak Grove so we have no evidence that the murder even occurred."

"In that particular case," C.B.M. said, his eyes brightening, "the murder would not had happened."

"Arguably," Lizzie nodded, "but one that could not be proven one way or the other. But as I pondered this solution, I couldn't help but be troubled over the loose ends. Why would Browbeat want to involve the Animal Suffrage League, or Borden & Almy's, or the Widow Borden, or any of us, for that matter? The only common connection among the Minuscule Monk, Mr. Root, Miss Turpin and Mr. Pratt is Herr Hugo von Trotter, the Truth Telling Dog."

All eyes in the room looked downward at the small beast, who alternatively panted and swiped his nostrils with his tongue, looking back at them as if expecting, at any moment, a bit of food or a loving pat between the ears.

"In this first chamber of the mystery," Lizzie said, "the killer has one name. But in the second chamber, as we shall see, he may have another. Or several."

Chapter Nineteen

The Second Chamber

"I needed to think again about this mentalist act," Lizzie confessed. "While I intuitively felt that Herr von Trotter's powers were viable, I could not be sure that we were interpreting his actions correctly. There were times we questioned him and he seemed to react inconsistently. Sometimes his responses went against all common sense, and then other times he seemed to be acutely aware of who was telling a lie. If you would all indulge me for a moment, I want to perform a test to prove my theory.

"Balderdash!" She pointed a finger. "See how his eyes dilate, his mouth goes still and snaps shut, his nose quivers with anticipation. Here we have a dog braced for action. Hugo," she said, kneeling downward. "Am I a Queen of Egypt in her tomb?" The dog stared at her, even tilted his head a bit sideways as if puzzled by her question.

"Hugo," she said again. "I am not a Queen of Egypt in my tomb." The dog continued to stare.

"Hugo," she said a third time. "I am a Queen of Egypt in her tomb," to which Herr Hugo von Trotter broke out into a violent series of barks that tossed his body about like a log in a river current. "Balderdash!" Lizzie said, bringing an end to the demonstration.

"Do you not see?" she asked. "My first statement was a question. One does not lie or tell the truth when one asks a question. The burden of truth is on the person answering, and since Hugo is not possessed of a mind capable of understanding the question, he does not know the meaning behind it. He was only sensitive to the fact that I was *not* telling a lie. My second and third statements differed only in the use of the word 'not.' In the first statement,

I was telling the truth, that I am not a Queen of Egypt. In the last statement, I was lying, stating that I am a Queen, when in fact, I am not. Significantly, I knew that I was lying. His response would have been different if I had stated something that I believed to be true, but was in fact a falsehood.

"This pattern is extremely relevant to our case. Earlier, I made the statement to Herr von Trotter that Jack Pratt *is* the murderer of Albert Duey. His violent reaction led us to believe that my statement was a falsehood and that Jack Pratt was *not* the murderer. However, it was only a falsehood because I did not believe it at the time. I personally had my doubts that Jack Pratt killed Albert Duey, and the dog sensed my doubts. The dog did not know who killed Albert Duey any more than I did.

"Then Deputy Wixon made the statement that Jack Pratt is *not* the killer, the opposite in meaning of my own statement, and the dog declared it to be a falsehood as well. This was because the good deputy honestly believed Jack Pratt to be the killer and did *not* believe him *not* to be the killer. You see, the dog senses the difference between an untrue statement believed, and a true statement not believed."

"You mean," C.B.M. marveled, "the dog can puzzle out a double negative?"

"Only in a sense," Lizzie continued. "He can sense when we do not believe what we are saying."

"Remarkable," Andrew said, pulling at his beard. "So the words of the statements we posed to him are meaningless…" Then he thought, rubbing his hands together. "This means that…" he said, and thought again. "Why, thinking back on things, this means that Manchester Root was posing a lot of monkey dash in front of this beast and getting any response he wanted us to hear."

"By posing a question in a specific way," Lizzie disclosed, "Root guaranteed that the dog would remain silent. He swore that he did not kill Albert Duey, which was salient enough, but he went on to insist that he did not know anything about Albert Duey's death in the basement. But as we shall see, in this most mysterious chamber of the Egyptian Tomb, things may not be as they seem, and that statement may indeed be a lie couched in a way that was perceived by the dog as a truth."

"How can that be?" Mr. Almy asked, trying to reason it all out. "If the dog is one hundred per cent capable of sensing a lie, and the statement was a lie, how can it be perceived as a truth?"

"Very easily," Lizzie said, smiling. "That is where the mirror of the Thesinger Box comes in. We are posed exactly upon its edge and do not yet see it clearly."

"But my dear Lizzie," the Widow Mrs. Borden said. "How can you see a mirror clearly? Every time you look at it, you see yourself, not the mirror." She noted Andrew staring at her stupidly. "I personally think my mirror is hiding from me," she declared.

"Good point," C.B.M. said. "I wish I had thought of that one. Yes."

Root sagged in his couch, his eyelids fluttering. "You may think me an unscrupulous cur," he said. "My only defense is that I had no choice. My fear of Benny Browbeat was incalculable. You are not aware of what brutality that man is capable."

"But you are not the only person who used the dog in that manner," Lizzie continued. "Many of us were unwitting victims of the logical contradictions that plagued our understanding of his responses. Yet, others, like Mr. Jack Pratt, went as far as Root to set the stage for his own innocence. He stated, 'The dog's silence proves my innocence.'"

"But the dog sensed that as a lie," Deputy Wixon was quick to point out.

"Yes, Hugo did. However, Pratt made one fatal mistake. He added to the end of the sentence, 'I am not lying.' And the dog took argument with that, being that it was not true. Jack Pratt was lying."

"Lizzie," Mr. Almy said. "Think of what you are saying. In the last few moments, you have accused both Manchester Root and Jack Pratt of being murderers."

Lizzie shrugged. "Herr Hugo von Trotter is the only voice in this room we can trust for now, and he has unlocked for us the second chamber, one in which there is not one killer, but several. For just as it is quite possible that everyone was framed by one individual for the murder of Albert Duey, it is equally possible that everyone committed the murder, and is trying to frame one man."

An abrupt hush fell over the lobby, and a quick cross-firing of glances generated a veneer of paranoia and unease. Lizzie broke the silence: "We return to Root's statement that he did not know anything about Albert Duey's death in the basement. The dog perceived that to be a truth. But it may not have been a truth. That's a contradiction. How do we resolve that contradiction? How do we make it a statement that would appear a truth to the dog, but a lie being told by Root?"

"Do not do this, Miss Borden," Manchester Root said, his face completely covered by his sausage-like fingers. "I will be ruined."

"If you killed that man," Andrew said, "we don't care a fig for your reputation."

Root lifted his torso with a tremendous exertion, pulling himself to the edge. "Hugo!" he shouted, and then caught the attention of the animal's large languid head. "Balderdash! I did *not* kill the man found in the basement!"

The dog took another swipe at his nostrils.

"There!" Root said, with a hand flourish. "I rest my case, your Honor. And when you have the time, Miss Borden, please show us your legal certificate before leaving the courtroom."

"It would serve you well, Root," Lizzie intoned, "if you would stop playing these games immediately. Your statement just now remained a truth because you did not mention the name of the man who was murdered. I will make a statement right now, one that would provoke a response from the dog."

"A waste of time," Root huffed.

"Need I remind you that the dog is still in a truth-telling way? See how his nose quivers, how his eyes glisten? He is waiting to hear the next statement."

Root's face betrayed his discomposure by inducing a bead of sweat on his brow. "Then be done with it," and he fell back onto the lobby couch.

Lizzie bent over the dog and said plainly, "The dead man in the basement of Borden & Almy's was Albert Duey." The dog immediately convulsed in a rampaging yelping. Lizzie raised her hand and silenced him. "Mr. Root," she said out the side of her mouth, keeping her rapt attention on the dog's head, "can you please state the opposite?"

"If you wish," said the defeated Root. "Very well. Hugo…the dead man in the basement of Borden & Almy's was *not* Albert Duey."

The silence was thundering, until Lizzie ended the session with a simple and thinly stated "Balderdash". After a moment of collective breathing, Deputy Wixon limply commented, "So it was *not* Albert Duey who was found murdered in the basement."

"*Not* Albert Duey," repeated Andrew.

"It was *not* Albert Duey," Lizzie confirmed. "The mirror has fooled us all along. We are now in the second chamber, having left the first one with its clean logical solutions behind us. In this chamber of the mystery, the body in the coffin was *not* Albert Duey."

"Then who was murdered?" Mr. Almy choked, as if reluctant to ask.

"There are several in this room who can tell us the answer to that question," Lizzie stated. "But the people who know the truth may actually *not* have killed the man who is not Albert Duey."

C.B.M. grinned. "Now you are barking up my tree. This second chamber seems very agreeable to me."

"I am sure of it," Lizzie said. "In this chamber, someone else came to Fall River posed as Albert Duey in order to obtain the Minuscule Monk, not to bring the Monk into the city. The Monk may already have been here, and this man was coming to get him. The body at the train station was a substitute, a real dummy, wax head and all."

"Two dummies?" Andrew said. "Pratt had one. At the Academy Building."

All eyes turned towards Pratt, who raised his palms calmly. "I did not kill that man, and you can fetch the dog on me to prove it."

"Then what were you lying about?" Andrew asked.

"I will reveal that," Lizzie said. "Many people had motivation enough to get rid of the man who was killed, and many people could have done the deed. But I propose that the murder was not performed by any of them. That cleans up many contradictions."

"That cleans up contradictions?" Mr. Almy said. "My God, Lizzie, that's the most contradictory of all. They all did the crime, but none of them did it?"

"Not if they hired someone," Lizzie smiled. "And who better to perform the deed than the hired gun who murdered the Monk, the dirty little coward, the Monongahela Mite. Surely our adventure in the cemetery this evening must have proven that here was a dangerous killer, highly trained and effective, an assassin of the first order, located in Fall River, small enough to climb in through the basement window, the Monkey Man of Anawan Street."

The small man in the corner stirred a bit, lifted his large blank eyes over the edge of his gag, and blinked.

"Is it time to take off his oral restraint?" Lizzie suggested. "Do we dare?"

"I'm willing to take the gamble," Andrew said. "Mr. Jack Pratt, would you oblige? Just be careful he does not try to bite you; we don't yet know how deadly his venom may be."

Pratt stepped forward, his face resigned to a dismal fate, and withdrew the handkerchief that bound the killer's mouth. Below was a ragged walrus moustache over a set of pursed lips. His eyes remained inscrutable.

"I am honored," came a melodious, comforting voice, "to meet the famed Girl Detective of Fall River. I have indomitable faith in the fortitude of your occupation and those who have the acumen for its performance, and I am duly in thunderstruck adulation. We of the rapscallion class have more of a fondness for those who hunt us and reveal our machinations than you may think."

"You speak quite well," Mr. Almy said, "for a savage killer."

"Not savage," the gunslinger cautioned. "By no means savage. I am to be likened more to an artist, direct and purposeful in my brush strokes, striving for harmony and elegance of design. Until now, of course."

"But you let yourself be caught," Lizzie said. "I can hardly believe you would have fired all those random shots in the darkness and make it so easy for us to catch you."

"Oh, you didn't catch me," the Mite said. "I am here to clear up this mystery and put the adventure to an end. After that, I shall be gone. Like magic, what?"

"You are tied up with rope," Deputy Wixon laughed. "We walked you through the streets like a captive bound to a chariot wheel. How can you possibly get out of this?"

"I have calculated nine different ways in which I can escape," the Mite said with pride. "Given enough time, I will find the means to pursue one or the other."

"Now that you've told us," Officer Wixon added, "we'll be doubly and triply careful when we transport you."

"Yes, true," the Mite said, staring at the rope about his torso. "But I have negotiated far worse. As I said, I take pride in my technique."

"We will see," Lizzie continued. "But I must congratulate you on the feat you performed at Borden & Almy's, one worthy of the best stage magician. You created a Thesinger Box the size of a room and managed to leave us all profoundly baffled."

"That was one of my masterpieces," the Mite said, grinning. "A critical moment of my career. My employer was stumped as well, and I suspect to this moment cannot even puzzle it out."

"Ah," Andrew said. "Now we get to the saucy bit. Who did hire this maniac? Was it Root? Turpin? Pratt? Mrs. Borden? Perhaps it was even the talking dog himself!"

"Truth-telling dog," Root corrected him.

"In all my cases," the Mite explained, "I hide behind my employer. I am not in it to make a legend, and my insertion in the Minuscule Monk street song is particularly perturbing, considering that it makes mention of cowardice, a quality which I am sorely lacking. But there I banked upon the remoteness of the outpost, the obscurity of the saloon, the general fear of discovery in the hearts of those present. Surrounded by drunks, desperados, rogues and murdering rascals, I did not think any of them would 'squeal,' as they say in New York. I took pride that I could assassinate the Monk in front of a hundred people, and depart from the scene a free man, barely remembered, impossible to describe."

"But you were described," Lizzie reminded him, "and inserted into the song. The doggerel mentioned your moniker."

"Yes, because there was a man present I did not expect. A balladeer, a guitar player who travels the West seeking out legends of the pistol he can put into cheap broadsheets to be cranked from the hurdy-gurdies and generate a large sum of cash in return. Such a man is a fast conduit to the whistling masses across America, one who can never hold a secret, a man who obfuscates reality to the point where his wretched street doggerel bears little resemblance to the events it pretends to portray, but nonetheless seizes the public imagination." He raised a small finger to his cheek and chuckled. "An entire continent believing a lie, such is the American character."

"So who is your employer?" Andrew asked hastily, his hands

curling towards fists.

"That cannot be revealed," the Mite said spitefully. "But I can say, he does call himself many names."

"Jimmy Pell," Lizzie whispered. "Yes, I see it now. The Jimmy Pell from the Terrible Trio was not involved at all. That was a blind drawn over our eyes by Mr. Root. Je m'appelle. 'I call myself,' in French. Perhaps you too speak French, Mr. Mite."

"Please," the Mite said softly. "Call me by my proper name: Jean Michel Sauniere Etranger-Gestang de Bordeaux. I have set foot only once in the Monongahela Valley, to assassinate an anthracite tycoon. The landscape was vile; I have no desire to wax nostalgic about its tepid ways."

"Regardless," Deputy Wixon said, "now we have a name to arrest him under. And he will be arrested, and he won't be leaving his cell any time soon, no matter what bluster he hurls at us."

"So where does this leave us?" Andrew asked strangely. "We know who killed a man that we know was not Albert Duey, in a way we haven't figured out yet, hired by someone whom we don't know. How is that a solution?"

"We are close," Lizzie promised. "But I encourage you to think clearly about this. Monsieur Etranger-Gestang has told us that his employer is known by several names. Jimmy Pell is a placeholder for several appellations."

Deputy Wixon snapped his fingers. "I knew it! They all hired the Monk. Every last one of them. Root, Turpin, Pratt, the Widow Borden, her crazy son."

"Wait a moment," C.B.M. said, holding up one hand. "I had nothing to do with this. I was hired by Root to spy on Pratt, and to discover where he was keeping the wax dummy. Beyond that, I feel as if I were played like a fiddle, the same manner in which he played the dog for your befuddlement."

"I believe you," Lizzie encouraged him. "It does seem as if you were used to throw off our investigation, although I'm not sure how we could have believed anything you claimed. You actually told us that the murder never occurred, that it didn't exist."

C.B.M. looked nervously at the two coffins. "Well, to be fair, for a small amount of time there, it didn't exist. I suppose when you rediscovered the body, it came back into existence."

Manchester Root sighed loudly, puffing his cheeks. "Why couldn't I have listened to my father when he told me to spend my life minding my own business?"

"At this point in the investigation," Lizzie said, "there are only two further possibilities. That everyone associated with the League took part in the hiring of the Mite for the purpose of murder, or that each and every one of those individuals who hired the Mite was unaware of one another's association with him. There would be a case where many people contracted the deed, and thought, in turn, they were the only ones doing so."

"And what about the planted evidence," Mr. Almy said, frustrated. "Who would go so far? Unless they planned it all together."

"No," Root groaned. "Not all together. The Mite approached us, one by one, and we all made a deal, independently and in ignorance of each other's intentions. And yet…" He paused and closed his eyes for shame that tears may stream and the authority of his words might sadly decline. "We cannot entirely blame the Mite. We all saw the opportunity; we all knew of the Mite's presence; we all acted in the same manner."

"And that is what has led to our downfall," Miss Turpin said, her voice cracking. "We all saw the need to cast suspicion on the other. I knew of the felt hat that Mr. Root had purchased during his travels in Germany. It was a family heirloom, topping its own pedestal in the League's conference room. I asked the Mite to steal it and plant it upon the body."

"My father's Homburg," Root sniffled. "He told me it would be a symbol of wealth and power, that statesmen and presidents would adopt it as their signature head wear."

"And I thought of the strip of vellum in the mouth," Pratt said resignedly. "Miss Turpin carried that poem everywhere. Everyone saw it with her. The suturing of the lips was not my idea but a finishing touch conjured by a madman!"

"And I arranged for the theft of Pratt's clothing," Root said, and turned his shamed eyes from the taxidermist's angry stare.

"There you have it then," Mr. Almy said, clapping his palms together. "The Fall River Animal Suffrage League had laid a trap for a person unknown who was bringing the real Minuscule Monk to Fall River. The Mite was hired by them all to commit a murder, but none of them knew the other to be setting up for the crime. They all told the Mite to plant evidence to implicate one another, something no one expected. Now I am certain that this solution is the most plausible, although it has a high degree of improbability all over it. The only part I am completely baffled over is the identity of the murdered man. If it is not Albert Duey, who is it, and why did you all want him dead?"

Lizzie walked slowly to the two coffins and placed herself between them, touching her hands upon the unfinished wooden surfaces. "Two coffins, both built by Borden, Almy and Darling between noon time yesterday and noon time today. One holds the murdered man, the other holds something unknown. I have prevented anyone here from opening that coffin on the chance that we would put our higher intellect to work and puzzle out the mystery. It makes everything more interesting, doesn't it?"

"Do you mean to suggest," Andrew said, "that Albert Duey, the real Albert Duey, is in the other coffin?"

"Perhaps," Lizzie said suggestively. "But we would not know until we have opened it."

"The suspense is killing me," the Widow Mrs. Borden said, clapping her hands. "I have waited all evening for this trick."

"Open it now," Deputy Wixon shouted. "I have troubles enough not reporting a corpse to the Marshal." He glared at the two coffins and choked. "Possibly two!" he finished.

"Do we want to lay wagers?" Lizzie joked. "How many people would care to wager a dollar that Albert Duey is in the second coffin?"

"I still want to know the name of the man in the first coffin!" Mr. Almy said. "Lizzie, you can't do this, it's cruel. We are in the midst of very serious business, and you are playing games."

"Games?" Lizzie said. "I assure you I do not see this as a game. But I also assure you that I have absolutely no idea who is in the second coffin, and I am just as anxious to see it opened as you."

"Then do it," Root said. "Put us out of our misery."

Lizzie hovered over the second box, then darted both hands under the lid latch and prised the top open till it tumbled downward revealing the body within.

Nestled in the narrow confine was an exact replica of the wax dummy of the Minuscule Monk, its wide eyes staring, its mouth crushed into a permanent scowl, the skin dark and brown, and its tiny hands resting on a leather vest. The body was angled down near the foot section of the coffin, for it had shifted in transport. Its limbs were pressed to its sides as if it were made from a single log of wood.

"The Monk!" Jack Pratt howled and leapt forward. "The real man!" He stormed the coffin, almost knocking it from its base, and tore with his fingers at the face. "See how he is hard as rock! Oh, why cannot you all see?! He was here all the time! The Mite! The Mite! He stole it, he kept it!" Then his eyes grew dark and he turned on the small man with the walrus moustache. The two studied each other ominously. "Let me have him," Pratt growled. "For ten minutes, alone."

"Quite a remarkable performance, Mr. Pratt," Lizzie said. "Although I do encourage you to lower it a notch, as the theater critics advise. You need not parade false sentiment before us."

Pratt's exuberance collapsed into silence within an instant and his face went slack, his hands by his side.

"What?" Root thundered. "That is not the Monk?"

"No more than the replica harbored by Pratt at the Academy Building," Lizzie explained. "They were both made to dupe Benny Browbeat. In fact, if all my suspicions are correct…"

She turned to the first coffin and withdrew its lid, revealing the corpse previously known as Albert Duey, its face discolored and distorted. "We now enter the final chamber of the Egyptian crypt where the mummy awaits, the real mummy, not the clever fake meant to baffle the grave robbers. By opening this coffin, we are one step closer to the heart of the affair."

"But who is he?" Andrew asked. "If he's not Albert Duey, then who the blazes is he?"

"We can answer that first by asking each of us who we are. For that task, I call upon the talents of Herr Hugo von Trotter, once more." She snapped her fingers to get the canine's attention. "Balderdash!" she shouted. "We will go around in a circle and each say the statement, 'I call myself…' or more appropriately 'Je m'appelle…' and then add our name. For example, I will begin: Je m'appelle Lizzie Borden. Yes, see how Hugo stares, calmly and without fear, but still braced for subterfuge. Now we may move on to Root."

The large man dipped his head and managed to announce, "Je m'appelle Manchester Root."

"Je m'appelle Evangeline Turpin!" the tall secretary said hastily, and without any prompting. "And no other!"

The dog remained poised, his ears wavering and whiskers twitching while he was brought before one human after another. The last one, on the end, was Jack Pratt, who grumbled and fidgeted with his hands.

"You may as well prepare the cell for me now," he said. "For I cannot make such a statement about being Jack Pratt without that hound spewing saliva."

"What!" Deputy Wixon said. "You're not…"

"Of course not," the man said. "There's no way out of this trap; I surrender. All I can say in my defense is that we rid the world of a very bad man. And no one can fail to applaud us for it."

"Then we have the honor of addressing…?" Lizzie said, her statement trailing into a question.

"I may as well have nailed a sign to my forehead," he said. "For I am the elusive Albert Duey. And that is a truth that no dog can rid me of."

"Great Gods," Mr. Almy said, stepping backwards. "Great blistering Gods!"

"All this time," Andrew said, his jaw bristle flaming. "You could have spoken up, if you are no guiltier than the others. There would have been no shame in it, no matter what you call yourself."

"I was protecting you all!" Duey shouted, his shoulders heaving with frustration. "The misery that will descend upon you now. No, this wasn't in any of my plans. Everyone was supposed to keep his trap shut! The body would silently disappear and then we would have done with this. Suffering wounds, why can't any of you mind your own damned business?!"

"You conspired to murder a man," Deputy Wixon said. "How is that not our business?"

"You have broken the social contract," Mr. Almy said stunned. "A sacred contract!"

"With whom?" Duey shouted. "With a fiend? A man who would have slashed your throat on Mulberry Street for a handful of pennies? Do you realize who that body is, and what service I have done to the world?! We now walk upon an Earth that is blissfully free of Benny Browbeat."

Lizzie glanced over at the corpse and examined its face. "All correct," she said. "You have confirmed my suspicion."

"You dare take the credit for that?" Manchester Root said, mustering the breath in his body. "I hired the Mite, and I did the deed."

"It was I!" Miss Turpin said. "Why are you so blind?"

"All of you did the deed," Lizzie said, her voice rising above their protests. "All— and none of you. You tried to double-cross one another, and tried to ensure one another's silence. But the one who was most silent in this entire business was the Mite. He knew he was doing the same assassin's job for three distinct clients, all of whom knew nothing about any other, and all of whom planned to implicate one another in the crime. So standing here at the hub of this fantastically spinning wheel is the Monongahela Mite. Here he stands; he is unbound, unfettered. He who has been so eloquent in speech and so verbose, let him speak now upon this matter."

The small man raised his whiskered face, a strange grin forming upon his half-hidden lips, and two tiny fists rose into the air.

"Go kiss my bottom's beard!" he spat.

Chapter Twenty

The Last Chamber

"I'll savage him, I will!" Manchester Root was screaming. "I may be swimming in bullets, but I can still murder him!"

Deputy Wixon grabbed the Mite's rawhide vest with both hands, raising him into the air. "Careful," Mr. Almy cautioned. "He is quite dangerous."

"No man speaks such words in front of women," Deputy Wixon scowled, and he shook the body as if he were trying to mix a drink within a metal shaker. The small man squirmed and fell to the side. The deputy, seizing the opportunity, completed the turn, grabbing the Mite by his ankles, and dashing him against the floor.

"Put him down," Lizzie ordered. "He is our only hope."

"And what for? He murdered one man; he tried to kill us at the cemetery. God knows how many men he has assassinated for money."

"Twenty-seven," came a thin voice from the capsized gunslinger.

"There you have it," Deputy Wixon said boldly. "The dog is still in truth-telling fashion and did not bark."

"The Mite is merely a hired man," Lizzie said. "And a human being, may I add, with all the protected rights to a fair trial by a jury of his peers."

"His peers?" Deputy Wixon huffed. "Where are you going to find twelve people like him? Perhaps Phineas Barnum can make some recommendations."

"Wixon!" Lizzie screamed. "You are an officer of the law! Come to your senses."

With glacial slowness, the deputy lowered his victim to the

ground, then raised his hands to his face. The Mite carefully wriggled his body away from his attacker.

"Don't be ashamed, Wixon," Andrew counseled. "I would have delighted to see that thing's neck snap."

"He is not a thing!" Lizzie said. "He is an erudite Frenchman who has worked as an independent contractor, albeit for evil purposes. Of course, we should put him under arrest and have him account for his crimes, but it will be the justice of civilization that will decide his fate, not our passionate outbursts."

"He swore he would get away," Duey said warningly, placing a boot heel on the Mite's torso, pinning him to the floor. "Every minute you keep him alive, he's one step away from escape. And then none of us may sleep at night."

"I don't suppose," Lizzie said, trying to compose her troubled audience, "that anyone here now doubts that the Mite murdered Benny Browbeat of New York, who was lured to Fall River with the desperate hope of obtaining possession of the Minuscule Monk. And I don't think we are in any disagreement that the various members of the Fall River Animal Suffrage League had hired the Mite to do the deed. I take it by your uncomfortable silence that we all agree.

"So given all these certainties, we now must turn back the clock to yesterday. The Monongahela Mite arrives in Fall River in a circus wagon. He is accompanied by a driver posing as Professor Bildung who lectures at City Hall in Egyptian mummification. We do not yet know this man's identity, perhaps we never will, but he is merely an instrument, a hired hand despite his erudite knowledge about antiquity. He may be a huckster from the West, a man who works often with the Mite. Perhaps he is Jimmy Pell of the Terrible Trio? Regardless, the wagon is a perfect cover for transporting both a dead body, a coffin, and a midget gunslinger. Bildung and the Mite camp in the wagon at its secret location in the graveyard.

"Also yesterday afternoon, Benny Browbeat arrives at the train station pretending to be Albert Duey. How does he think he can get away with this? He must have knowledge that Duey is living under an assumed name, and known to all as Jack Pratt, the Immortalist.

"Benny also brings with him a coffin with a waxen dummy of the Monk, a clever forgery that resembles one already in the possession of the real Albert Duey. How did two replicas of the Monk come to exist? And how did Benny Browbeat know to bring one? He must have had a contact in Fall River, albeit a deceiving one, someone who knew enough about the Suffrage League and could have planned this entire escapade from top to bottom. Someone who could have persuaded three people simultaneously to plan Benny Browbeat's murder, who directed them to the Mite, and could lure their victim here with bait of a most palpable kind. What was that bait? And why was the murder necessary? So the vendetta against the Terrible Trio can be ended? So the money in the punter's pot can be obtained without having to produce the real Monk? Only this person knows."

"And you know who that person is?" Mr. Almy said. "You have kept us waiting long enough."

Lizzie rubbed her chin. "I have been pondering this all day. Complications arise when we consider a dog who reveals to people when they do not believe what they are saying, and a young amateur detective who tries to prove that something that you do not think about does not even exist. Between the two of them, we have moved from sure footing to the plane of the metaphysical, as elusive as reality itself."

"Such is life," C.B.M. said solemnly.

"Nonetheless, when you put the two of them together," Lizzie said, "you have the tools and the technique to deceive and throw any investigator off the track. If you know how to set these two players into motion, you can lead even a girl detective into a dead end."

"Root," Andrew said. "My God, it's Root. He made the arrangements with Browbeat. He set this all into motion."

"Did I?" Root asked. "And why do I monopolize that honor? Two other people hired the Mite!"

"But only you know where the Minuscule Monk resides. The real Minuscule Monk."

"How can I?" Root blurted.

"Need I remind you that Herr von Trotter is still active?" Lizzie said happily. "How will you fool us then? Will you merely blurt out a double-negative? Or will you put your metaphysical detective to work to have us believe that the Monk does not exist? Which of those deceptions will you play, Mr. Root?"

"Neither," said the flustered man. "I am full of lead, and I do not feel capable of resistance. If you must trap me at my game, at least explain to me how you knew?"

"We did ask you about the Monk's location, and you answered, 'I know not where the Monk resides, but as sure as I am Manchester Root, I will help you find out.' Upon those words, Herr von Trotter became befuddled and whimpered. I took that to mean that you had told both a lie and a truth in the same sentence, cutting off abruptly the dog's seemingly mentalist abilities. I tried this half-lie, half-truth on the dog myself by declaring myself Emma Borden, the Girl Detective of Fall River, and obtained the same whimpering results."

Root shook his wide face. "Perhaps I'd best give up the game and take you on a tour of your final chamber. There you will find your precious mummy." He motioned for Miss Turpin to help him to his feet, but with a huff, she walked far away from the couch, open contempt on her brow. Mr. Almy and Andrew came forward and with considerable exertion, lifted Root to a standing position and offered him his cane. "Come," he said. "We will have done with this mystery. Mr. Almy, Deputy Wixon, would you be so kind as to swing aside the Labrador?"

The furniture salesman and the deputy puzzled for a moment over his words, then nodded to each other and set to work moving the heavy pedestal under the proud stuffed mascot. It rotated only with some effort and revealed a rectangular entryway towards a lower level accessible by a steep stone staircase.

"I'll be dangled," Deputy Wixon commented.

Miss Turpin smirked. "The most effective hiding place…" she began.

"…is one that is in plain sight for all to see," Lizzie concluded. "Let us descend."

C.B.M., having lit his oil lamp, took the lead, followed by Manchester Root, his hand clutching his gut, helped down the steps, by Borden and Almy. Albert Duey carried the Mite, who wiggled and made guttural noises, having lost all the verbal eloquence he had previously exhibited. Lizzie cradled Herr von Trotter in one arm and delicately sustained the Widow Mrs. Borden's frail hand with the other. Deputy Wixon took the tail, carrying his own lamp, placing one foot before the other as they descended.

When they had all reached the hard dirt floor of the basement, they instinctively gathered in a circle, as if the corners of the room were menacing enough to be dangerous. Manchester Root hobbled on his own steam to a huge cabinet that dominated the center of the floor and withdrew a turnkey from his cavernous pants pocket.

"You may condemn me," he said, as he stood poised to open the cabinet. "Yet, do not judge me. I do not defend the execution of a savage beast, be it a Missouri bushwhacker or a New York gangster."

The door to the cabinet swung open, and the assembled stood mouth-gaped, staring at an incredible scene. The interior was about six-feet-square and illuminated only by the globe lamp that Root held in his hand. In the exact center was a man seated on a stool, a large, heavy man that at first seemed like a pot-bellied stove, such was his girth. His scalp was smooth and hairless, and stuck in his left eye was a shiny monocle that caught the glare of the oil lamp. His face was dark and contorted, the nose abnormally flat, his chin twisted sideways. A yellowish-brown hand rested on one knee, while another was balanced upon the silver gleaming head of a sturdy wooden cane.

"Behold my father," Manchester Root announced, "displayed in the aspect he maintained in life. In the exact manner expressed in his probate. Such was my father's fear of death that he encouraged me to create this chamber of immortality that he may rest his weary legs, so weakened from his heavy flesh, and lord it over the only creature in life he truly despised."

Everyone stood speechless taking in the sight; then came a gasp from Miss Turpin. Her shaking finger pointed towards the dead man's feet, where rested a bound figure, a small child-sized man dressed in the exact manner as the two waxen dummies that had played so large a role in the day's affair. It was swathed in the leather vest and cowboy pants of a Western shootist.

"That is he," Duey said, restraining himself. "Here, all the time."

"Perhaps," Root said sadly. "You may know him as the Minuscule Monk, but to my father, he was the hired gun who killed my brother in the Lawrence massacre of 1863. The poor innocent man was playing with a kitten at the river's edge and, so legend has it, the Monk took his life with a Remington rifle. Dad spent his remaining years in a miserable search to find the killer."

His eyes moved solemnly to Duey, who withdrew towards the shadows at the edges of the room. "Then this man came into my life, reinvented as the itinerant immortalist, Jack Pratt, with whom I made a devil's deal in blood! Duey was committed to bringing the Monk's body to New York and flinging the lifeless creature at Benny Browbeat's feet, to redeem himself of his treachery and to collect on the punter's pot.

"But I had a more satisfying scheme in mind. Why not lure Benny Browbeat to Fall River, collect the money and rid this world of the demon barber of Leonard Street once and for all. Duey gave me custody of the Monk and in return I betrayed him. The miserable beast that I am! For my father's sake I stole the Monk from Albert Duey!"

"I've never heard you admit it before," Duey said, his face lengthening. "I always believed it, but never thought I could prove it. I joined your ridiculous organization hoping that I would eventually be able to steal it back!"

"But why," Lizzie asked, "did Benny Browbeat come to town pretending to be you?"

"Ah," Duey sighed. "You ask me to recall a very painful scene. After killing the Monk, I had his body preserved with arsenic and then took it back to Kansas where Jimmy Pell had resumed his surgeon's practice. There it remained for several years, underneath the floorboards of the cabin where I was once nursed back to life. It was our waxen spoof that circulated through the West, displaying the Monk to the depraved tastes of the lowest dime museums and carnivals."

"Communicating our victory to Browbeat was too dangerous. No, it was no longer the punter's pot that we desired, but justice on all points. That would take time, and time meant money. So we reaped the benefits of the carnival fake and reduced the risk to the Monk's real mummy. We guarded it with our lives."

"How did Root get involved?" Lizzie asked.

"Every anniversary of the massacre, the town held a solemn church service and a memorial on the banks of the Kaw River for the first victim, Lancaster Root. It was only a matter of time before Lancaster's father inquired about the death of the Monk. Rumor was that the Monk was still alive, and only I could put an end to that. I went to Fall River with the Monk in a steamer trunk and made a Devil's deal with Manchester. He offered to act as a liaison with Browbeat, to lure him to the city so we can murder him."

"What happened to Jimmy Pell?" Mr. Almy asked. "Is he mixed up in this as well?"

"Hardly," Duey said. "I went back to Kansas several weeks ago and found him dead in his cabin. He had been handled roughly before he died, no doubt tortured to reveal the location of the Monk. Our waxen replica was missing from its hiding place."

"So Benny Browbeat murdered Jimmy Pell," Deputy Wixon said, his face brightening, "and came to Fall River from the West, your wax spoof in a coffin, pretending to be Albert Duey, a professor of Egyptology."

"That is the part that is hard to reason out," Lizzie admitted. "There was already a professor of Egyptology in town, the driver who brought the Mite." She peered down at the captive gunslinger and asked, "Who drove your wagon?"

The small savage remained silent.

"Perhaps it no longer matters," Lizzie sighed. "We can only now assume that Benny Browbeat called ahead and ordered a coffin from Borden & Almy's under the name of Jimmy Pell. Into this box he intended to place the dead body of Albert Duey. By a strange coincidence, the survivor of the Terrible Trio and Fall River Animal Suffrage League had ordered a coffin in which to place Benny Browbeat.

"The mystery all comes down last night's midnight scene in the furniture store's basement. What happened? Our conspirators arrange for Browbeat to rendezvous at the store which had been broken into by the Mite. Perhaps our driver overpowered him, forced the prussic acid down his throat, followed by the key and the vellum. After a quick change of clothes, the careful planting of various taxidermy tools, and the crowning of the victim with the Homburg hat of H.B.E. Root, the scene was complete. The conspirators are now murderers and the murderer a victim."

"It doesn't add up," Deputy Wixon said, shaking his face. "Why would the Mite betray them all? Even his own clients?"

"We may never know," Lizzie said.

"Torture him," Duey growled. "Just as he did Jimmy Pell."

"No," Lizzie said. "We are not living by frontier rules. He must be handed over for due process."

"The Monk!" Evangeline said, reaching angrily toward the tethered mummy. "Let me have the Monk! I'll grind him to dust!"

"Impossible!" Root sobbed. "He is at my father's feet, where he belongs."

"He is *my* demon!" Duey shouted. "You stole him from me!"

"Saved him from being sent to New York," Root countered. "You would have handed him over to Browbeat for the punter's pot."

Duey held up two fists and advanced towards the wounded Root. "He killed *me*, so he's *mine!*"

"He killed my brother," Root spat. "So he's *mine!*"

"He is also mine," Miss Turpin moaned. "The Monk murdered my father on the streets of Five Points at the command of his gang leader, Benny Browbeat."

"But you said you were a seminary girl," Mr. Almy said, amazed.

"So I was," the thin woman said shamefully. "A wealthy uncle rescued me from the Five Points in an act of mercy. My family was not so lucky. I came to Fall River a proper woman, leaving the darkness of those times behind me. When Manchester first came to me, he promised revenge. He told me that I would, one day, stand before the fiend himself and bestow him one final indignity."

She stepped toward the mummified gunslinger, knelt down and peered at his dead eyes. After a mocking laugh, she spat in the dead man's face.

"Ah, Evangeline," Root sighed. "We have accomplished our mission. The barber and the Monk are both dead. Their bodies are at our mercy. Even Death cannot remove that from us now."

"You were doing this for your father and your brother?" Lizzie asked Root. "Not for the money?"

"Good heavens, not for money," Root exclaimed. "I am not so base. Not like some people I have the dishonor to work with. H.B.E. Root was a man who guarded himself from many temptations, but revenge for my brother's death was not something he could shake off so easily. He thirsted for revenge. With all living creatures made by God, he exercised Christian compassion and charity. He cared for the animals, for the insects even, for anything that moved and breathed in creation. He was a man who could not brush a fly from his hand lest he damage its wings. Tenderness and mercy were his watchwords. But, with the Monk he only wanted to wrap his hands around the beast's filthy neck and choke him to death. Often he described to me how he would squeeze until the eyeballs popped, the tongue lolled. After such a murder, he would rest in the earth forever knowing only one certitude: he never harmed a hair upon any human being's head." He paused for breath. "Except the Minuscule Monk," he added.

"So the Monk in Browbeat's coffin was made of wax," Andrew said, "and you promised to swap it for the real Monk. That was your trap to catch Browbeat."

"In effect," Root nodded. "Such were my instructions to the Mite."

"Such were *my* instructions to the Mite," Miss Turpin echoed.

"As were mine," Duey echoed. "This is the last time I hire an assassin without letters of reference, I swear." He spiraled across the floor, sidestepping Root and the cabinet, to where Deputy Wixon stood with the Mite by his side, and began to kick at him with his brogues. "Damn your eyes!" he shrieked. The Mite tried to shuffle his hog-tied legs, but the rope about his neck pulled him towards the officer.

"Now hold on, Duey," Deputy Wixon commanded, holding up a restraining hand. "This man is going to jail."

"Then let me alone with him for one minute," Duey hissed, "and I'll save the city the cost of his incarceration!"

"Feed him to the dog," Miss Turpin snarled, losing all her decorum. "Tear him to shreds!"

"No," Root said. "Let's be done with this!" He glanced at his father's crushed face. "Please forgive me," he intoned. "Under your guiding hand, you have led me to a life of success and comfort. But your one weakness, your hatred for the Monk, which grew to an abnormal obsession, was inherited by me as well, and it has become my undoing. Forgive me, Father! Oh! I am a fiend!" He raised a clawed hand to his chest and screamed, his body thundering downward, crushing itself against the floor with a sickening thud. Many ran to his side and all was chaos as they struggled to raise his head, relieve the pressure on his throat, and open his shirt to let him breathe.

"Take hold!" someone shouted, and then an oil lamp crashed, and much of their illumination vanished. A scuffle ensued to light another lamp that hung from the far wall, and after a frazzled moment Lizzie stood with its shutter angled upon Deputy Wixon, who stood with startled brows, his legs bowed and his mouth agape, his hands holding a broken piece of rope and the Mite's cow leather hat. The small man was gone.

For some strange reason that Lizzie could not fathom, Herr Hugo von Trotter stood in a proud poise before them all, darting his head forward and snapping violently at the air. Amidst the clatter and confusing mixture of human bodies, growled shouts, unwholesome exclamations and cries of despair, someone unknown was telling a lie.

Chapter Twenty-One

The Sentinels

Two days after the tragic affair in the basement, Manchester Root was buried in Oak Grove Cemetery, but not before a wake was held at the Fall River Animal Suffrage League. Hundreds of people turned out for the event, filing into the receiving hall in double line, having waited outside in the thundering rain, only to spend a single moment in respectful prayer before the large corpse in the oversized coffin on its funereal brace work. On the side of his last resting chamber was the embossed signature: Borden & Almy's. Root's placid face was shadowed by the distended muzzle of the stuffed Labrador that loomed over the coffin, as Root had stipulated in his will.

It was in the midst of this long parade lasting several hours that Lizzie Borden, standing at attention by the coffin with her father, Mr. Almy, C.B.M. and his mother, as well as Deputy Wixon and a rather embarrassed and displeased City Marshal, realized in one of her flashes of intuition, that the crowds were not coming out to see Manchester Root because they had thought highly of his work or his position in their town, but because they had heard only mangled and insufficient reports of the events surrounding the capture of the Monongahela Mite. They stared at Root like those pedestrians who gaze transfixed at a horrible train wreck or a streetcar accident, peering with desperate eyes in the hope that they will see something freakish or morbid. Manchester Root's dead presence in the coffin was eerie enough, but the viewers seemed a bit disappointed. What did they expect? A shootout with a gunslinger? A dog that could talk? A crew of murderers? No, there was nothing to see but a dead philanthropist whom many had previously assumed insane.

immortalization of a soul, a funeral rite performed over a vessel that had carried the intangible spirit that had been Manchester Root—his now liberated Manchester Root-ness so to speak—through fifty-two years of life and through much struggle. Or, perhaps it was not so liberated. Was it still within the flesh, still feeling pain, still sensing the material world with all its outrageous plenitude?

Perhaps not. The truth seemed so arbitrary and depended so much upon which philosophy caught your attention while browsing through the library at City Hall. Lizzie still felt the urge to travel to the Far East and join an archeological expedition into the Valley of the Dead Kings to fathom the secrets of immortality. She still wanted that, more so than ever, after excavating a very private tomb in Fall River, one with three chambers, and a very real set of human remains, and perhaps a bit of its soul left within.

The coroner's jury ruled that Root had not been murdered but had died of a heart attack, and that in his basement he had kept his own father's stuffed body preserved for eternity. The newspaper accounts focused on the ghoulish descriptions of the mummified corpses and the death of the New York gangster. The City Marshal, as predicted, had been furious that Deputy Sheriff Wixon had not reported the discovery of Browbeat's body the moment he first laid eyes upon it. But after much discussion, mostly with Lizzie behind closed doors in the Marshal's office, a deal had been struck and a scenario had been agreed upon to present to the public, who were now hopelessly mired in rumors and distortions of the actual events.

The Fall River Herald had published their morning edition with the headlines:

EXTORTION RING DESTROYS BENEVOLENT SOCIETY

ANIMAL ADVOCATE KILLS GANGSTER BARBER IN SELF DEFENSE

LOSES HIS OWN LIFE IN BASEMENT OF HORRORS

TALKING DOG SOLVES MYSTERY

The Marshal, in a remarkable display of grace, dignity and loyalty to the Bordens, held a meeting with the press in the lobby of the Central Police Station. Fully uniformed, sporting white gloves and a tall helmet, he encouraged them, practically begged them, to ignore all rumors and unsubstantiated details that they ordinarily would feel worthy of front page headlines, and write columns that portrayed the violent murder of Benny Browbeat as an act of defense. The gangster barber from New York, who held no positive favor with any journalist in the East, had attempted to blackmail, and then kill, the members of the Fall River Animal Suffrage League. The latter, fearing the troubling lawlessness that follows such a man as Browbeat, had hired the Monongahela Mite as a bodyguard. No one had been present at the actual murder; indeed they did not even know where or when it had occurred, which was true enough, but the innocent people who had hired the Mite were guilty of a single crime: not reporting it immediately to the police.

This official version of the events surrounding the death of Benny Browbeat and Manchester Root was, Lizzie noted, the Fourth Chamber of the vast Thesinger Box that Fall River had become. In some ways, it was the most mysterious chamber of all.

Manchester Root had paid for his actions with his life. The Monongahela Mite was currently in custody, having been caught trying to mail himself in a steamer trunk from the central post office. He was being deported to the West, where there was enough evidence stacked against him, no doubt several times his body height, amassed by sheriffs and lawmen across many counties and frontier towns, to send him to the gallows many times over. All Fall River wanted was for the New York gangsters to come collect their fallen leader and for the Mite to be shipped back, accompanied by a U.S. Marshal, to the Dakota Territories for what was known simply as "processing." The irony did not escape anyone that Benny Browbeat remained a victim, guiltless of any crime, at least within the boundaries of Fall River.

Lizzie neglected to mention Professor Bildung to the Marshal. What would be the point? The complications with Jewel the saddle horse of McDermott's stables and the unnamed man with the eye-patch and mutilated face were best left undiscovered. But Lizzie often did wonder upon it. The man had lectured so eloquently, as if he were intimate with the twin specters of Death and Immortality. Whoever he was, he had been a wandering philosopher, a prophet of old, a *memento mori* in the persona of a man, the sole character in the cast to escape unscathed from the affair in Borden & Almy's basement.

After much deliberation with the only surviving member of Manchester Root's family (a sister was found living in Philadelphia, long resigned to her dear brother's perceived lunacy, but saddened to hear he came to such a violent end), it was decided to bequeath her the League's building, complete with the stuffed bodies of H.B.E. Root and, more famously, the Minuscule Monk, who, as far as could be predicted, would remain at the feet of the Root Patriarch for as long as the building stood. He would suffer the fate of a demon bound to the will of a mad magician who had surrendered to sadism. It was beyond Lizzie Borden's powers to know whether such an arrangement suited the two souls that had once inhabited, and may indeed still be inhabiting, their bodies. If anything, it was a testament and a tribute to all the dead of Bleeding Kansas and a deadly river bank where Root blood had flowed, once upon a time.

In all his explanations to the press, which to Lizzie's great surprise were enthusiastically accepted and followed, there was no talk of the Minuscule Monk, and no talk of Lizzie Andrew Borden the Girl Detective. The upper echelon of Fall River had decided to honor Andrew Borden's request that the disclosure of the affair be contained and that his family honor be upheld.

Evangeline Turpin (humbled and shaken) and Albert Duey (again posing as Jack Pratt, immortalist for the League), both scared out of their wits, agreed to lie to anyone who asked them to give an account. Root's sister paid them a small stipend for the services they had rendered her brother, and one day the two vanished, some say into the West, having concluded that the death of the Monk and Browbeat healed nothing, provided no closure, and that starting a new life together in Lawrence, Kansas, now a thriving city full of life and prospects, may bring them ever so much closer to the death of their demons. Lizzie liked the think that Lawrence, once a victim of murder, had been raised from the dead and now could boast of a master immortalist for its dearly departed pets and a Latin instructor for its women's finishing schools.

Within a week, Miss Root had announced that her late brother's peculiar organization would be renamed the Fall River Animal Rescue League, and would tend to the suffering of its itinerant bestial population. Lizzie managed to persuade her father, no great lover of creatures, to put up seed money for its new kennels and veterinary staff. Andrew was dismayed to find that his own portrait had been commissioned, painted and eventually hung in the office once inhabited by Manchester Root, replacing the one of H.B.E. Root. The new owner even offered Andrew a position on their board of directors, one he accepted reluctantly since the second seat had been offered to Herr Hugo von Trotter, the canine mentalist. Andrew feared that attendance at the board meetings would be hazardous to his sanity, at best.

There was no one more jubilant over the conclusion of the affair than C.B.M. Borden, who began to pay social visits to the Borden's house on Second Street with his dazzled mother in tow, to chat away with Andrew, whom he considered to be a very wise and noteworthy man. Whatever Andrew thought of the young scion was anyone's guess, since his thin lips and his marble eyes never brightened when C.B.M. walked into the room.

"This is absolutely remarkable," C.B.M. commented one afternoon while lighting a cigar in the Borden's sitting room. Andrew reclined onto the edge of the sofa, snuffing out the match that he had extended to his guest. The mantle clock chimed the noon hour as a pillar of smoke rose towards the ceiling, its whispery lines billowing into a light cloud. Herr Hugo von Trotter sat placidly in his owner's lap, panting heavily, his eyes contently squinting.

"Indeed, this animal has hit upon a validation of my life's work," C.B.M. declared, patting the dog between the ears. "He has displayed a way in which anything can be a truth just because you believe it to be so. And it is a falsehood if you believe it to be so, completely independent of *a priori* or *a posteriori* knowledge. I must write to the Bishop Berkeley Society immediately and announce this major philosophical breakthrough! If they have not banned me from the listings yet, for my garrulous tongue and outspoken opinion—"

"Charles," the Widow Mrs. Borden said, from her place in the arm-chair across the room. "We've been through this before, a thousand times. Don't be so naïve about *a priori* existence. We really must define our terms and agree about our ontological assumptions!"

"Mother!" C.B.M. cried. "Not now! You're embarrassing me!"

Andrew growled, sinking further into his sofa, as if he had despaired of getting back the privacy of his sitting room.

His brooding was interrupted by a knock on the front door, and they all stared towards the hallway while the current Maggie, a small-boned Irish girl whose name Lizzie had long since forgotten, let in a large cumbersome man who was shouting some nonsense about needing to see Mr. Borden. He bolted into the room, a round face under a piggish derby hat. His erratic stride and maniacal gaze, and his unctuous act of holding out his calling card before him as he strode, announced boldly that here was a newspaper man.

"Borden!" he said, stomping into the sitting room. "You, Borden! I'm O'Neil, from *The Globe*, blast you!"

"How dare you, sir!" Andrew said, struggling to his feet and taking the man's card. "This is my home."

"Never mind that, is this him?" He leaned over and sniffed at Herr von Trotter, who returned a mercurial and mystifying gaze. "Is that the talking canine that solved the Browbeat case? Confounded Columns, I'm the first one to see it!" Herr von Trotter's muzzle pushed forward, and his nostrils quivered with anticipation. "Go on!" O'Neil ordered. "Tell me the name of the real killer! Speak it, you monster! What's wrong with that mangy brute?"

Lizzie stepped forward between the bellowing newsman and the confused animal. "I ask you to calm down, sir. Perhaps we can talk about this like sensible people."

"Sensible?" O'Neil said, outraged. "What's sensible about this? An oath of silence at City Hall, nothing from the police except for that farce of a press conference, no one giving interviews, all these rumors that no one can either deny or verify? Not only is nothing sensible, but nothing has been concluded. My readers want to know the truth, and I swear by my movable-type case that I'll give them the truth or my name isn't Godwin O'Neil!"

Lizzie digested his words for a moment, and then turned to her nervous companions. She picked Herr von Trotter up by the back of his neck and rotated him into her arms, where he tried to climb upwards into the safety of her embrace. "Mr. O'Neil, I shall give you the truth. You are looking at a truth-telling dog. No, he does not speak, but he can read your thoughts. Look into his eyes, look into them deeply. See how they are dark and bottomless, and all you can see is a shiny reflection of yourself?"

Herr von Trotter strained his neck forward to get a sniff at the reporter's nose, but the man withdrew, an uncanny discomfort overwhelming his face. "What's he thinking?" O'Neil demanded.

"He is thinking what you are thinking," Lizzie explained, "and if you continue your investigation into this affair, he will repeat it all to the reporter from *The Herald* who is coming here in the afternoon."

"No," O'Neil said, "you can't do that! You can't judge my thoughts! Neither can that dog!" Looking frantically about and sensing that he had not an ally present, he began to scurry towards the front door, his feet pounding the floor board. "Get him away from me!" he shouted. The Maggie, a sharp enough girl, had anticipated his flight and had opened the door to accommodate his evacuation. After slamming it shut, she muttered, "What the feck is he so hockeyed about?" and everyone in the sitting room broke out into hearty laughter.

"I never thought I'd say this," Andrew said, relaxing back into his couch, "but I like that hound. I say keep him around for a while."

"I've always been fond of him," sighed the Widow Mrs. Borden. Her lower lip trembled as she conjured a distant memory. "He reminds me of a lapdog I had back when my husband was alive. We called him Mr. Blodgett, after Dickens, you know. He strutted like a major and I delighted to watch him. But there were times, yes, I believe there were times when the dog was penetrating my thoughts and telling me things about myself that I didn't even know to be true. I would wake in the middle of the night and Mr. Blodgett would be on my sheets, staring at me, like I was obligated to respond to his mysteries. That would go on for hours, and I wouldn't have a clue what he was getting at."

"What happened to Mr. Blodgett?" Lizzie asked.

"That is the most curious thing; no one knows. When we received word that Mr. Borden had been gored by an elk, Mr. Blodgett fell into a profound funk. He didn't eat for days, and he looked as lazy and as melancholy as myself, being that I was in mourning for my dear husband. Then one morning, Mr. Blodget just vanished off the face of the earth. Not a trace. His dinner bowl was half-empty, and he hadn't even touched the scraps and bits of bone I had thrown into his cubby. The servants couldn't find him. There weren't even any dog prints leading off the property."

"That is tragic," Lizzie nodded. "I'm so sorry to hear it."

The Widow Mrs. Borden's eyes glared into the past a few moments more, seemingly lost in some train of thought, and then snapped back into the present. Her cheeks flushed, as her eyes brightened. "No matter, I'm just convinced that this had been a turning point in my life. Both faithful husband and dog gone in a trice. I don't think I ever really accepted it, you know. Perhaps that explains why I prefer things that aren't there over things that really exist. The absence of a thing is always more real to me than the thing itself. I know that may seem peculiar, but you must allow this aging widow a few indulgences, if you please."

C.B.M. motioned for Lizzie to pass Herr von Trotter to him and began to stroke him with a warm hand. "Mother," he said, "I have been trying to make the world not exist for quite some time now."

The Widow's aged face smiled. "I always wondered what it was that you weren't doing. Such a generous act which I hope you won't commit again."

"My pleasure," the boy grinned. "I don't suppose a son can fail to perform any greater gesture of love for his own mother."

Lizzie Borden was now secure within her world. The Case of the Minuscule Monk had been solved, and all within twenty-hours. There can be little doubt that Lizzie was the most excellent girl detective in Fall River, perhaps in all of New England.

The men sat and laughed, lighting cigars, enjoying the freedom of the afternoon and their deliverance from care. Their happiness, however, had little to do with any abiding peace within themselves; rather it was related to the deal that had been made with the Marshal and City Hall. They were all off the hook. No one would ever again question why a dead barber from New York appeared in the basement of Borden & Almy's; or why taxidermy tools and a Homburg hat had been found on the corpse; or how a group of upstanding citizens of Fall River could have become implicated in murder, extortion, deadly revenge and foul conspiracy. They could afford to smoke their cigars and enjoy their laughs, for tomorrow they must inevitably die.

Lizzie touched the breast of her jacket. Within the lining she had sequestered the *Memento Mori* with its dreaded but true words. The vellum rested within a pocket she had sewn into her clothing to facilitate her Fancy taking, that peculiar habit she had of borrowing items from shops and markets. She would abstain from this practice for now, keep only the vellum against her heart. The poem had entered her life as an intimacy between her and her father, then incubated within the mouth of a corpse; but it had become for her a form of magical protection against all that was evil. Fall River, as far as Lizzie Borden was concerned, was safe, for now.

So be it. The *Memento Mori*, Lizzie's most treasured souvenir of the entire affair, was hers once more, both its words and its wisdom.

Herr von Trotter, tired of being handed back and forth like a tennis ball between humans, wriggled his body, twisted out of C.B.M.'s lap and clattered to the floor boards. He didn't like being in this room, not with the Box Builder sitting on the couch, the one who smelled like wood shavings. A strange shadow hovered over the man's head, ready to swing down and make him as lifeless as the Labrador who stood forever pointing his nose upwards in the lobby of the Fat One's building.

With a few hind kicks and a manic dipping of his head, he took off across the floor, pressed his nose against the swinging door that entered into the kitchen area, and shot towards the back staircase, all the time running his nose along the floor, diligently sniffing and cataloging all odors that he could detect with his wet nose.

He paused at the top of the basement steps, perhaps a bit wary of the darkness below, but as his eyes adjusted, he felt a confidence that propelled him down the stairs, a small beast clomping downward into the depths of the house. Once in the cellar, he looked at the long hallway leading to the ash pit, the wash room, the coal bin, the fruit cellar. Their entrances were dimly lit from a lamp that hung above his head.

Onward he strode, bravely into the interior, his head swaying to see the shadows and shapes that populated the cellars. As he approached where the Bordens kept their firewood, he paused, confronted by two figures who stood in silhouette, guarding the coal bin like sentinels before a dark tower.

They were shaped like humans, but smaller, perhaps half the height. Both had on wide hats and wore furry chaps on their legs. Both had blackened faces and thick flaring moustaches. They smelled not of human flesh, but unburnt candles and camphor. Herr Hugo von Trotter had seen these half-men before. One had been in a wooden box under the trap door in the big hall and the other had been in the dead box at the cemetery, and for some reason the humans had killed each other to get their hands on these strange half-men who smelled like candles. In a way they were whimsical, but Herr Hugo didn't like them. They were lies. Not just untrue, but unnatural, created by humans to cause damage, to deceive, perhaps to steal and exploit.

Herr Hugo von Trotter knew about such men and their deeds because it was exactly that type of man who had raised him from a pup, and lied to him, over and over, to get him to eat abominable food that hurt his stomach, who beat him in drunken rages, who kicked him in the gut and sent him twisting down staircases. That horrible untrue man was so long ago, but Herr Hugo remembered with his body as truthfully as he remembered with his mind, and his body remembered the pain of being kicked and beaten. It was all lies. Men and their lies, he hated them.

There are humans who don't beat me, he thought, *like the Wizened Woman and the Mannered Boy who treat me like royalty, build doors for me, feed me more than I need, play pat-head and rub-tummy to my heart's content. But the Wizened Woman lies to me when she feeds me empty bowls and tosses sticks that aren't there. The Boy is lustful and deceives others with his words, but he cares about me. He is a tricky one who must be watched.*

Then there is the Curious Girl, the one they call Lizzie. She is a truth teller; she hates lies as well. I could feel it when she holds me, that she cares about people, and cares about the truth. I want to see more of her, want her to pat my head and rub my tummy. Perhaps she too will build a door for me and let me come and go as I please. I need to be around humans who speak truth. It means I won't get beaten any more.

The most disturbing thing about these humans, Herr Hugo von Trotter thought disdainfully, *are their eyes. They are either filled with darkness and danger like the dead black marbles of these two half-men, or full of light and safety, like the Curious Girl. I can stare at them for hours trying to tell them, but they just don't understand. Yet they know what is true in their hearts. They do feel it, even if they don't fully think it. It is the ones who don't even get that far, the ones who would murder and destroy without blinking an eye, without feeling a thing, those are the bloodletters and bad men that I bark at. It is my only defense.*

But this girl Lizzie Borden, she's another guardian of the truth. I will keep an eye on her, see how she progresses in her ability to sniff out the truth and howl at the untruth whenever possible. There is hope for the world yet with such sentinels guarding the gates. Let these wax ruffians stand guard over their blackened coal bins. I will offer my efforts to those who live in the light of day.

So he turned, his claws scattering on the dirt floor, and left the two bad half-men in their absurd hats and strange moustaches to sit in the dark and wait out eternity in the prisons of their own untruthful bodies.

The Rider

At seven o'clock in the evening of June 12, 1875, in the port town of Fairhaven near the Delano estate, law enforcement officials stopped a man upon a large chestnut roan who appeared to have lost his way. He was a stranger, in an advanced state of agitation, who could not give a coherent account of how he came to be upon that road at such an hour saddled upon such a horse. When pressed for his identity, the man tried to make an escape but was stopped in the act by the bravery of one police officer who brought him to the ground even from atop his horse. A distinguishing characteristic of the man in custody was that he was missing one eye and wore a black patch over his face to hide the socket. He was also wearing a golden silk swatch over his nose, which upon closer inspection proved to be partially mutilated.

He remained in custody in Fairhaven for several hours until his identity was finally established to be Gabriel Blake of New York City, and who had a long criminal record from his time in the Five Points. Over the next two days, arrangements were made, and Blake was dispatched back to New York, there being no charges that could legally be brought against him.

The horse that he rode at the time of his capture was kept in a Fairhaven stable while inquiries were made in surrounding towns. The Fall River police responded that a Mr. Ian McDermott, a stable master of that city, had reported a missing roan, claiming it had been stolen from his stables the day of Blake's arrest. McDermott pointed out that a large white diamond on the roan's forehead had been painted over to obliterate identification. Mr. McDermott could give no explanation as to why Mr. Blake would want to steal his horse and declined offers to bring the perpetrator back to Fall River for prosecution.

"What's done is done," Mr. McDermott concluded. "I'm not even sure about anything anymore. This horse may not even exist for all I know."

The true meaning of Mr. McDermott's statement, as well as the motivation for Blake's thievery and every aspect of the incident, remains, to this day, a total mystery.

www.ingramcontent.com/pod-product-compliance
Lightning Source LLC
Chambersburg PA
CBHW020756250626
47155CB00003B/1099